TYME'S END

Also by B. R. Collins

The Traitor Game
A Trick of the Dark

TYME'S END

B. R. COLLINS

BLOOMSBURY

LONDON BERLIN NEW YORK SYDNEY

Bloomsbury Publishing, London, Berlin, New York and Sydney

First published in Great Britain in January 2011 by Bloomsbury Publishing Plc
36 Soho Square, London, W1D 3QY

ISBN 978 1 4088 0647 0

FSC
Mixed Sources
Product group from well-managed
forests and other controlled sources
Cert no. SGS - COC - 2061
www.fsc.org
© 1996 Forest Stewardship Council

Typeset by Dorchester Typesetting Group Ltd
Printed in Great Britain by Clays Ltd, St Ives plc, Bungay, Suffolk

1 3 5 7 9 10 8 6 4 2

www.bloomsbury.com/childrens

2006

I

I've had enough. There's only so long anyone can stand being shouted at, and I'm way past it. We've been arguing for ten minutes, our voices getting louder and louder, and now I don't trust myself to speak. It's fifty-fifty whether I'll swear or burst into tears, and I don't want to do either. I shove past Dad, out on to the landing.

Dad shouts, 'Where the hell are you going?'

'Out.'

'Don't you dare, young lady – I'm *talking* to you –'

'Stop telling me what to do! I know you think I'm a waste of space, you don't have to keep telling me. Leave me alone.' I grab my jumper off the banister and run down the stairs.

'You come back here *right now* –'

'I want to go out.' I look over my shoulder. 'I need to get out. I can't stay in this bloody house for one more second. So *leave me al—*'

'Bibi! We have a guest coming tonight.' He's talking slowly now, like I'm very, very stupid. 'Look, we can talk about – I'm sorry I shouted. But I do – I need to do the laundry now. So please will you take the sheets off your bed and give them to –'

'He's not a bloody *guest*! He's a *customer*. Jesus! You make it sound like a brothel.'

'Bibi, don't you dare talk to me like –'

I grab my keys, go out of the front door and slam it behind me. I hear Dad's voice rise in a kind of helpless howl, and if I wasn't so angry I'd laugh. I shove my hands into my pockets and turn right.

Sam is kicking a ball against the wall at the end of the street. I walk straight past him without turning my head, but he jogs after me, still dribbling the ball. He says, 'Oooh, leave me *alone*, you're not my *real* father,' in a high-pitched voice that's meant to be me. He's giggling.

'Piss off, Sam.'

'*Oooh*. You're not my *real* father.'

'And you're not my real brother either, so shut the hell up.'

'I could hear it from here,' he says, bending to pick up the ball. He grins up at me, shaking his fringe out of his eyes. 'Suppose one day you ask Mum for something and she's like, no, you're not my real daughter?'

'Piss *off*. *They* adopted *me*. *I* did not adopt *them*. And you don't understand.'

'No,' he says, sighing. 'No one understands you. I *definitely* don't.'

I reach out to hit him, but he's already drifted back, kicking the ball from foot to foot. He gives me a little distracted wave, without looking up. I swallow, hard, because I can feel my anger draining away and misery taking its place, and I turn away. I go left then right again, hurrying down the High Street because I'm determined not to cry in public. There are tourists jostling with cameras outside the church, and I push past them, not caring if I walk through their photos. Someone says, 'Oh, excuse *me*,' and I clench my jaw, half wanting to turn and apologise, half wanting to swear. I go past Eddie's shop and he salutes, grinning. I raise my hand without meeting his eyes, and then break into a run. Any moment now I'm going to start crying . . .

I sprint across the road, past the gates of Tyme's End and the gaggle of foreign students yelling to one another. Some of them are rattling the padlock, but the gates are rusted shut, and they're wasting their time. I swerve round them, swearing under my breath, and go round the corner. It's much quieter, suddenly. I look both ways, then run at the wall where it's cracked, dragging myself up and over and through the gap in the bars. I drop awkwardly into the brambles and feel a thorn draw a stinging line across my forehead. I struggle forward, until I'm standing waist-deep in the grass under the trees. The light is grey-green and dim, like water, and it's very quiet. I take a deep breath and the tension ebbs and fades. I'm on my own. There's a bloody great wall between me and Dad and Sam and Mum – wherever she is right now.

I clench my fists, throw back my head and shout. The birds swirl upwards in a clatter of wings. I swear through my teeth – it's better than crying, anyway – and shake my head. Bloody Dad. When I think about it, it's so stupid – fights about tidying my room, going out, *laundry*, for God's sake – but Sam's right. It always ends up with *you're not my real father*.

I hate myself for saying it to him, but I can't help it. Every time. It's like a reflex. Afterwards, I resolve never to say it again, but it just comes out. And it hurts. I can see it on his face, like I've kicked him on the shins – but the funny thing is that I feel it too. He *isn't* my real father. And Mum's not my real mother either.

And Sam's right – one day they might turn round and say it back.

I feel my stomach tightening again, and I make myself take another deep breath. It's OK. I'm here, now. I'm safe, on my own.

I concentrate on not thinking about Mum and Dad. I walk forward slowly, wading through the thigh-deep bracken, and come out on what used to be the lawn. I stand in the long grass, looking at the house. Tyme's End. Where would I go, if I didn't have Tyme's End? I'd have to stay at home. I feel a rush of protective-ness, and a strange sort of pride, because Tyme's End is mine. Not really, of course, not legally – H. J. Martin left it to some historian, who died ten years ago, and *he* left it to someone that no one's ever met – but who else comes here? Who else likes it as it is, half falling down, rotting and sagging and crumbling? The tourists stare through the gates, but the drive's too overgrown to see anything, and they don't know about the broken bit of wall. And they wouldn't want it, anyway, the way it is. They want it to be restored and given to the National Trust. They want a car park and toilets and a gift shop. Even my parents have got the *H. J. Martin's House Should Be Open To The Nation* petition displayed on the table in the B. & B.

They don't know I come here, of course. They'd

have a fit, because it's probably the most dangerous place in Falconhurst. When I'm inside I have to tread carefully, because the floorboards are soggy and the stairs sag and complain when you stand on them. Everywhere you look there's green stuff growing. There are rats. There's a wasps' nest in one of the attics, like a huge humming pillar of papier mâché. And everything's covered with tendrils of ivy – no, not tendrils: trunks and branches, it's grown-up, kick-ass ivy – and the floors stink of mould and water runs down the walls, and where there was wallpaper there are crumbling brownish scrolls of it peeling away, and where there was only plaster there are huge damp bubbles on the walls, like they're boiling slowly sideways. On the ground floor almost all the windows are boarded up and on the first floor loads of the panes are cracked or missing. Tyme's End is dying, slowly. And I love it. I stand in the long grass, watching a rag of old curtain flutter in one of the top windows, and feel a savage surge of gladness that it's here, and so am I. And finally the anger fades, and I imagine myself screaming at Dad about sheets, and I start to laugh.

When the giggles are over, I straighten up and walk through the grass, round the side of the house, to the open door. As I slide through the gap my top brushes the crooked wood, and suddenly I can smell the air in the house: the scent of age, and damp, and seventy years' loneliness. It's musty and a little bit bitter. I take a big breath, opening my mouth so that I can nearly taste it.

Inside it's silent. I stand still, just listening. My heartbeat is the only thing I can hear. Sometimes there are odd noises, or odd silences – moments when your nerves tingle as if you heard something, although you know you didn't – but today the house is dormant, almost welcoming. I go through into the dining room, then into the hall and up the stairs. The staircase creaks ominously, but I'm used to that.

Upstairs I turn left. The corridor's dark, and the air leaves sticky cobweb traces on my face. I walk towards the bedroom at the corner of the house, and as I go through the door the sun comes out from behind a cloud and the whole room lights up. There's not much here – a bed, a desk, wardrobe, everything old-fashioned and covered in a layer of gritty dust like ash from a volcano – but it's cleaner than anywhere else, and hardly any of the windowpanes are broken. A few months ago I nicked the groundsheet from Sam's play-tent, and now I can sit on the bed without my clothes stinking of mildew afterwards. I've got a tin of biscuits, and a couple of books, and a plastic bottle of whisky and Coke for emergencies, and a torch. Not that I'd ever be here at night – but once, years ago, when I got stuck here in the rain, it was so dark I got the creeps. I thought I heard someone moving around downstairs, and I sat there with my eyes closed, practically wetting myself with terror, until finally the sun came out again. After that I didn't want to be here without a light.

In summer I drag the bed over to the window so that I can sit and look out. The groundsheet is still rumpled from the last time I was here, which was yesterday, and my book is splayed face-down on the windowsill. I put the biscuits within easy reach, sit on the bed and find my place in the book. But it's hard to concentrate. I still feel like hitting someone or crying.

Outside the trees are swaying from side to side, like they're warning each other about something. The sun goes in again and the warmth fades out of the room.

I kneel up and lean my elbows on the windowsill. It's going to rain. I press my forehead against the glass. A breath of cool air from the broken pane slides over my lips, like there's someone sitting next to me.

A noise makes me look round. It's the draught, riffling the pages of my book. It's one of Eddie's from the ten pence box, an old blue hardback with yellowing pages. It smells of libraries. It's a ghost story about a violin and it's quite good, but my favourite thing is that it's got a little handwritten conversation in the margin. At the moment the spiky handwriting is telling the blunt pencil that writing in other people's books is vandalism. I watch the pages turn by themselves. The air pauses, like it's found a good bit, then gets bored and carries on flipping through.

I look out of the window again, and the first spots of rain spatter the glass. The sound of it is half comforting, half spooky, like someone tapping on the window with their fingernails. I move sideways, away from the broken bit of the window, so I won't get wet, and lean against the wall, propping the book on my knees. The curl of wallpaper hanging above my head bounces and rustles. I listen to the quiet inhuman sound of the rain. I let my eyes focus on the page in front of me and after a while I start to read.

When I lift my head again I don't know how long I've been reading for, or why I've stopped. But there's something . . . I frown, trying to work out what distracted me. I feel uneasy somehow; jumpy.

I tip my head back and look at the ceiling. The

damp has drawn a map in the plaster, a network of cracks like country roads. Something's wrong.

There are footsteps downstairs.

I sit up as quietly as I can, and a shiver goes down my back. I pray that I've imagined the sound, or that it's my heartbeat. But it isn't.

Maybe it's just someone who's come in to get out of the rain – a tramp, or a kid, or a tourist. But the local kids don't come here. No one comes here. Even tramps only come here in winter, when they're desperate.

I'm cold all over. I'm on my feet but I don't remember standing up. Oh, God. There *is* someone downstairs. The light has gone grey-blue, shadowy, like dusk.

I stand very still, praying for the noise to stop, praying that I've imagined it – like before, like all those times before – but it carries on. Deliberate, slow footsteps. I shut my eyes to imagine somebody walking like that, and then wish I hadn't. I can see him – the paces are heavy, definitely male – too clearly: someone who's been here before, wandering slowly through the house, familiar room after familiar room, the owner checking that everything's in order.

I don't believe in ghosts. I don't believe in ghosts. I do *not* –

Oh, shit.

There's a silence, just long enough for me to relax a tiny bit. Then a door slams. Another pause, then more footsteps, measured, getting very slightly louder, as if they're coming towards the stairs.

I feel panic start to creep over my skin like frost. Oh, God. I shouldn't be here. Part of me wants to hide

– I look instinctively at the corner next to the fireplace, where I'd be out of sight of the doorway if I pressed up against the wall – but I don't think it would be any good. I have a horrible, irrational conviction that whoever is downstairs knows I'm here, that he's taking his time, letting me hear him approach. A door scrapes and groans. Then an interminable silence. I tell myself that this time he *must* have gone away, but I know I would have heard him move. No, he's standing still, waiting, watching.

Then the stairs creak. I know the sound so well I can tell that he's coming up two steps at a time – not quickly or eagerly, but as if he's been here before, he knows that they're too shallow to go up one by one. I look stupidly at the window, but even if I could get it open the mullions are too close together to let me through.

The other staircase.

I dig my nails into the palms of my hands, trying to screw up my courage to go out into the corridor. If he's coming up the main staircase – if I run – I could get down the back stairs and out through the side door without having to pass him. But I have to go now, or he'll be at the top of the staircase and it'll be too late. The fear's like nausea, swelling until I'm not sure I can control it. It's like a nightmare, one of those ones where someone's chasing you and you can't run. Come *on*, Bibi! This would be a good moment for the emergency whisky and Coke, but I don't have time. There's the complaining creak of someone putting their weight on the banister and a little cut-off sound like someone hissing through their teeth.

I have to move.

And I do, suddenly, my limbs not obeying me properly, so that I stagger awkwardly over to the doorway and pull up short, breathless, shocked by how much noise I'm making. But now my body's unfrozen I can think more clearly, and even though I'm shaking I'm not quite as scared as I was. Now it's almost a game: I have to slide silently away down the corridor like a ghost, before . . .

OK.

The corridor's dark, and the rain is pattering on the windows like something's trying to get in. I step carefully out into the shadows, and plaster crunches underfoot. There's a kind of hollow singing noise coming from the door opposite me. I know it's the wind in the chimneys, but right now it makes the hair on my arms prickle. I don't want to look left – if there's someone coming up the stairs, I don't want to see him – but I can't help it. It's so dim that the air looks grainy, like old film. There's nothing there. I keep looking, frozen, because I can hear someone breathing and it's not me. But no one's there. I swallow, and my throat is so tight it makes a little squeaky gulp. In the silence it's as loud as a scream.

The footsteps pause. Then, very slowly, I hear him coming up the last few stairs, round the corner.

He's there, standing in the half dark, staring at me.

I should run. But I can't. I think my heart has stopped completely.

We stand perfectly still, looking at each other. I'm frozen, as if time has paused, but suddenly the fear has faded into the background. I feel faintly surprised that nothing terrible has happened. There's no sense of pervading evil, or malice, or even a cold draughty feeling. It's almost a relief.

I can make out just enough of his face to see that he's opened his mouth, as if he's about to speak. His face is a dead kind of white that stands out in the murk, like a drowned body coming to the surface.

Then he says, 'Who the hell are you?'

I know instantly from his voice that he's a real person.

My whole body is covered with a sort of fizzing heat; I don't know if I'm embarrassed or relieved or incandescent with rage. I say, 'Who the hell are *you*, creeping around like you own the place?'

He makes a noise that might be a laugh. Somehow, from the way he does it I can suddenly tell that he was as scared as I was, if not more. He says, 'I *do* own it. Get out.'

'There's no need to be rude.'

'You're trespassing.'

'I wasn't doing any harm.'

'I don't give a damn what you were doing. You shouldn't be here. Get *out*.' He sounds breathless, not quite in control. '*Now*.'

I stare at him, imagining him falling backwards, stumbling down the stairs, slipping and breaking his neck with a satisfying crunch. Who the hell does he think he is? But there's nothing I can do. I grit my teeth and stare at him just long enough to make it clear that I don't *have* to do what he says. Then I say, 'Fine. Let me get my book.'

'No.'

'What?' I can't believe it. It's not exactly an unreasonable demand.

'Forget the bloody book. Just – you're not welcome

in this house, understand? I don't care if you've got a Shakespeare folio in there. Get out *now*.'

'Or what?'

'Or I'll make you, you stupid little cow.' His voice is tense, like he's trying to concentrate or like the words aren't ones he'd normally use.

'Oh, yeah? You and whose army?' I cross my arms and glare at him, trying to ignore my own voice in my head: *You're not my father* . . .

He looks back, his eyes narrowed. There's an odd flicker of something in his eyes, almost like he wants to laugh, but his fists are clenched. Then he lunges for me and grabs my arm. It hurts and I yelp, but he doesn't loosen his grip. 'Right. You want me to call the police? Come with me *now*. I won't tell you again.'

'Shit, that hurts – get off me – you can't –'

'I think you'll find I can,' he says, swinging me roughly round and pushing me forward so that I'm walking in front of him. I might be able to get away, but I think he might actually hit me if I try. I can smell something clean, like washing powder, and I realise it's his clothes. It's strange that I have time to notice it, because he's bundling me down the stairs and I have to concentrate not to fall. I can feel the tension in his fingers, grinding the muscle of my arm against the bone, and when I glance back at him he's biting his lip and doesn't meet my eyes. I don't think he realises how tightly he's holding on to me.

'I can walk by myself, you know,' I say.

'Once you're off my property you can do whatever you want.' He knows exactly where he's going: he steers me through the dining room and out through the side door. I wait for him to let go, but he keeps walking, shoving me in front of him round the side of the house and down the driveway towards the gates. There are tourists there, taking photos. He slows down and stops, still without letting go of me. We stand side by side, watching people pose in front of the *TRESPASSERS WILL BE PROSECUTED* sign. He says, 'Go on, then.' He sounds very tired. Suddenly he seems to realise that he's still gripping my arm like grim death. He catches my eye and for a second it's like he's forgotten how angry he was; he smiles, rolling his eyes, mocking himself. 'Go on. Never darken my door again.'

I look at the gates, then back at him. Now we're in daylight I can see what he looks like, and I kind of wish I couldn't, because he's younger than I thought, tense and pale but not bad-looking. 'What do you mean, *go on*? They're padlocked.' When he looks blank, I add, 'I thought you *owned* Tyme's End. Wasn't it you that padlocked them?'

'Then how did you –?' He stops. 'Right. Of course. Over the wall, the same way I did.'

'There's a gap in the –' I stare at him, and suddenly I feel a giggle rising in my gut. 'Hey. The same way *you* did? You're such a liar. If you owned the place, you'd hardly climb in over the wall.'

'No, really, I would,' he says. That flicker of amusement comes into his eyes again, although it doesn't reach his mouth. 'I wanted to avoid the tourists. Can you imagine, if I just turned up and unlocked the gates, after ten years, with them all standing there?'

We look at each other, and then we start to laugh. Suddenly it's like we're friends. He says, 'I know, I know, it's ridiculous,' and I say, 'Yeah, it is a bit,' and we carry on laughing. He still hasn't let go of my arm, but I don't mind any more. I want to tell him how scared I was. I want him to tell me how scared *he* was. But we just laugh, and we're making so much noise that after a while he pulls me sideways on to the lawn, the way we came, out of sight of the gates.

I wipe my face and belatedly realise it's still raining.

I take a long, juddery breath, and say, 'You gave me a hell of a fright, when you came up the stairs. I thought you were the ghost of H. J. Martin.'

His face changes. He lets go of my arm. He says, 'You'd better go home.'

I say, 'Oh. I only meant –'

'And don't come back. The next time I catch you here, I'm calling the police.'

For a moment I think he's joking. But he stands still, his hands in his pockets and his face hostile, glaring at me until I turn to leave. I look back once, as I'm scrabbling to get over the wall, and he's still there, thigh-deep in grass, rain sliding down his face, watching me run away.

II

There's a knock on my bedroom door. I say, 'Go away,' because I don't want to talk to anyone, especially Mum or Dad, but the door opens anyway.

It's Sam. He says, 'Mum says, the guest is eating with us, so can you be presentable by seven o'clock. Which means basically now,' he adds, like a helpful translation service.

'For God's sake!' I say. 'This is meant to be a bloody bed-and-*breakfast*. Why do they have to have dinner with us? If we have to give them dinner, why can't they at least eat it on their *own*, in the breakfast room?'

Sam just blinks at me through his fringe. 'Don't ask me. It's not my fault.'

'No one else does it. It's ridiculous. And he's not a *guest*, he's a *customer*. Guests are people we have a choice about.'

'If you want to say that to Mum, you can do it yourself.'

'Fine.' I roll my eyes. 'Yes, I'll be presentable at seven o'clock. But he hasn't actually got here yet, has he? He might not even come.'

'He dumped his stuff, so he's probably coming back. And he must have said he wanted dinner or Mum wouldn't have –'

'All right, stop being logical,' I say, and Sam grins. He looks pointedly at his watch, and I check the clock on the wall. Ten minutes. I'm in a manky old T-shirt because my other top is still wet from the rain, but I can't be bothered to change. I pull my hair back into a ponytail with a rubber band and squint at myself in the mirror. 'How's this? Will I put him off his food?'

'No more than you would normally.'

I kick out at him, but he moves deftly out of range, still grinning. I say, 'I am so glad I'm not related to you, you little toerag.'

'You *are* related to me.'

'Only very distantly.'

'Well, it's mutual, anyway.' He puts on his mock BNP voice. 'Bloody wogs, coming over here, stealing our parents . . .'

'Shut up, Sam.' He's only joking, and normally I'd laugh, but right now it's not funny. 'Stop being a racist little git.'

He opens his mouth, then closes it again and shrugs. 'You coming to have dinner or what?'

I just stare at him until he leaves. Then, defiantly, I grab my baggiest, most frayed hoody, and follow him downstairs.

Mum's laying the table, glancing up between bits of cutlery to check the clock. She says, 'Bibi, I told Sam to tell you . . .' Then she catches my eye and stops. 'Darling, will you get the napkins out for me?'

I get the napkins out. 'I still don't understand why

you can't just let them eat at the Cloven Hoof.'

'Your father enjoys cooking, darling. You know that.'

'He could cook for *us*. On our own.'

'Yes, but this is one of the reasons that people come back. The family atmosphere, the convenience of eating here – and he's on his own. Why don't you sit down and –' The front door clicks and creaks open. 'Bother.' She winces at the half-laid table. Then she goes through the door into the hall, and I hear her say, 'Do come into the dining room. Would you like a glass of wine? God, it's filthy weather out there, isn't it? But I hear they're predicting a heatwave.'

She comes in first. 'Bibi, darling, this is Oliver. Oliver, this is my daughter Bibi, and Sam, her brother, and of course you've met Chris, my husband –'

Oh no.

It's him.

I meet his eyes and suddenly I feel sticky all over, like someone's drenched me in glue. I clear my throat and say, 'Ah . . .' It's meant to be *hi*, but it comes out wrong.

He smiles. He looks casual, polite, like he's never seen me before; but I can tell he recognises me. 'Hello.'

Oh, God. If he says something – if Mum and Dad find out I've been in Tyme's End – they won't ground me, they'll probably expatriate me. I want to wink at him, but my face won't move properly, and anyway that's all wrong, he'd just think I fancied him. Oh, *shit*. I say, 'Who are you? I mean, sorry, what was your name?'

'Oliver. Oliver Gardner.' He's got a faint American

19

accent; I don't know why I didn't notice it before.

Mum has somehow got the rest of the table laid in record time. Now she's waltzing in from the kitchen with a bottle of wine and pouring a glass for him. 'Oh – I meant to ask before, when you booked – any relation? To the biographer, I mean. Oliver Gardner is one of my heroes, you know. A great writer. He inspired me to be a historian. We've got all his books.'

'Oh. Yes. He was –' Oliver reaches for the wine, and takes a sip, licking his lips before he starts to speak again. 'Yes, he was my grandfather. I was named after him.'

'Goodness. How wonderful.'

'He was a –' He takes another gulp of wine and frowns into the glass as if he can see something at the bottom. 'Yes. Wonderful.'

'Such a pity he didn't come to live at Tyme's End . . . I always hoped to run into him at the supermarket or something –' She laughs, for no reason. She's trying so hard to make him feel at ease that it's embarrassing. 'Of course he must have needed to live somewhere a bit more metropolitan – for his research, and – well . . .'

There's a silence. I sit down at the table and try not to look at Oliver, in case he looks back. I'm suddenly very conscious of my manky sweatshirt and messy hair.

'Well.' Mum pours herself a drink and then, as the pause lengthens, she leans over to adjust the angles of the knives and forks on the table, aligning them exactly. 'So, you must know Falconhurst quite well, then?'

'No. Actually . . . no.' He swirls his wine round in

the glass, making a tiny red whirlpool. He doesn't look up.

'Oh.' Mum catches my eye and gives me a tiny, unexpected smile.

Sam says, 'So are you on holiday?'

'No.' He keeps rolling the stem of his glass between his fingers, until the wine sloshes up and on to his hand. Then he seems to see it for the first time and puts it down on the table with a determined click. He looks round at us. 'Sorry, I'm still a bit jet-lagged. No, I'm here to – on business, I suppose. I own – I inherited Tyme's End. When my grandfather died. I – I couldn't face coming back, before now.' He pauses and grins, without amusement, mocking himself. 'It's taken me ten years to screw up the courage.'

Mum blinks and fumbles quickly at the tablecloth. 'Oh – yes, of course – I mean, we never knew exactly *who* – but I should have –' She's gone red round her ears. 'Oh dear, I hope I wasn't being tactless. I . . . we were so sorry to hear about his death. It was in all the local papers, you know.' She stops.

Oliver nods and shrugs. It looks like he's trying to smile. 'It was a long time ago.'

'It must be –' she says, in a spurt, and for a nasty moment I think she's going to say *wonderful* again. 'A great responsibility. Tyme's End, I mean. A house with so much history.'

He makes a kind of quiet choking noise. 'Yes.'

Dad says, from the kitchen doorway, 'All the tourists would love to see it open to the public, you know. And the historians.' He smiles at Mum. 'All the rabid academics, like Meg here. Still a lot of stuff being written about H. J. Martin. They're desperate

21

to have a proper look round, get it restored. Any thoughts in that direction?'

Mum says, 'Christopher!'

'Only asking, darling.' He's drying his hands on a tea towel, and he flaps it jocularly in Oliver's direction. 'No offence. It's your house, naturally. I'm only giving you an idea of local feeling.'

'I'm going to sell it.'

I swallow. For a split second, I can see Tyme's End in front of me. I can smell damp, and things growing, and freedom.

'Right.' Dad drapes the tea towel over his shoulder. 'I didn't mean you should *donate* it, necessarily, only that –'

Oliver looks up, straight into his eyes. 'I don't give a damn who I sell it to. I'd raze the whole house to the ground if it wasn't listed.'

There's a few seconds of silence. Then the cooking timer goes off, bleeping urgently into the pause as if it's been waiting for the right moment. Dad opens his mouth and goes back into the kitchen without saying anything.

'Oh,' Mum says.

Sam says, 'Because your grandfather died there?'

'No, because I –' He stops. He picks up his wine glass again and takes two sips in rapid succession, wiping his mouth with his other hand. His fingers are shaking very slightly. I remember, all of a sudden, the way his arm felt against mine when he was pushing me. 'Yes,' he says. 'That's right.'

I say, 'You can't sell it.' The words arrive in my mouth without my knowing how they got there.

He looks up sharply. He's got hazel eyes and tiny

22

creases under his lower lashes. Somehow the fact that he's good-looking makes me angrier. He says, 'Why not?'

'Because –' I glare at him. He stares back at me, raising his eyebrows. 'Because – you *can't*. Someone'll buy it and turn it into flats for commuters. It'll be shit. How could you do that?'

'I'm sorry,' Mum says. 'It must be a difficult –'

'Excuse me,' he says. He stands up, very quickly, and his chair scrapes loudly over the floor. 'No, *I'm* sorry. I don't think I want dinner. The jet lag –'

And then he's gone, nearly tripping over the rug. I catch sight of his hand on the door frame as he steadies himself. It's an odd, pale, yellowy colour: like ivory, or something very old.

He doesn't come back.

The fight goes on far longer than it should. It starts off reasonable, almost *gentle*, with Mum asking me what the matter is. We sit and talk very quietly – because after all Oliver is in the guest room and the walls aren't that thick – about how rude I am, and how this is a business, and how being childish and obnoxious doesn't make anyone feel more sympathetic, and I can't possibly be *really* unhappy, it's just a phase everyone goes through, and maybe I should get a summer job so I have something to take my mind off it. By that stage we're shouting. Dad tells me I'm self-absorbed and selfish and self-dramatising and everything else that begins with *self*. Mum says, 'Bibi, we only want you to be happy, but I think your father's right,' and then winces, like she's just stubbed her toe on something. I make her wait for it. Then I open my mouth and say, very clearly and slowly, 'He's *not my father*. And *you're* not my –' Out of the corner of my eye I see Sam mouthing the same thing, like he's lip-synching to a film he's seen hundreds of times.

I storm out. I slam my bedroom door and lean a chair against it – that's more symbolic than anything, because it wouldn't stop anyone getting in if they really wanted to – and pummel my pillow until I feel a bit calmer. Then I get my special box out from under my bed and spread everything out on my duvet. I curl up in the middle of it and hold my favourite photo a few centimetres away from my nose, so it dissolves into a warm blur of ochre and brown. I stay very still. I shut my eyes and pretend I'm somewhere else. I get pins and needles in my hand from holding the photo too tightly.

I can't sleep. I hear Sam doing his teeth next door, and then the TV goes on and then off again, and the taps run and the toilet flushes until it's nearly midnight, and everyone else has gone to bed.

Finally I get up – carefully, so I don't crease any of my bits of paper – and turn the light off. I stand there in the dark. I feel better now that no one else is awake.

The rain's stopped, and I open my window to get some fresh air. It's warm and I can smell the water evaporating off the lawn. Every so often there's the swish of a car from the road, or the roar of a motorbike. Once there's a motorbike that cuts out, abruptly, at the loudest point. I stand still and listen to the silence, but the noise starts again after a few minutes and chugs away into the distance.

I yawn. Suddenly I feel sleepy.

The front door clicks, softly. If it had been a bit louder, I wouldn't have noticed it.

Oliver.

I wait for the footsteps to come up the stairs, but they don't. He must have been going *out*. I put my bedside light on and check my watch: just gone midnight. Where . . . ?

The warm breeze makes my curtains billow and dance, smelling of summer rain and darkness. One of the sheets of paper on my bed twitches. Outside there's silence, nothing but empty streets and gardens.

But I think I know where he's going.

I cram my feet into my shoes without untying the laces and check my keys are still in my jeans pocket. Then I'm running down the stairs, keeping close to the wall so the floorboards don't creak. I go out into the street and shut the door behind me.

I'm almost too late. He's just disappearing out of sight, turning left at the end of the street. I follow, dodging in and out of the pools of light from the street lamps, but he's looking down at the ground and doesn't glance up, even when he comes to the turning towards the High Street. He goes right, past Eddie's closed-up shop, the way I went this afternoon. He stops in front of the gates to Tyme's End, and I slip sideways into the porch of the Cloven Hoof in case he turns round. A car goes past, but once it's gone the world seems quieter than ever, like we're underwater. He stands there, his hands in his pockets, just watching. If it wasn't the middle of the night he'd look like a tourist, or a casual passer-by, pausing for a few desultory moments to read the *TRESPASSERS WILL BE PROSECUTED* sign, wondering who owns Tyme's End these days.

He crosses the road slowly, as if he doesn't care if he gets runs over, and goes right up to the gates. He reaches out and touches the padlock, shakes it a little, so it chinks on its chain. It's like he's checking how securely it's locked. Then he leans forward and rests his forehead against the bars.

He stays there for so long my heart stops thumping and my breathing goes back to normal. I take a few steps forward, so that if he looked round he'd see me, but he doesn't move. I keep going until there's only the width of the road between us.

He's mostly in the shadows, and his clothes and hair are dark, so it's as if he's blurred at the edges. His hands and neck are very pale. I can see the shape of his back through his jumper, the breadth of his shoulders.

I open my mouth because I want to say something, but I can't manage to speak. I feel strange, like I'm not quite real. I'm scared that if I called out to him he wouldn't hear me.

More than anything in the world I want to go up behind him and touch the bare nape of his neck, where his jumper dips. I don't know why. I want him to turn and see me and –

Somehow I know he's going to turn round a split second before he does.

He frowns. For a moment we stare at each other, silently. Then we both speak at exactly the same time.

I say, 'I wasn't following you. I just wanted to say I was sor—'

He says, 'Leave me alone. Go away. *Go away.*'

I run home without looking back. I stumble through the front door and slam it. I nearly bolt it behind me, so he has to stay outside all night. He's got Tyme's End, after all; he can stay there, with the rats and wasps and my emergency whisky and Coke. But I have just enough self-control not to do it. I pound up the stairs to my room, not caring if I wake Sam up, and slam that door behind me too.

I don't cry. I refuse to cry.

I *wasn't* following him. Not like that. I just –

I shut my eyes and think of Tyme's End, quiet, waiting for him beyond the locked gates. I remember that moment, just before he saw me, when I felt like a ghost. I wanted to touch him. I wanted him to –

I curl up on my bed without taking my shoes off. I arrange my papers around me, building a landscape of computer printouts and pictures from magazines, desert and dusty villages and bright Mediterranean sea and tower blocks and beaches. I do it so that when I narrow my eyes it's as if I'm looking out of a blurry aeroplane window, gazing down at the place where I was born. Then I put my favourite photo in front, so the background merges into the rest of the pictures. Now my mother's standing there with me in her arms, and behind her the country is spread out in widescreen Technicolor. She's grinning at the camera. I stare at her and try to remember what it felt like to be held like that, to be so small she could balance me on her hip.

I keep looking, until I've almost convinced myself I'm there. I concentrate, blocking out the noise of the road and the scent of the rain still coming through my window.

After a long time I fall asleep. I don't hear Oliver come back in.

*

The next morning I'm sitting behind the counter in Eddie's shop, my head in my hands and my sunglasses on, because the light's streaming through the front window and my eyes don't feel up to the challenge. I feel hungover, even though I'm not. I didn't sleep very well; I had uneasy, sticky dreams that left a kind of damp taste in my mouth and made me struggle to escape from my duvet. Now I feel like death – and I don't look much better, according to Eddie. He was whistling a second ago, but I made a noise like an animal caught in a trap and he shut up. Now he's piling books on top of each other with exaggerated care, making a point of how quiet he's being. He glances round at me and smirks. I ignore him.

Leila comes through from the back office with a cup of tea. She puts it in front of me. 'There you are, lovely. Toast?'

'Don't give her toast, she'll get crumbs in the till.'

'No thanks, Leila,' I say. I don't want breakfast. When I left the house Mum was cooking a full English, presumably for Oliver, and the smell made me want to throw up.

She pats my hand. 'No problem. Any time, honey. We foreigners need to stick together.'

Right now, I could do without people telling me I'm a foreigner. But she means well, and she's just made me a cup of tea, so I only smile.

Eddie says, 'I'm a foreigner too, if it comes to that.'

'Being Welsh doesn't count,' Leila says.

He mock-scowls at her through his beard. 'Try telling Owen Glendower that.' He squints at my tea and then turns back to Leila. 'And where's mine?'

'No, maybe you're right.' Leila winks at me. 'They're not like those polite English people. Always wanting something, the bloody Welsh.'

'It's easy to be polite when you've stolen everyone else's country. Now – *tea*, woman! And make it –'

The bell tinkles and Eddie stands up to peer round the bookcase into the front area. I slouch down and close my eyes behind my sunglasses, because I can't handle someone I don't know, not first thing in the morning, when I feel this rough.

Eddie says, 'Good morning. Do excuse the mess – I've just had a delivery.'

'That's OK.' The voice hesitates. It's a soft, American-sounding voice. Oh, crap. I slide even further down, so I'm almost hidden behind the counter. 'Um . . . I just wanted to look around.' He clears his throat. 'It says outside, second-hand books?'

'That's right, boyo. Section through there – see the doorway?' He never calls anyone *boyo* in real life, but he likes to make a point of it for the tourists.

Either Oliver doesn't notice me as he goes past, or he's ignoring me. I'm glad. I glance up and then force myself to turn away, because it's not as if I care what he looks like. He doesn't seem to see me.

Then he stops. He reaches sideways to the nearest bookcase and pushes against the books with his fingers in a strange, tense, distracted way, as if he's trying to keep his balance. He's looking at Eddie's half-built display. He doesn't say anything, but he's pressing so hard that the top joints of his fingers bend backwards.

Eddie looks up from his unpacking and says, 'New

book. Just in. One for the tourists.' Then he adds, hastily, 'We get a very high class of tourist, you know, very educated, not just your average –' He's probably about to say *your average American*, because he stops. He pulls another armful of books out of the box and proclaims, '*Mapping the Sands: The Strange Inner Life of H. J. Martin*. Nice cover. I mean, they all use that photo, but the blue's good, unusual – normally they're sort of yellowish.'

A pause. Eddie looks from him to me, raising his eyebrows, and I shrug, knowing he can't see through my sunglasses. Finally he says, 'Well. Feel free to have a look if you want.'

Oliver takes one of the books from the display and flips through it awkwardly. His fingers slip and fumble with the pages. He stops in the middle, on a page of photos. I count to ten slowly. Then he puts the book back in the display case and looks round, as if he's seeing the H. J. Martin section for the first time. He clears his throat. 'How many – you've got a lot of biographies of H. J. Martin.'

'Well, yes. That's what a lot of people come for. Bit of a pilgrimage site, Falconhurst. I do the books, Malcolm down the road is the Secretary of the H. J. Martin Society. Steeped in history, this bit of the world.' Eddie staggers to his feet with an armload of books. 'Not you, then? He was a fascinating man, though. I recommend *The Owl of the Desert* if you're at a loose end while you're here.' Eddie grins, pointing to the de luxe illustrated edition in the window, which costs a good thirty quid more than the paperback classic. Then his smile slips. 'Now I may be wrong, but haven't you been here before? A long time ago? I seem to remember –'

'No, I don't think so. I don't remember. Possibly.' A pulse is beating in Oliver's temple. He rubs at his face with his hand, as if he's trying to hide it, or his expression.

'Oh, well.' Eddie walks past him and starts to prop the books up one by one, until there are dozens of them, all with black-and-white faces on the front. 'Great writer, H. J. Martin, interesting man . . . One of the most controversial and intriguing figures of the twentieth century.'

I know for a fact that he's quoting the blurb of *The Owl of the Desert*. He looks wistfully at the book in the window and back at Oliver, then sighs and gives up. He adds, more casually, 'The grave's in the churchyard. Pity the house isn't open to the public.'

'Is it? A pity?' His voice is tight, but Eddie doesn't notice.

'We've got a petition somewhere, if you fancy signing it. Thousands of names. Not that we've ever had a bloody answer. But you have to think, sooner or later –'

'You're probably wasting your time.'

'I doubt the solicitors pass it on to the owner, frankly. Every month we send off the new names, get a nice little note back – yes, thanks very much, all duly noted. But there's never been anything else. And the house – have you seen it? It's a disgrace. I mean, even if it wasn't of historical interest it's scandalous, letting a listed building go to seed like that. Must have been worth a bomb when the old man died. It was in a decent state then, but *now* –'

Leila comes through the door with a mug of tea.

31

'Eddie! Let the poor gentleman look at the books. He doesn't need a rant.'

'It's all right, I'm just browsing.' Oliver smiles at her, but it seems to take an effort. He glances at the books again and takes an odd, lurching step sideways, as if he's trying to get past the display. Unexpectedly, he catches my eye.

For a second I think he hasn't recognised me, or that he has and he's going to smile at me or say hello. Then he turns sharply on his heel and strides towards the door to the street. Eddie rocks backwards, surprised.

Suddenly, for no reason, I feel my throat constricting. It's stupid. I don't care what he thinks of me. I don't *care*.

I say, 'You could just give him the petition now, Eddie. Now that he's actually *here*. Then at least you'd know he'd seen it.'

Eddie frowns and does a kind of double take. 'Er . . . ?'

Oliver pauses, so abruptly it looks like it was involuntary, on the doorstep. I see his shoulders move as he takes a deep breath.

'He owns Tyme's End. That's him. The mysterious owner. Why don't you just hand the petition over right now?' My voice comes out hoarse and spiteful.

'Oh.' Eddie and Leila swap a glance. 'Er . . .'

'He told us last night. He's staying with us. He's going to sell it.'

'Well, that's –'

'To the highest bidder. He doesn't care who gets it. So it'll probably be converted into commuter flats. Won't that be nice?'

Oliver puts the flat of his hand on the door, spreading his fingers out on the glass so that a mist grows between them like mould. Without turning round, he says, 'That's right. Won't it be nice.'

Eddie says, 'Oh. Well, maybe – if I could give you Malcolm's phone number – the H. J. Martin Society might –'

'Tyme's End is *mine*. I don't want it, but that's the way it is. So –' He does turn round, then. His eyes are narrowed, shining brown-green, and he's looking straight at me. One dark lock of hair has fallen over his forehead. 'Jesus! What's your problem? Why don't you mind your own business? Just – *leave me alone*.'

He slams the door. The bell tinkles and clinks and finally rattles into silence.

'Oh dear.' Eddie coughs. 'I can see why he wouldn't want everyone in the village to know that –'

I pick up my mug with both hands and take a sip, but it doesn't taste of anything. I put it carefully back down on the counter. 'Sorry, Ed. Sorry, Leila.' My voice doesn't sound like mine.

Leila says, 'Honey, are you –'

But by then I'm out of the door.

I can't go to Tyme's End, and I don't know where else to go. So I go home.

III

I get in through the front door and Mum and Dad are talking about me.

I don't realise at first. I go through to the kitchen, because I'm hungry all of a sudden. There are some leftover sausages sitting on top of the fridge and I eat one of them in two greasy, salty bites. It makes me feel queasy, but I take the other one and eat that too. I sit down at the table and put my head on my arms. I feel like crap.

Dad's voice comes through the doorway. I didn't know they were there, so it's not like I'm eaves-dropping, and anyway he's talking so quietly I only catch one word in three. 'It's only . . . no friends in the village and . . . holidays . . .'

Mum says, 'I know . . . summer job . . . but . . . miserable . . . don't know what to *do* . . .'

'Teenager, Meg . . . but guests . . . can't let her . . .'

Mum raises her voice. 'We don't know that's why he's leaving.'

'Oh, come on. She didn't exactly make him welcome. Jesus, Meg, it's like she's going out of her way to sabotage everything.'

'Maybe she needs more attention.'

'She already gets more than Sam, and *he's* – oh, Christ, Meg, I'm not saying she's –'

I raise my head and look at the wall in front of me. I say loudly, 'Not saying she's *what*?'

There's a pause. In the corner of my eye I see a blurry shape come and stand in the doorway, but I keep staring at the wall.

Mum says, 'I suppose you were listening to all of that?'

'I was having breakfast. What was I supposed to do? Put my fingers in my ears?'

Dad says, 'Our guest has decided to leave.'

'So?'

'So,' Mum says, 'we were trying to arrive at an understanding of what might have influenced his decision.'

'You mean you think I drove him away.'

'No, of course not, darling.' Her voice is soft and careful. 'He said himself that it wasn't anything to do with you.'

'Right.'

'But the fact remains,' Dad says, 'that he paid for four nights in advance. And then this morning he came and told us, very politely, that he'd changed his plans.'

'So he changed his plans. People do, you know.' I sound too aggressive, but I can't help it. They're right, and I hate them. Of course it's my fault. After what happened last night, and just now with Eddie and Leila, who *wouldn't* cut and run? 'Sorry you've lost all that money. Why don't you feed me on bread and water for the next week, to make up for it?'

'Don't be so stupid, Bibi –'

'He wouldn't take a refund,' Mum says. 'He said that as we'd reserved the room for him –'

'Great. What a perfect bloody gentleman.'

Dad hisses through his teeth and swaps a look with Mum. 'Bibi, we're trying very hard to be reasonable. The B. & B. pays your school fees, you know. If –'

'And Sam's. And his are more than mine.'

'Yes, but Sam –'

'Isn't adopted.' I spit the word at him.

'Oh, for crying out loud! Sam isn't being a *complete bloody pain in the arse.*'

'Having to spend your own money on someone else's kid,' I say. 'Sorry, that's rough. I can see why you're so miserly. I expect you're wishing you'd never agreed to take me in –'

'Bibi,' Mum says, 'this is not the issue. Stop trying to use it as a weapon. You know we love you just as much as –'

'Or would do,' Dad says, 'if you weren't being so obnoxious. I am so *tired* of all this. Actually, sometimes I *do* wish I'd never –'

'Chris! Don't be so –' Mum says; but it's too late.

I look up at them both and the silence grows. I can still taste the sausages. I feel sick.

Dad takes a deep breath. 'Come on, Bibs, you know what I mean. If Sam were behaving like this, I'd wish I'd never had *him.*'

I stand up and walk to the door. Neither of them tries to stop me.

I say, 'I'm sorry if I made Oliver go away. I didn't mean to.' Then I turn round and walk down the hall

36

and out of the house. I shut the front door with a cool, distant click. I make my way carefully down the street, as if it's in danger of collapsing under my feet at any moment. The sky is a high, cloudless blue. The sun blazes into my face. I tilt my head back and wrap my arms round myself, squeezing until my shoulders start to ache. But I still feel cold.

At least if Oliver has gone, it means I can go back to Tyme's End.

The High Street is full of tourists, even more than yesterday, because Saturdays are always the worst. There are already a couple of people sitting outside the Cloven Hoof with pints of real ale and OS maps. But I'm not really here; I walk steadily, slowly, and somehow everyone gets out of my way. Eddie's shop is doing good business. I see someone come out, already getting his copy of the new H. J. Martin biography out of the bag, turning it over in his hands so that the cover reflects the sun. I keep walking and he glances up and stumbles out of my path just in time.

I go past the gates to Tyme's End and round the corner. I'm still treading lightly, gliding, as if I'm trying not to touch the ground. I don't want anyone to see me, or hear me, or touch me. I pretend I don't exist.

I stand in front of the cracked wall, and for a moment it occurs to me that I could go somewhere else. I could even go home.

It isn't *home*, though. If anywhere is home, it's Tyme's End.

It's like someone else puts my hands on the top of

the wall. I don't particularly try to move, but I find myself scrambling up and over the way I always do. I catch my finger on something and it starts to bleed, but it doesn't hurt.

I walk through the long grass and the sun beats down and I'm still cold. The strange, muffled, numb feeling stays with me all the way through the darkness of the sitting room and the corridor, up the stairs, and then I'm sitting on the groundsheet on the bed, bathed in sunlight from the window, and I pick up the corners of the groundsheet and wrap myself up like a parcel, because I'm freezing. I wonder about the whisky and Coke and whether this is an emergency, but the thought of it makes the stale taste of sausage flood on to the back of my tongue. I sit very still, as if I'm inside a blister of calm that might rupture at any moment.

It isn't that Mum and Dad are angry with me. *I*'d be angry with me if I were them. I *am* angry with me. It's not that we fight. All my school friends fight with their parents. It's not that. It's just –

I don't belong here. I don't belong with Mum and Dad and Sam. And no matter how much they love me, they can't change that. Leila's right – I'm a foreigner. I always will be. But I don't belong anywhere else, either. None of this is *mine*.

That's why I like Tyme's End so much. It's ship-wrecked, like me.

I take deep breaths. I don't want to cry, even now that I'm on my own. I'm scared of how miserable I might be, if I let myself think about it. I say aloud, 'Don't be so self-indulgent. Don't be so self-dramatising. For God's sake, Bibi, don't be so *stupid*!'

It almost works. I sit up a bit straighter and put on Sam's don't-you-know-there's-a-war-on? voice. 'Gosh, Bibi, I think you're being jolly ungrateful. If it were me, I should simply *jump* at the chance to be English. Just because you were born somewhere else doesn't mean you can't be almost as English as the rest of us. You're here now, so why don't you buck up? I agree, it's a bit unfortunate, but if you try to put the past behind you, we'll agree to say no more about it.'

If Sam had said it, it would have been funny. But somehow, when I'm on my own, it sounds flat and empty and echoes in the room like it wasn't a joke.

I try to laugh, and then I'm crying, instead.

I don't know how long I cry for. I put my head down on the groundsheet and sob into the plastic. After a while I have to move because there's a little puddle of tears and snot and spit collecting in the dent underneath my face. I wipe my face with my arms and sit up and take deep breaths but then the tears well up again. I tell myself it's because I didn't sleep properly and I didn't have a proper breakfast, but that doesn't make me feel any better. I think of Mum and Dad's faces, and Oliver when he told me to go away, and the way I ran off without answering when Leila asked me if I was OK, and in the end I stop trying to be sensible and let myself cry. The last tiny bit of my brain is glad I'm here, not at home, and I can make as much noise as I want.

I curl up and put my hands over my face. I can feel the bedsprings quiver underneath me when I move. The frame of the bed squeaks, and the plastic makes a sticky kind of crackling noise. I can't breathe smoothly; when I inhale it's like my lungs have to keep changing gears.

In the end I quieten down. I lie and stare out of the window at the tops of the trees. They glow a bright, unlikely green. The sky is still completely blue. When I blink the world blurs and wavers. Then the water rolls out of my eyes and it's clear again. It's almost restful, letting things go from soft-focus to real and back again.

I don't know how I know I'm being watched. The feeling grows gradually, like a seed. At first I don't move, but it gets stronger and stronger. I'm not scared, but I stay still, like I'm playing dead. But in the end I have to look.

It's Oliver. Of course. He's standing in the doorway, leaning against the frame as if he's been there for a long time.

I sit up and wipe my nose and say, 'All right, all *right* – I'm going –'

'It's OK,' he says.

'I'm *going*, I just came to – I thought you'd . . . What?'

He shrugs and scrapes at the ground with his toe. For a split second he looks about fifteen. 'I – you were crying. I couldn't help hearing. Sorry.'

There's nothing sensible to say to that, so I don't answer.

'Listen, I –' He puts his hands in his pockets, without looking up. 'I came to get your book for you. I thought it wasn't fair of me to make you leave it here, so . . .'

My book? I want to laugh. I say, 'Oh. Right. Thanks.'

'I was here anyway, I mean, but I thought – but obviously you came to get it yourself, so . . .' He tails off. 'I was going to apologise for being rude to you.'

'Were you? Why?'

He opens his mouth. Then, suddenly, he looks straight at me and grins. 'I have no idea. Good point.'

I grin back at him; I can't help it. Then I realise what I must look like and wipe my face on my sleeve. When I can see again he's sitting against the wall, fumbling in his pocket. He sees me looking and says, 'Cigarette?'

'I don't smoke.'

'Me neither.' He takes the cellophane off the packet and taps a cigarette out into his hand, then lights it. He's got a heavy silver lighter that throws a reflection into the corner of the room. 'This is my first for ten years.'

'So why –?'

'Bloody England. I can't handle it. No, not England, just this bit of it. I can't –' He stops all of a sudden, as if he's said too much. 'Never mind. Don't start. It's a horrible habit.'

'Yeah, I know.'

The corner of his mouth twitches, and he glances at me through the smoke.

I think he's going to say something – ask me what the matter is, or say something meaningless and comforting, or talk about something irrelevant like the weather – but he doesn't. He just sits there and smokes, so there's no sound but his breathing and my sniffles. He's staring at the floor, and he turns his head every time the house creaks. But the pause doesn't feel awkward. I let it go on until I can't imagine either of us speaking, ever.

The sunlight from the window creeps further into the room, and the smoke wavers and spreads out.

Eventually he stubs the cigarette out on his shoe, looks round for an ashtray, and finally puts the dog-end back into the packet.

I say, 'Were you really going to apologise to me?'

'Yes. Well, I was going to leave your book with the people at the bookshop, and if you'd been there, I might have. Apologised.'

'Oh.'

This time the silence does make me uncomfortable, even though he's not looking at me. I say, 'You were only rude because – I mean – sorry. About following you, and telling Eddie that you owned Tyme's End. I was – it was a bit –'

He looks up expectantly, as if he's waiting for the end of my sentence.

I screw my face up. 'Vile. Me. I was vile. I didn't mean to be, I just –'

'Thank God you think so,' he says, leaning forward. 'I thought you were being vile too. But I thought maybe it was just me, and I was overreacting. That's a weight off my mind.' He has to be joking, but he doesn't sound like he is.

'Wait. You thought I was vile but you were still going to apologise?'

'Um. Yes. God, how English.' He shakes his head, mocking himself.

'I thought you were American.'

'No.' He raises his eyebrows. 'No. I went to the US when – ten years ago. When my grandfather died. This is the first time I've been back.'

'Oh.'

More silence.

He says, 'I didn't *watch* you crying or anything.'

'What did you do? Close your eyes?'

He catches my eye and smiles, making a funny movement with his head that could be a nod or a shake. Then he says, 'I'm sorry. If I – if whatever upset you had anything to do with me. If I got you into trouble with your parents.'

'They're *not my* –' It's automatic. I stop, but he's watching me like he's listening. I lace my hands round my knees and say, more quietly, 'They're not my parents.'

'I thought maybe . . .' He trails off too, as if he's scared of saying something wrong. 'You don't look much like them. I did wonder.'

I laugh, but not because it's funny, exactly. 'You mean I look Middle Eastern and they look English?'

'N—' He bites his lip. 'Um, yeah. Essentially. Yes.'

'No shit, Sherlock.' I roll my eyes at the look on his face.

'I didn't mean –'

I shrug, and he doesn't finish his sentence. Then I look out of the window at the sunlight on the trees, and hear my voice as if it's coming from a long way away. 'I'm adopted. It's sort of complicated, because Mum – the one you met – is my real father's cousin. Was, I mean. He had a heart attack. My mother was an Israeli Arab. I was born in Tel Aviv. But after my father died she moved to England to be with his family, and she . . . Mum helped out with me when I was small. And then she – my real mother went a bit . . . funny. I mean, I don't blame her, with me to bring up.' It's a joke, and I grin fiercely at him, but he bites his lip and meets my gaze without smiling. Something about his expression makes me want to cry again. I clear my throat. 'I don't think she spoke English all that well, and she didn't like it here much, and . . . Anyway, there was an accident. She walked out in front of a car, on a really fast, busy road.' I hunch my shoulders, like I've frozen in the middle of a shrug. 'So Mum and Dad took me in. It wasn't that they wanted to adopt kids, it was just that I needed someone to look after me, and they didn't want me to go into care.'

'They must have loved you already.'

I glance at him for signs of irony, but he's looking out of the window as if he's thinking about something else.

'Either that or they felt guilty.'

'I don't think the one necessarily excludes the other,' he says, tilting his head as if he's trying to get a better view of the sky.

I open my mouth to snap at him. But he isn't trying to make me feel better, the way everyone else does. He's not saying stupid, comforting things that neither of us believes. It's as if his attention is on something else, so he can say casual, careless things that might actually be true.

It's because he doesn't seem to feel sorry for me that I can say, 'The driver of the car said she looked him straight in the eye, and – just walked out in front of him. He was going really fast, and . . . He said he thought she was crazy.'

He looks at me then.

'I'm not supposed to know that. I heard Mum and Dad talking about it, when I was small. They didn't know I was listening.' I swallow. 'Do you think – if someone wanted to kill themselves, do you think they might . . . ?'

'Accidents do happen,' he says slowly. 'They drive on the right, don't they, in Israel?'

A pause.

'Yes,' he says. 'I suppose someone might do that. It's possible.'

'I'm not saying she meant to – I just –' Suddenly my throat fills up with a hard slippery lump, like wax. I swallow but it won't go away, and I know that if I carry on talking I'll start to cry. I've never asked anyone that before. There's never been anyone I could ask, who'd give me an honest answer and not care too much if I got upset.

His hand makes a short movement, as if he's about to touch me, but he doesn't. 'Is that what you think happened?'

'No. No, it isn't. But I don't *know*. If I knew, one way or the other . . . I hate it that I don't know and I'll never know.'

'Yes,' he says. 'That does pretty much suck.'

He sounds so matter-of-fact that I laugh.

'On the other hand, you do have two parents who love you. Presumably.'

'They're not my real parents.'

'Yes, you said. But they love you. That's something.'

I say, 'It's not enough.'

He flicks a glance at me. 'Yeah. I know how you feel.' He digs for his cigarettes, and an odd smile plays round his mouth. 'You poor little orphan.'

I stare at him. I think how stupid I was to think that

he was actually being nice. I say icily 'How could you possibly *know how I feel*?'

'I feel – I felt – the same. I never knew my parents either. My mum got cancer when I was two, and my dad –'

He stops and lights another cigarette. It's only when he's put his lighter back in his pocket that he meets my gaze. There's a pause, as if we both need time to take in what he said. Then he smiles, a bit too quickly, and flicks the ash off his cigarette, even though he's only just lit it.

Suddenly I'm scared to say anything in case I make a mess of it. Suddenly I have an urge to go and sit next to him. But I stay where I am, just watching him.

He stares down at the rectangle of sunlight from the window. He reaches out and runs his middle finger along the edge of it. The ribbon of cigarette smoke streams up through the light, blue-grey, almost opaque.

'I met my father a couple of times. The last time was when I was about thirteen. He didn't die – he chose to leave. I don't know if that's better or worse. But I had my grandfather. And he was – he loved me a lot. Well, as far as I know.' He laughs softly. He digs at the floor with his fingernail, as if he's trying to scratch the sunlight away.

'But – you didn't think it was enough?'

'What?'

'You said, just now. That you felt the same way as me, about – I mean, when you met your dad – what was it like?'

'I –' He looks up. His voice cuts out, like a car stalling. For a second it's like he's looking straight through me, that he can see someone else where I'm sitting. It's a weird, horrible sensation. Then his face changes – snaps shut, like a padlock – and he gets to his feet. 'How did we get on to this? Look, I – I'm sorry you're adopted. Poor you. It must be terrible. Now get your stuff.'

'I only –'

'Come on. You can't stay here.'

'I wasn't being nosy, you started talking about –'

'Right. Well, now I've stopped.' He goes out into the corridor. There's a rucksack leaning against the wall, and he swings it on to his shoulder. 'I don't even know why I told you that.'

'Because you were trying to make me feel better?' I kneel up on the groundsheet, putting a hand on the windowsill to steady myself. The strange, intimate silence that filled the room a minute ago has dissolved so quickly I can't remember what it felt like.

'Probably because I know I'll never see you again. Did you have anything else apart from your book? If so, you'd better get it. You're not coming back here.'

I reach for my book and hold it against my chest, hugging it. I say, 'You can't stop me coming back. You're leaving.'

'Do your parents know you spend so much time here?'

I squeeze the book tighter and tighter. I say, 'You can't. You won't. Don't you *dare* tell them –'

He shrugs stiffly. 'You shouldn't be here. I don't know if it's structurally sound any more. If the roof came down you could be very seriously –'

'That's bollocks.'

'Did you bring anything else, or is that everything?'

I glare at him. He doesn't seem to care. He stares straight back at me, with that closed, unsympathetic look on his face.

I stand up, go to the space by the fireplace, and take out my tin of biscuits and bottle of whisky and Coke and my torch. His forehead creases when he sees the torch, as if it worries him, and I open my mouth, ready to say, 'Yes, fine, I know, I *really* shouldn't be here alone in the dark.' But he doesn't say anything, so I just pick everything up in my arms and say, 'OK.'

He steps aside so that I have to walk in front of him, down the stairs and out into the sudden heat and sunlight.

If it wasn't for the weather, we could've gone back in time, to yesterday. Oliver stands in the long grass and jerks his head towards the cracked bit of wall. 'Go on.'

'Are you going to tell my parents that I come here?'

'Not if you promise to stay away.'

I don't say anything. We just look at each other.

'Goodbye, then,' he says. He drops his rucksack on the ground and crouches to adjust the straps, frowning.

'Are you really going back to America?'

'Yep.'

'What about – never mind.' I turn to leave, and then turn back. 'So you're still going to sell it? Tyme's End?'

'I'll get the solicitors to sort it out. I only came back because – I needed to see it. I wanted to find out if –' He stops.

'I thought you hated it. I thought you wanted to raze it to the ground.'

'I do,' he says, and rubs his forehead with one hand. 'I do.'

I glance over my shoulder. There are tiny dark green rags of ivy fluttering in the attic window, and I can hear birdsong. Oliver follows my gaze and takes a long, deep breath. Under the tobacco I can still smell the clean washing-powder scent of his clothes.

I hear myself say, 'Give Tyme's End to me.'

'What?'

'If you don't want Tyme's End, give it to me.'

The words sit in the air as if someone else said them. *Give it to me.* I want to laugh, but at the same time I'm filled with a kind of irrational certainty. It's as if Tyme's End itself is telling me something.

Give Tyme's End to me.

And for a brief, clear moment, I know – absolutely, without a shadow of a doubt – that he will.

49

IV

Oliver looks at me, and his eyes widen. He stands up slowly and starts to laugh.

'I'm serious,' I say.

He's still laughing, but there's a funny constricted note in his voice. 'I can't, Bibi. I'd love to but I can't.'

'Why not? You don't need the money, or you wouldn't have left it ten years and let it end up like this. Please –' I sound like a five-year-old begging for sweets. 'It's the only place I feel at home. Please. I love it. You don't want it. *Please.*'

For an odd, weightless moment I wait for him to agree. He puts his hands in his pockets and turns to look at Tyme's End. It's as if he can see someone there.

Then, without moving his eyes, he says, 'What do you know about H. J. Martin?'

At first I think it's a rhetorical question, until he turns to look at me. His expression doesn't give anything away.

'What?' There's a pause. 'About H. J. Martin? Not a lot,' I say. He waits, as if he's expecting me to say something else. I rub one foot against the side of my

50

other leg, trying to scrape the grass seeds off my jeans. When I look up he's still waiting. I clear my throat, feeling stupid. 'He lived here. Um. He fought in the Second World War. In North Africa. He –' Oliver winces and glances away, and I stop. 'What?'

'*First* World War,' he says. 'The *First* World War. He fought in Egypt and the Middle East.'

'Egypt is North Africa.'

'All right. Go on.' His face is neutral, impassive, as if he's deliberately not letting me see what he's thinking.

'He got killed on a motorbike on the road – the B2168. There's a stone marking the place. Er . . . there's a museum about him in Falconhurst.'

Oliver nods. 'Is that the extent of your knowledge?'

'He's buried in the churchyard. He wrote a book called *The Owl of the Desert*, which is a really bad title for a book.'

'It's a quotation.'

'So is "to be or not to be", but that doesn't make it a good title.'

He hunches his shoulders and laughs, although there's a kind of scratchy note in his voice. Then he says, 'And that's all you know.' It's not quite a question, so I don't answer him, and he takes a long breath and hisses out through his teeth. 'Bibi, Tyme's End isn't – I know this sounds weird, but – Tyme's End isn't just a house. It's *his* house – it was his house.'

'I thought it was your house.'

'Legally, yes. That's not exactly what I mean.' He pulls at his lower lip with his finger and thumb, looking back at the house over his shoulder. His eyes are narrowed, as if he's looking at something a long

51

way away, trying to focus on it. 'I –' He breaks off, with a short gulp that's almost a laugh. 'Never mind.'

'No,' I say. 'What *do* you mean?'

'Nothing.' He picks up his rucksack and reaches roughly for my arm. 'Nothing. No, you can't have Tyme's End. Now, go away.'

'Are you – you're not saying it's *haunted*?'

And I giggle. I can't help myself. It's not that it's funny. It's just that he must be at least twenty-five, and the sun's blazing down, and he's biting his lip and looking nervously over his shoulder for ghosts.

His grip on my arm tightens until it's painful, and he swings me round so that we're face to face. This time I think he knows he's hurting me.

'You're right,' he says. 'Of course I'm not saying that. What happened in the past stays in the past. Don't you agree?'

'I –' It's hard to speak because my throat's tightened up. I'm not scared of him, but – 'I don't understand.'

'No.' He lets go of me all at once. 'Why would you? You're just a kid. An ignorant, bad-mannered kid. You don't know about the past, and you don't care. It's all so simple, isn't it? What happens to *you* matters, and what happened to other people a long time ago doesn't, and you don't even realise that they're sometimes the same thing.'

I stare at him. His eyes are narrowed against the sun and his irises are so dark I can't tell where they end and his pupils begin. He's looking at me as if he hates me. I say, 'I'm not ignorant.'

He makes a tiny, dismissive gesture with one hand.

'OK.' I turn round and walk away, towards the saplings and the brambles and the cracked bit of wall.

The tears are threatening to come back, but I squash them down. The biscuit tin digs into my wrists. I must look ridiculous, with my biscuits and torch and big sloshing bottle of Coke. I concentrate on not dropping anything, because I don't want to think about what Oliver just called me. I don't know why I care – it's not like he's a friend of mine – but I do. I'm *not* ignorant. I'm not bad-mannered, except when people are rude to me first. And I'm not, I'm *not* a kid.

I squeeze the tin too tightly. The lid makes a kind of clanking sound and pops up at one corner. The torch starts to roll off and I try to grab it. And then everything drops into the grass, biscuits scattering everywhere, torch hitting the ground with a worrying thud, a book bouncing off my shoe, the bottle landing flat on its side and gulping gently to itself. A bookmark has lodged itself in a clump of grass. I look down at the broken debris of crumbs and laugh, painfully, until I'm scared Oliver will think I'm crying.

He says, 'Is that Coke, in the bottle?'

'Mainly.' And I'm furious, so miserable I can hardly speak, because I went to all the trouble of filching it and I never even drank it. And it's all his fault. And Tyme's End will be sold, and –

I sniff determinedly, and swallow hard, but it doesn't help.

'Oh, shit.' He breathes in through his teeth. 'OK. This time it *was* me that made you cry, right?'

'I'm fine. Leave me alone.'

'Sure you are.' A pause. 'I'm sorry. I didn't mean that. Not all of it, anyway. It's just – you say you love Tyme's End, but you wouldn't if you – it's not – it's . . . Oh, hell,

I don't know. How can you live here, in Falconhurst, and not even know what war H. J. Martin fought in?'

'That stuff's for tourists,' I manage to say. I'm on my knees, trying to gather everything up, but I keep dropping things. 'I'm not a tourist.'

'No, but –' He stops. Then he's opposite me, picking up my books. He passes them to me, and then reaches for the Coke bottle. 'Mainly Coke, you said?'

'Yes. With whisky. It's for emergencies.'

'Ah.'

He doesn't say anything else. I don't say anything else. We both stare down at the whisky and Coke, watching the bubble rock from side to side like a spirit level. Then, as if we're synchronised, we look at each other at exactly the same moment, and I know we're both thinking the same thing. He presses his lips together like he's trying not to smile. I'm taking deep breaths, trying not to cry, except that now I'm trying not to laugh either.

Then, in a sticky, snotty sort of voice, I say, 'Actually, I think this might qualify. As an emergency.'

'I can't believe I'm doing this,' Oliver says, taking the bottle from me, drinking, and passing it back. We're sitting in the shade, our backs against the wall, side by side with our feet in what used to be a flower bed. The noise from the High Street is muffled by the trees, but we can still hear kids shouting to each other and the occasional whine of a siren going past. 'How old are you, anyway? Seventeen? Eighteen?'

'Sixteen, actually.'

'Oh, bloody hell.' I glance at him, and he shakes his head and gestures to the bottle. 'You're not even old enough to buy that for yourself. If I gave it to you it'd be illegal.'

'Big deal.' I take a mouthful, and another. It's warm and it's gone flat, but the whisky is going straight to my head, and I'm glad. I feel exhausted.

'Yeah, OK,' he says, and waits, his palm out-stretched, for me to give it back.

'So how old are you?'

'Twenty-seven. Old enough to know better.'

I smile, tilting my head back until it rests against the wall. There's silence, except for the kids shouting outside the gates and Oliver swallowing. We're not touching, but I can feel the heat of his shoulder where it's only a few centimetres away from mine. I want to slide sideways until I'm leaning on him, but I concentrate on staying upright.

I say, 'If you hate the place, why do you keep coming back to it?'

He runs his thumb round the top of the bottle, not quite wiping it. At first I don't think he's going to answer me, but he says, 'I told you, this is the first time I've been back since – this is only the second time I've been here.'

'No, I mean, last night you came and just stood and looked through the gates. And yesterday, and today . . . If you hate the place, why are you here at all?'

A pause. He takes three gulps of whisky and Coke in quick succession. Then he passes the bottle back to me. I hold it between my hands, lacing my fingers together like I'm praying.

'Because – something bad happened to me here,' he says. 'I don't like the house, but – I have to be here.

When I'm not, it feels – it's worse. I can't leave it alone. Does that make any sense? I don't *know* why I'm here.'

'Is that why you want to sell it?'

'I want to get rid of it. I don't ever want to think about it again. I want to – delete it. Completely. Even when I went to America, I used to dream about it. Nightmares, I mean. I can't –' He stops and grits his teeth, looking sideways at the bottle in my hands. 'God, listen to me, I'm already half-cut. Forget it. I don't want to talk about it. I want it never to have happened.'

I raise the bottle to my lips and take another sip, tasting the harsh sweetness of the whisky and Coke and something else that could be Oliver's spit. I swill the liquid round in my mouth until my gums start to tingle from the alcohol. Then I swallow. 'What did happen?'

He glances at me, then turns his head to look at the house. I can tell from the shape of his cheek that he's smiling, or grimacing, but I can't see his eyes. 'You don't mind asking straight questions, do you?'

'Should I?'

He doesn't answer.

I slosh the last of the whisky and Coke around in the bottom of the bottle and wonder how we managed to drink it so quickly. I hold it sideways for Oliver, but he doesn't take it. I wait for a few seconds, then drink it myself. I put the empty bottle neatly against the wall and fight the impulse to burp.

Suddenly Oliver leaps to his feet. 'You're right,' he says. 'What the hell am I doing? This is stupid. I need to get over it.'

That wasn't what I said, but I don't say so. I look up at him and then stagger to my feet. The world slides ninety degrees to the right, wobbles, then steadies itself. The sunlight is hot on my face.

'Come on,' he says, and starts to walk away.

'Where are we going?'

'Mystery tour.' He looks over his shoulder, grins, and breaks into a jog. He's left his bag, but I don't tell him that. I follow him. The grass swishes around my legs and the seed heads hit my hands, stinging, like little insects.

He waits for me at the wall, and when I don't manage to get over first time he links his hands and makes a foothold for me, without saying anything, as if it's just good manners. I still have a bit of a struggle getting over and when I start to giggle he does too. Once I'm over I forget to move out of the way, and he has to jump to avoid me. He says, 'Oh, God, you're sixteen and I've got you drunk.'

'Don't be ridiculous,' I say. '*I* got me drunk. You had very little to do with it.'

'Right.' He's laughing at me, but I don't mind.

'Anyway, I'm not as think as you drunk I am.' I sway theatrically and grab at his arm.

'Bibi –' he says. Then he catches my eye. 'Very funny.'

'I thought so,' I say, and I don't let go of his arm.

I don't know where he's taking me, but we walk together down the High Street in the sun, weaving our way between the tourists in wide curves.

'Do you think you could not hold my arm like that? I feel like you're arresting me.' He peels my fingers away from his elbow.

'Oh. Sorry.'

He looks down at me, and for a second I think he's going to say something else. Then he links his arm through mine. I don't know if he's being nice or taking the piss, but somehow I don't care.

We walk in silence. I concentrate on keeping in step with him. It's hard, because he's taller than me. I feel giggly and excited and strange. For a while I think I must be really, properly drunk. Then I realise I'm happy.

To be honest, I might be drunk as well, because it's only when we're outside the church that I realise where we must be going. I look up at him, but he doesn't meet my gaze. He steers me down the path into the churchyard, towards the back of the church and round the yew tree. There are a couple of tourists in the far corner, talking quietly – a woman staring at the headstone, the other one with his face raised to the sky. I open my mouth, but there's something about the greenness everywhere and the silent graves that makes me shut it again without saying anything. The man takes a photo. The woman says something and they both laugh. She's got a tiny bright yellow flower behind her ear. They start to walk away, as if they've looked for long enough, and the man takes her hand. Then she turns back and flicks the flower on to the grave. It spins as it drops, like a bright yellow propeller.

Oliver is watching them. There's a crease between his eyebrows. He looks like someone reading an exam paper.

But even once they've left, he doesn't go over to the

headstone. He disentangles his arm from mine and takes a couple of steps in the other direction, until he's looking at the War Memorial. He says, 'What's your surname?'

'Hope.'

He smiles at me unexpectedly, then looks back at the memorial. 'No Hopes. No Gardners either.'

'Why should there be?'

He shrugs. 'I always check. Don't you?'

'Every time I go past a war memorial?' I'm being sarcastic, but he nods. 'Er . . . no. I'm pretty sure I haven't died for my country. Is that what we came here to find out?'

I shouldn't have said that, because he stops smiling. 'No.' He tilts his head towards the dark headstone where the tourists were. 'No, *that*'s what we came for.'

I stand and wait. He walks over to it slowly, and stands looking down at the grass and the tiny yellow flower. His hand beckons me over.

HUGO JOHN MARTIN
1894–1936
WATCH YE THEREFORE:
FOR YE KNOW NOT WHEN
THE MASTER OF THE HOUSE COMETH.

The silence in this part of the churchyard has a different quality to it: fragile, echoing, like glass. I shake my head and tell myself that's stupid, but I can't get it out of my mind. It's like the air in this corner is thinner. It's harder to breathe.

I say, 'It's not exactly *beloved husband and father*, is it?'

Oliver smiles, but it doesn't reach his eyes. 'He wasn't anyone's husband. Or father.'

'Oh. I just meant – it's not very . . . comforting. The *watch ye therefore* bit. It's a weird thing to choose.'

'I think my grandfather chose –' He stops. He makes a quiet, shocked sound, like someone's just punched him in the stomach.

'Oliver?' In a distant part of my brain I notice that it's the first time I've said his name. I have a stupid, embarrassing desire to say it again.

'My grandfather. Chose it. He inherited everything, so I guess he –' He reaches out as if he's going to lean on the top of the headstone, and then draws his hand back quickly. 'I forgot that. He must have – Jesus. I suppose that means he – God, he *knew* –' He's slurring his words.

'Are you OK?'

'Yes. Yes, I'm fine. I – something just – occurred to –' He looks at the gravestone, and his mouth moves silently. The look on his face is too complicated to read, as if he's shocked and angry and afraid and – somehow rueful, like someone who's run for a bus and missed it by half a second. As if the epitaph is telling him something he wishes he'd known before.

He starts to laugh, painfully, as if someone's told a joke at his expense.

I say, 'Er . . . Oliver?'

'He *knew*,' he says, as if I'll know what he's talking about. 'My grandfather *knew. The master of the house cometh* . . .' He rubs his face, laughing through his fingers. 'But what the hell – how –?'

The silence grows in the space between his words.

60

It isn't fragile any more: it feels heavy, merciless, like snow.

Through his hands, Oliver says, 'Of course. How – simple. He knew because – because he –'

I wait. When he uncovers his face again he looks calm, like a mask.

'Right,' he says.

'Right,' I say, mimicking him.

'Right.' He looks back, just once, at the headstone.

> WATCH YE THEREFORE:
> FOR YE KNOW NOT . . .

Then he walks away. He waits for me at the lychgate, but although he gives me a kind of smile he doesn't take my arm again.

He leads me back the way we came, down the High Street. At first I think we're going back to Tyme's End, but when we pass the cracked bit of wall, instead of clambering over it, Oliver keeps on walking, a few steps ahead of me, and we follow the road as it winds away to the right and the wall disappears behind a screen of trees and bracken. It's quiet, and the woods rustle around us, full of little noises from the undergrowth. I look up and the leaves are like stained glass, blurred out of shape by the sunlight, all green and gold. I want to ask Oliver where we're going now, but it seems wrong to break the silence. He's striding ahead, his head down, and I have to gallop for a couple of paces to catch up with him.

'It's beautiful,' I say, breathless.

He frowns, as if I've said something in a foreign

61

language, and then looks round at the web of sunshine on the road, the high trees. 'Yes,' he says. 'I guess it is.'

There's the swish of a car, and I look round, but it's coming from a crossroads ahead of us. Oliver pauses for a moment, listening. I stand by his side and he glances at me. He looks paler than he did before, pre-occupied. For the first time it's easy to believe that he's twenty-seven.

'You'd better walk behind me,' he says. 'This road is dangerous. If a car comes –'

'I'm not a kid.'

I think he's going to argue with me, but he doesn't. He shrugs and keeps on walking. I feel a perverse surge of disappointment.

We turn left. This road is straight, flat, a wide band of sun-dappled grey narrowing to a point between trees. Oliver speeds up, still walking with his head bowed, his shoulders incongruously hunched as if it's pissing with rain. His hands are in his pockets. The breeze presses his T-shirt into him so that I can see the shape of his back. He breaks into a kind of jog, without taking his hands out of his pockets. He's running in an odd, awkward way, as if he's going up a very steep hill. As if he doesn't want time to think about where he's going.

Then he stops. He leans forward to catch his breath. There's a little shadow of damp in the small of his back. I can feel the sweat sliding down the back of my neck too, like fingers. I'm thirsty.

'Over there,' he says, clearing his throat and tilting his head towards a little clearing a few metres from the edge of the road.

He doesn't move. I look at him, then pick my way

through the bracken, stepping over fallen branches and avoiding bits of bramble. The stone is a kind of flattened prism of sandstone, not quite a plaque. *H. J. MARTIN WAS FOUND DEAD ON THIS SPOT, 21st JUNE 1936.*

I stand in front of it, not knowing what to do. If I were with Mum or Dad I'd say, 'Big deal.' I look round at Oliver, hoping that he'll say something.

He doesn't meet my gaze. He's got a distant expression on his face, like he's listening to something I can't hear. He says, 'No one knows what happened.'

'I thought it was a motorcycle accident.'

His eyes flick to mine and away again. 'It was. But – he shouldn't have come off. He wasn't going particularly fast. He knew the road, and it's straight and level, and there wasn't any traffic. It was early in the morning, but it was probably already light. No one even knows where he was going.'

I'm about to say, 'So?' but I manage to stop myself. I say instead, 'People have accidents. They just do.'

'Yes,' he says, but he doesn't sound like he's agreeing.

I say, as gently as I can, 'Does it matter?'

'What really happened? Does that matter?' He takes a step towards the memorial stone. 'I don't know.' He reaches out, even though the stone isn't close enough to touch. 'You said, about your real mother – if you knew, one way or the other . . .'

'That's –' I breathe in. 'That's different.'

'Why?'

'Because – that matters to *me*.' I wish he'd look at me. 'She was my mother, and – this is different. This happened seventy years ago. He'd be dead by now anyway. And it's not like you knew him. Everyone

63

who knew him must be dead by now.'

He stays where he is. I don't even know if he's listening to me. The trees whisper around us. I wish I knew what he was thinking. I wish I knew why he'd brought me here.

All of a sudden he twists to look at me, so quickly that twigs crack under his feet. His eyes don't quite focus on my face. 'If you knew, for sure, one way or the other – suppose you knew, for sure, that she'd killed herself . . .'

I say, 'Yes?'

But he doesn't finish what he was going to say. He says slowly, 'I think it does matter. I wish it didn't. But I think it does.'

It's hard to keep track of what he's saying. 'You mean, if my mother had –?'

'No.' A split-second shake of his head. 'Of course, but that's not what I mean.' He gestures at the memorial. *H. J. MARTIN WAS FOUND DEAD ON THIS SPOT*. 'Suppose it wasn't an accident? Suppose it happened because –'

He stops. He shakes his head again, as if there's an insect buzzing in his ears.

I swallow. The heat surrounds me, suddenly oppressive. My mouth tastes stale and sour, tacky with sugar. I say, 'Shall we go back? I'm thirsty.'

It's as if he hasn't heard me. Maybe he hasn't.

'My grandfather knew H. J. Martin. They were friends. My grandfather was Martin's heir,' he says, and his words are quiet, precise, without any trace of the American accent he had before. 'He inherited Tyme's End, and – and a lot of money. A huge amount of money. And he –'

There's a pause, filled with birdsong and a siren from a long way away. I feel dizzy, unreal, as if I'm not really here. And Oliver is staring into the middle distance as if someone's standing in front of him.

'I think my grandfather murdered H. J. Martin,' he says.

There's another split-second silence. He turns to me and he's smiling, like he knows that what he just said is ridiculous, melodramatic, unbelievable.

I say, 'Er . . .'

And then suddenly he spins on his heel, ducks behind a tree, and I hear him vomiting.

V

I don't know what to do. I push my hands into the back pockets of my jeans and kick at the bracken, so that if he looks round he'll see that I'm not watching. He coughs wetly, and I hear liquid splattering on to the ground. There's a pause, and I think it's over. Then he gasps and makes a kind of rasping, barking noise. He spits, and makes another noise, halfway between a sigh and a groan. I look at him, in spite of myself, and he's wiping his mouth on his forearm. He glances up but I can't tell if he's seen me or not. He pushes his hair off his forehead with his other hand, and it sticks up, clumpy with sweat. He stands up, bracing himself against the tree. He says, 'God. Excuse me.'

'Are you all right?'

He smiles, coughs, and spits again. He digs at the earth with his toe, wincing. 'Of course. Can't you tell?'

'OK,' I say. 'Stupid question.'

'I didn't mean that,' he says, but it doesn't sound like he cares much, one way or the other. 'Look – let's go.'

I nod. He walks past me and down the road the way we came. I follow him. I feel faintly sick too, as if it's contagious. I want a drink of water. My T-shirt is sticking to me.

'I'm sorry,' he says, without looking round, so the words are almost blown away by the warm breeze. 'I shouldn't have brought you here. It was a really bad idea.'

I hurry to catch up with him, feeling the sweat break out on my forehead. 'Wait. Will you *wait*, please, Oliver –'

He slows down and stops, but he's still staring straight ahead. There's a long blotch of damp on the side of his chest and I can smell alcohol.

'What you said,' I say. 'About your grandfather. Did you –'

'Forget it.'

'So you didn't mean it?'

He looks at me. His expression is so hostile it's bewildering, as if the last few hours haven't happened. 'Just *forget it*.'

'But –'

'It doesn't matter. Isn't that what you said? It doesn't *matter*. What difference does it make to anyone? They're both dead. And there's no evidence. No evidence that would – there's *no* evidence. What are you going to do, run and tell the H. J. Martin Society?' He holds my gaze until I look away. Then he whistles tunelessly through his teeth, and adds, 'They're nutters anyway. Half of them think he's going to come back in England's hour of need, like King Arthur.'

I wait until I trust my voice not to crack. 'I'm not

going to tell anyone. I just – is it true?'

He takes a deep breath. 'Is it true that I believe it, or is it *true*?'

'Do you believe it? That your grandfather murdered H. J. Martin?'

He thinks for a moment. Then he says, 'Yes.'

We keep walking. I feel like the ground is sliding in the opposite direction, like a treadmill, so we're going slower than we should. The silence goes on and on, and things rustle and watch us from the bushes. It's too hot and too quiet. I can't think of anything to say. It's as if Oliver is somewhere else, and the gap's too big to shout across.

At the cracked bit of wall, he turns to me and says, 'You'd better go home.'

'My stuff's still over there.' I point towards the place where we sat to drink the whisky and Coke.

He stands aside without answering and gives me a businesslike hand to get over the wall. I want to stand on the other side and watch him climb over after me, but I trudge through the long grass and collect my biscuit tin and torch and books and empty plastic bottle. Oliver's shadow falls on my hands and I pick up his rucksack and pass it to him. He doesn't thank me.

I stand up with my arms full of stuff. He's got his rucksack over his shoulder. When I look at him, he glances away.

'You've got to stop coming here,' he says. 'I'm going to get someone to do something about that wall, and the railings. You won't be able to get in.'

I stare at him. 'What?'

'I'd better be off. Nice to've met you,' he says,

picking a stalk of grass and rubbing it between his fingers. 'Apologise to your parents for me.'

'What? You're going now?' I say.

'Yeah.' He still won't meet my gaze. 'Thanks for the drink.'

I don't say anything. There's nothing I can say.

'Right then,' he says. 'Can you get over the wall with all that stuff or shall I help you with it?'

I want to throw it at him, bit by bit. I imagine hurling the biscuit tin last of all, how it would hit his head with a resounding clang. 'You're going,' I say, keeping my voice flat. 'Right now.'

'I should catch my train.'

'What time does it leave?'

'It –' He hesitates. 'I'll go down to the station and get the next one. They go every half-hour or so, don't they? Bibi, I should –'

I don't know why, but the way he says my name goes straight to my gut, like a knife. It punctures something I didn't know was there.

I hear myself say, 'Don't go. Not right now. Please don't. Stay a bit longer. Stay until this evening. Please.'

'Bibi, I have to – look, it wasn't a good idea to –'

'Please. *Please*.'

Finally, he looks at me.

'You don't have to go right now,' I say. I can feel the biscuit tin slowly slipping out of my grasp. 'Please. It doesn't have to be horrible.'

'It's a complete disaster,' he says. 'I shouldn't be here. I should never have come.'

I can't think of anything else to say. 'Please.' My heart is beating so hard I can feel the fabric of my T-shirt trembling.

He looks down at me. He's squinting because of the sun, but his eyes are the colours of wood, amber and mahogany and green. He looks at me for so long I'm scared of what he can see in my face. Then he sighs and tilts his head back, defeated. 'I can't stay for long,' he says. 'I do, I really do have to go.'

I feel the air fill my lungs. 'I just –' I swallow. 'I just think you should buy me a drink, because it's your turn and I'm thirsty.'

He laughs: a helpless, abrupt laugh, like a release. 'Fine. Let's go to the pub.'

We look at each other. His eyes flicker, reading my face. Then he turns away.

As we walk I glance up at him. It's as if he notices my look, because he smiles and adds, 'I'm only buying you lemonade, mind.'

'Whisky and Coke,' I say. 'It's only fair.'

'Coke.'

'Shandy.'

'Oh, all right, shandy.' He reaches out and squeezes the back of my neck. 'Hey. How come I offer to buy you a drink and you *negotiate*? Honestly. The kids of today.'

I laugh. I walk very carefully, not making any sudden movements, because I don't think he realises that he's still got his hand on my neck and I don't want him to take it away. And he doesn't. He keeps it there, right up until we have to climb over the wall.

The beer garden of the Cloven Hoof is full of people – all tourists, though, no one I know – so I end up sitting on the wall under the horse chestnut tree while Oliver buys the drinks. The ground is covered with little scraps of brown flowers that stick to the soles of my shoes. I lean back against the trunk of the tree, looking up through the leaves. There's a wood pigeon somewhere, hooting and hooting as if it's trying to make everyone go away.

When Oliver comes back his face is wet, as if he's washed it, and he's carrying a tray with two tall glasses of water and a packet of crisps as well as our drinks. He balances it carefully on the wall and then levers himself up. He says, 'I seem to have done an awful lot of climbing on walls today. One of the waters is yours, so you don't get dehydrated.'

'Thanks.' I drink half of it in one go, and then reach for the shandy. Oliver does the same, and we clink our glasses. 'Cheers.'

For a moment it's like we're on holiday. Oliver lights a cigarette. I open the crisps – I'm starving – and realise I haven't had lunch.

We sit without talking until Oliver's flicked his cigarette away and I've finished the crisps. Then I close my eyes and lean back, half asleep, content.

'I'm not very good company,' he says, after a while.

I open my eyes and squint at him sideways. 'Aren't you?'

He hunches his shoulders, reaches for his cigarettes and then stops himself. 'I mean – God, you must think I'm crazy. *I* think I'm crazy.'

'No. Mysterious. Enigmatic. A bit angst-ridden. A tall dark stranger with a past.' I make a face at him.

'I can't think straight. I don't know what I'm doing here.'

I pick up my glass and tap the rim against my teeth.

'Having a quiet civilised drink with a friend?'

He shakes his head at me, but he's smiling. 'Not what I meant, but –'

I grin. Now we're here and not at Tyme's End, some of the tension that was in his face seems to have relaxed. And he didn't contradict me when I said *friend* . . .

He sits up straighter and finishes his beer. 'Enough about me. What are *you* doing here? Shouldn't you be with your own friends? Drinking cider on street corners or something? Isn't this a bit middle-aged?'

'None of my friends live in Falconhurst. Mum has to drive me to school, so . . . They all live miles away.'

He raises his eyebrows. 'What do you do in the holidays?'

'Sometimes I stay at their houses for a night. Or we meet in town, when Dad can give me a lift. Or I catch the train.' My voice has gone hard and defensive, although I don't know why. 'Anyway, I don't mind.'

'And the rest of the time? Don't you get lonely?'

'I like being on my own,' I say. 'I go to Tyme's End, and I read, and think, and –'

He's staring at me. When he sees that I've noticed, he looks away, with a kind of gentle, anxious expression that makes me angrier.

'I'm fine,' I say. 'I'm *fine*. I *like* being on my own. I –'

He doesn't answer.

'Anyway,' I say, 'it's not like there's anything I can do about it. So my friends all live miles away. It's not a big deal.'

He nods. I wish I hadn't mentioned Tyme's End. I finish my drink. I put the glass down next to his, but he's gazing at the ground and doesn't notice. He's drawing patterns in the withered horse chestnut blossoms with his foot.

He says, 'Tell me about your parents.'

It takes me a second to understand the words. 'What?'

'Your parents. Your real parents. What were they like?'

'I told you. My dad died, and my mum –'

'No, I mean, what were they *like*?' He kicks gently at a wad of pale brown petals on the ground.

'My dad was a engineer. He went to Israel after he left university. He was called Alan. My mum was called Munira. She was sort of dumpy-looking. She was clever. My grandparents were really proud of her.' I shrug. 'What do you want to know?'

'Do you remember them?'

'I – well, not my dad. And – you know when you think you can remember things, but you've been told about them so often you don't know if you're remembering or imagining them?'

'Yes.'

'Well, I can picture my mum like that. I think I remember her playing with me. I can picture her bedroom. I stuffed a lampshade with tissues because it looked pretty and she was angry with me. We saw a house on fire once.' I kick my heels against the wall, slowly: right, left, right, left. 'I don't remember her dying.'

'Do you have photos and things?'

There's something strange in his voice, like the answer means a lot to him.

'A couple. Most of them are in photo albums and I

can look at them, but I'm not allowed to take them out until I'm eighteen, in case I lose them.' There's a pause. I wish he'd say something. I can feel the matter-of-fact look on my face start to crack like varnish.

He nods. He reaches for his cigarettes again. I watch him take one out and light it. After he's lit it he turns his lighter over and over in his hands. His fingers leave smears on the silver.

'I've got a lot of . . . research,' I say. 'I call it that, anyway. It's stupid, but – I haven't shown anyone, ever. Maps and pictures and things. Because –' I'm glad he's not looking at me. 'They're nice, Mum and Dad, I'm not being ungrateful, they didn't have to take me in, and – but I don't belong here. It's not . . . *mine*.'

He tilts the lighter so that I can see his face, reflected. His eyes stare at me, pulled out of shape by a dent in the metal.

'I don't belong here,' I say again. I've never said it aloud before today. 'People look at me with Mum and Dad and Sam and they can *see* I'm not one of them. And here –' I look around at the tourists and the little kids playing on the grass. 'It feels like a foreign country.'

'You don't think you're English, because you weren't born here?'

'I know it's stupid. But – I come from somewhere else. That makes a difference. You said yourself, the past is important. Well, my past is somewhere else.'

He turns his head to one side, frowning, as if he's listening to something a long way away.

I say, 'What's wrong? What did I say?'

'Nothing. You think the past is – passed down in your blood or something.'

'Well –'

'We inherit history. We don't have a choice about how we think, or who we are. It's already decided for us.'

'That wasn't what I –'

'It's an interesting idea. Potentially racist, incidentally, but interesting.'

I twist to stare at him. 'Why?'

'Well, because if who you are comes from your parents and your ancestors, then you automatically have more in common with the people who come from the same genetic background.' His tone is intellectual, faintly amused. His accent is so English he sounds like someone from an old film. He catches my eye and laughs, but there's something uncomfortable in the way he's looking at me. 'I didn't say it was *wrong*. Necessarily.'

A silence.

I say, 'I wasn't saying –'

He reaches out and puts his hand on my arm. 'I'm sorry. You said – you put something into words. You made me think about something else. About – some*one* else. I wasn't taking the piss.'

I look down at his hand. His skin is pale against mine and his palm is warm and slightly damp. I feel as if I've got more nerve endings in that patch of skin than in the rest of my entire body.

'Really, Bibi. It's very . . . biblical. The sins of the fathers being visited on the sons, debts being passed down to people who don't even know what happened.' His voice negotiates the consonants like corners, a little too precise.

Oh, shit. After what he said about his grandfather . . . I can't believe I forgot.

I say, 'Oliver, I only meant – because of who *I* am – because of *my* past – I can't be happy here. I wasn't talking about anyone else.' I'm trying too hard, and my voice is shrill and unconvincing.

He isn't listening anyway. He flicks his fingernail against his empty glass and screws his mouth to one side, as if he's trying to decide whether to buy another round. He says, 'Can I see it? Your . . . research?'

'My –?'

He looks at me. 'I know it's none of my business. You don't have to say yes.'

'Why do you want to? It's not even really about my mum, it's just about –' I imagine my papers, the grubby computer printouts and tourist brochures for Israel and newspaper articles and . . . It means something to me, because – well, because it's a kind of promise to myself, a reassurance that I don't really live *here*, that Mum and Dad aren't really my parents, that some day I'll leave and never come back. But Oliver wouldn't understand. 'Why do you want to see it?'

'Because I –' He laughs shortly, tapping the glass over and over. 'I suppose – I want to know more about you.'

'Do you?' I catch myself on the verge of giggling and blushing and saying, '*Really?*' and control myself just in time.

He nods. He glances sideways, but his eyes don't meet mine. 'You remind me of – someone I used to know.'

Oh. I want to say, 'Who?' but there's something about his face that tells me he doesn't want me to ask. But it doesn't matter. I replay the words in my head: *I want to know more about you* . . . I say, 'All right.'

He smiles at me. 'Thank you.'

'My stuff's in my room, at home. Shall I go and get it now?' I despise myself as soon as I've said it, because I sound like an eager, helpful little girl who wants to be milk monitor. But Oliver doesn't seem to notice.

'If that's OK, yeah, good idea. I told your parents I was leaving this morning, so I don't really want to run into them.' He gestures at my empty glass. 'Another shandy?'

'Yes,' I say. 'I want it waiting for me when I get back. And another packet of crisps. Preferably prawn cocktail. Please.'

The corner of his mouth twitches. 'And the moon on a stick?'

I lean across and punch him on the arm. I don't do it hard, but I can feel solid muscle and the warmth of his skin on my knuckles. He says, unconvincingly, 'Ouch,' and grins at me.

I jump off the wall and make my way towards the side gate on to the High Street. I can feel Oliver watching me leave, but I don't look back. I'm scared that, if I do, he'll be able to see the way my heart is pounding.

By the time I get back the people eating their lunch have finished and gone, and Oliver is sitting at a table, smoking. I've got my special box in a bag across my shoulder, and it's heavy, but I stand where I am for a few seconds, looking at him. He hasn't seen me. His chin is propped on one hand and his hair is falling over his forehead. He taps the cigarette ash on to the table and I want to laugh at how perfectly he does it – how that is the only, the absolutely *best* way of tapping ash in the whole world.

I walk over to him. He doesn't look up until I sit down opposite him. Then he smiles and pushes a full pint glass towards me. 'Madam's shandy,' he says. 'Waiting for her, as requested.'

'Thanks.'

'My pleasure.'

I look at him for too long and I can feel myself starting to blush, so I sling my bag on to the table. 'Here we go,' I say. 'The Habibah Hope Archive.'

'Who's Habibah Hope?'

'Me,' I say. 'It means "beloved". "Darling".' A split-second pause. 'I mean, it means "darling" as well as "beloved". I wasn't calling you –' Oh, bloody hell.

'Really? How disappointing.' He laughs. I join in, but he looks at me in an odd way, as if I haven't done it quite convincingly. 'It's pretty. Habibah. Beloved. It suits you.'

'Yeah. Er . . .' I clear my throat and get my special box out of the bag, open it, and push it across the table to him. 'You said you wanted to see it.'

He nods, and the laughter goes out of his face. I wish I hadn't reminded him; for a second he looked young and ordinary and happy. He takes the box and starts to look at my things, picking them out carefully as if he's taken me seriously about it being an archive. I watch his hands, grateful for the way they treat everything like it's precious.

When I look at his face finally, he's frowning.

'There's a lot of stuff here, Bibi.'

I shrug. 'Whenever I see something that – seems

relevant, I cut it out. I like it when there's so much I can spread it out on my bed or the floor and nothing else shows through.'

'And how much of it is actually about your parents?'

'Quite a lot,' I say. 'There are all the Google maps of where they used to live in Tel Aviv, and the village where my mother was born, and –'

'That's not technically *about* them though, is it? It doesn't tell you anything that might – that would mean anything to you.' He's talking gently, seriously, like a teacher. If he were anyone else I'd tell him to piss off.

'Does it matter?'

'No-o,' he says. 'Just –' Suddenly he covers his face with his hands, rubbing his forehead, and I see his shoulders move as he takes a deep breath. Then he puts his hands down flat in front of him and looks straight into my eyes.

'Bibi,' he says. 'You live here. Here and now. You're not a foreigner.'

I open my mouth, but I don't know what to say. I reach for the nearest bit of paper, but the sun glares on the white and I can't take in what's on it. I say, 'But – this is about my parents. My real parents. It's important to me.'

'Of course. But –' He stops.

'*But?*' I pick up the sheets of paper and put them back in the box. One of the photos of my dad is on the table next to Oliver's elbow and I lay it carefully on top of the rest. My hands look weird, like someone else's.

'But.' He swallows. 'Does this – is it *useful*? Does it make you happy?'

79

'That's not the –' I stop, because I know I've answered his question. I can hear Sam's voice in my head, mimicking me – *You're not my real father* – and my own voice shouting at Dad, spitting *adopted* at him like an insult every time we have an argument. And then I run to my special box, my imaginary Israel with my imaginary parents, where I belong. Or to Tyme's End, to be on my own. I look up at Oliver and it's like he can see what I'm thinking.

I say, 'You said the past was important. You said it matters, that it makes us who we are. So this is me. What's wrong with that?'

He put the box to one side, gently, and pushes my shandy closer to my hand.

'Tell me! What's *wrong with it*?'

He looks over my shoulder. I almost turn and follow his gaze, because I could swear he can see someone there, that he's not talking to me.

He says, 'But we're stronger. We have to be stronger.'

Silence.

It's like something's happened. Something invisible and soundless, but . . . The world's changed in a hidden, quiet way that I can't see.

Oliver's still staring past me. For a second I feel disorientated, dizzy. Something's going on, and I don't know what it is.

I say, 'Sorry. What –? Can you explain what you just said? Subtitles for the hard of understanding?'

He laughs. He looks at me and laughs. And it's strange, it's the first time I've heard him laugh as if he means it, as if he's not thinking about something else at the same time. It's a warm, lovely laugh. It makes the hairs on my arms stand on end with sheer pleasure. I take a quick drink of shandy because I can't look at him.

He says, 'What are you doing now? This afternoon?'

'I'm –' I shake my head. 'Nothing. Why?'

'Why don't we get some food and stuff, and we can have a picnic. By the river, maybe. D'you fancy it?'

'Yes, I do fancy it,' I say, like an idiot. 'That sounds lovely.'

'Splendid.' There's definitely something new in his voice, a kind of excitement. He looks younger than he did. He stands up and points at my shandy. 'Are you going to drink that?'

It's like he's a different person. I laugh and drink as much as I can and offer him the rest. He downs it. Then he gives me his hand to help me up.

I take it and stand up, but neither of us lets go.

He brushes a strand of hair away from my face with his other hand. He says, 'Bibi . . .'

'What?'

'I won't sell it. Tyme's End. It won't be turned into commuter flats. Whatever happens, I promise I won't sell it.'

'Really?' I can't breathe properly.

'Really.' His eyes are steady, but there's something in his expression that I can't identify.

I think he's going to kiss me. But he doesn't.

He drops my hand. I follow him out through the pub on to the High Street. I can feel my face smiling and smiling, as if it's going to crack.

VI

The garage shop is cool and filled with an even, calming hum from the fridges. Oliver spins on his heel, his hands in his pockets, like a little kid. When I catch his eye he grins and shakes his head, laughing at himself. 'Wow!' he says. 'So much stuff. So much surprisingly posh food.'

'Only the best for us,' I say. 'Champagne. Caviar.'

'Hmm,' he says. 'I wonder if . . . Do you really like caviar?' He turns away without waiting for the answer, picks up a basket and shoves it into my arms. 'OK, here's the plan. I'll pay for it if you carry it. Deal?'

'Deal,' I say, and then start to giggle as he strides towards the chilled drinks cabinet and grabs a bottle of champagne and a bottle of elderflower pressé. 'I didn't mean champagne, necessarily. I was just –'

'I know,' he says, and holds the bottles out to me, already raking the nearest shelves with his eyes. 'Don't worry, the champagne's for me. You're a minor. You get the elderflower juice. Cookies? Chips?'

'Biscuits and crisps, you mean,' I say. 'Yep, sounds good.'

'Strawberries. Chocolates. Guacamole, caviar, French bread, watermelon –' He's not actually talking to me any more. 'Caviar? Caviar – hmm . . . sorry, looks like it's no go on the caviar. Cheese?'

I walk behind him like a handmaiden and curtsy demurely when he drops an armload of food into the basket. There's no way we'll get through all of it, but I don't say anything. My arms are already aching from the weight of the bottles. He says, 'You OK with that? I was joking, you don't have to carry it.'

'I'm fine. Ice cream?'

'There's a slight drawback to ice cream,' he says. 'What with the heat outside and everything. I bet you a fiver you can't guess what it is.'

I nudge him with my shoulder, because I can't let go of the basket to hit him properly. He steps sideways to avoid me, then catches my arm to stop me losing my balance. 'Oops!' I say, and laugh up at him.

'You're not drunk, are you?'

'Stop *asking* me that. I'm completely – I'm absholutely shober.' I roll my eyes. 'Honestly, Oliver. I'm not a kid. I'm not drunk, and even if I were –'

'OK, OK. I'm not listening,' he says. 'Come on, let's pay for this stuff.'

He gets his credit card out at the till and taps it on the counter while the attendant swipes the bar codes. 'Oh – Bibi, would you grab a couple of those containers for gasol— petrol? I have a feeling there's a lawnmower in one of the outbuildings – you know, one of the big ones, that you drive – and I might see if I can do something with it later.'

I get two petrol containers, and swing them up and on to the counter. They look odd beside the

83

champagne and strawberries. The attendant says, 'That's thirty-two pounds and eighty-seven pence, please.'

'Ouch,' I say. 'Oliver, are you sure? We could just get crisps and beer.'

'Don't be silly,' he says, punching in his PIN. 'It's a pleasure. Really.' He looks up and smiles, so I can't tell whether it's a joke. 'Stop worrying. I've got more money than – well, more than you, anyway.'

'Fair enough,' I say, and wait while he pushes his wallet into his back pocket. I follow his hand with my eyes and feel myself blushing, stupidly, for no reason. He thanks the attendant, passes me the bulging plastic bags, and picks up the petrol containers.

'Wait here, I won't be a sec,' he says. He smiles at me. I stay where I am, leaning against the counter and watching him through the window as he fills up the containers and comes back in to pay.

'Right,' he says. 'Let's go.'

'Where to?' I say. 'Tyme's End?'

'Dear God, you'd think it was the only place in the world,' he says. Then he grins. 'Yes. Well, sort of. Follow me.'

He walks out with a bounce in his step, glancing round but not waiting for me, so I have to hurry to keep up. The heat from the garage forecourt pours over me like warm oil. I feel softened and slippery. The bottles clink gently.

And we go back down the High Street towards the broken bit of wall. It's like I've spent the whole day just walking back and forth, tying an invisible knot round Tyme's End, with Oliver. It feels like a dream. I clench my fists tightly round the handles of the plastic bags, but the sense of unreality doesn't go away. When we climb over the wall I can't believe I've done this before, for real: it's more like I've been rehearsing it, hoping, waiting with bated breath for the moment when he takes my hand to steady me. I stagger and he laughs, and somehow it's easy, it's natural, to put my hands on his shoulders, letting him take my weight, to lean forward until our faces are only a few centimetres apart.

Then he swings me safely to the ground, gives me back the plastic bags, and leads me down past the house, through long grass and the beginnings of woods, to the most beautiful place I've ever seen.

I stop, and I open my mouth, and I hear myself make a noise like a hiccup, because this is exactly, *exactly* where I want to be.

To my right there's a wide, rocky stream, emptying itself shallowly over rocks into a still, narrow pond that's full of the reflections of trees. Over our heads the trees glow green – grass-green and jade and eau de Nil and moss-green, so many different greens I don't have words for them – and the flat water is bright with sunlight, rippling with lines and circles like an abstract painting, except in the shade, where it's murky brown, like water you've cleaned your paintbrush in. I see the flicker of a grey fin and a tiny ring expands on the surface, bright silver-gold.

I hear Oliver move, but I can't look round. The water rattles and gurgles over the stones, talking to me. The sunshine runs light, intimate fingers over my collarbone and shoulders. The only word I can think of is *yes*.

'Have you been here before?'

I shake my head. It's not true, because we used to come here when we were kids, years ago, to muck around in the mud and flick pebbles at each other. But this is different – this is –

I can hear Oliver smiling. He can't see my face, but I'm sure he knows, somehow, that I'm smiling too.

'Are you hungry?'

'I –' The stream says words to me, suggesting answers. I'm scared to go on talking in case I say some of them by mistake. 'Yes.'

'Good. So'm I.' There's the rustle of plastic and the crackle of packaging. Then Oliver walks past me, crouches by the stream and lays the bottles carefully down in the running water. He looks round at me. 'We can wait, right? For the champagne?'

'I thought I wasn't allowed any.'

'You can, if you're good.'

'I'll be very good.' I'm so hot. I can feel sweat on my face and soaking into my T-shirt. 'OK. Bagsy the strawberries.'

'You're not getting all of them,' he says, and we look at each other. Then we both dive towards the food, grabbing for the strawberries, giggling like kids. I realise I've still got my bag over my shoulder, and it slides sideways as we struggle and elbow each other, crushing the crisps. Oliver makes an indignant, protective noise, and breaks off to rescue them. Now I'm on my knees. I turn my back to shelter the strawberries, pick out a handful of the nicest, and then pass them back. He shakes his head in mock disgust, crams some into his mouth and stretches out next to me, leaning back on his elbows and chewing thoughtfully.

We eat in silence – a companionable, sparkling silence that makes me feel so happy I could cry. When I'm full I lie back – putting my bag on one side, so it doesn't dig into my ribs – and look up at the leaves shimmering green above us. Oliver's still eating. I hear him swallow.

At last, he says, 'Who would've thought it? How on earth did I end up having a picnic with a trespasser? How did you transform from such a vile teenager into someone who's actually rather lovely?'

I glance at him. He's looking into the middle distance, as if it's a real question.

'I was going to leave but I'm still here,' he says quietly, as if he's talking to himself. 'How did it – this – happen?'

I look up at the leaves and I feel giddy, like I've suddenly realised that the ground underneath me is quicksand.

'I guess I was just –' he says, answering himself, as if he's two people. 'Lonely. And miserable. And I hated being back here. And then, when I met you, when I saw you crying – I guess I thought you were – like me. You were the only nice thing in – well, in England.' He licks guacamole off his index finger. 'And you were the same. You were miserable, and then I turned up and took your mind off it.'

There's a silence.

I say, 'Actually, I think I just fell in love with you.'

More silence. The noise of the stream goes on, and the trees whisper, like people at a party who don't realise everyone else has gone quiet.

It seems like an eternity before he turns his head.

He looks at me. I wait so long I half expect to see the setting sun reflected in the water behind him. There are creases under his eyes as if he's smiling, but he's not, not quite. His irises are so beautiful I can't bear it.

He says, 'Yes. That's pretty much what I said, isn't it?'

We hold each other's gaze. I feel as if I've been turned into nothing, into thin air. I want to look at him for ever. What does he mean? Is he saying –?

Then we both crack up.

It's not funny, not really, but right now it feels like the funniest thing in the world. I laugh so hard the taste of strawberries surges into the back of my mouth, acid but still summery-sweet. I carry on laughing longer than is strictly necessary, because I don't want to be the first to stop.

Oliver's collapsed on to his stomach, his face cushioned by his arms, his shoulders shaking. In the end he says, 'Oh dear. Sorry. I wasn't taking the piss, I just . . .'

'It's OK,' I say. 'I know.'

He looks up. Only his eyes are visible above his forearms. His wrists are slim and bony, like something made out of marble. 'OK,' he says.

Another silence, and I don't know how I feel.

'I'm going to have a swim,' he says. 'Do you mind?'

'Why would I mind?'

'Because I –' His eyes crinkle, but I don't know if he's smiling or wrinkling his nose. 'I don't have – do you mind if I, um . . . I thought I'd just wear my boxers. I don't want to make you uncomfortable or anything.' A pause. 'No, forget it, I'm sorry, that's completely inappropriate, it was a crap idea, forget I –'

I'm laughing again. I can't help it. I say, 'Please, Oliver, I have seen boys in their underwear before, I'm not a *complete* virgin.'

His eyes widen.

'No, wait,' I say. I can feel myself blushing. 'I only meant – sorry, this is so embarrassing – I didn't mean I *wasn't* a – it's just that, you know, we have a life class at school and everything, I'm very enlightened. I'm not going to be traumatised by you in your boxers.'

He sits up. He's blushing too. He says, 'You don't know that yet. It might give you nightmares.'

'I'm prepared to take the risk.'

He nods, without looking at me. 'Well – anyway, I believe the convention in a life class is to let the model undress in private.'

It takes me a second to realise he's telling me to turn my back. I twist round, staring through the trees. I can see the outline of the roof of Tyme's End, and a glint of glass.

I wait until I hear a splash and an intake of breath. When I look round Oliver is doing a kind of flappy front-crawl, splashing and gasping. He stands up, so the water only comes up to his shoulders, and waves at me. 'It's lovely,' he says, spitting. 'I recommend it.'

I grin at him. 'Yeah,' I say. 'You're really selling it to me.'

He shakes his head, so that little globes of light fly through the air. I feel a drop hit my cheek. 'It's OK really, once you get used to it. It's a bit cold to start with, that's all.'

'I'm fine here, thanks,' I say. 'I'll just sit and watch you catch hypothermia.'

'Ghoul,' he says. 'Revelling in other people's misery.'

I smile at him without answering and he laughs. Then he sinks slowly, until his hair is floating on the surface like weed and a few little bubbles rise to the surface.

I lie back, reach for the little gold cardboard box of chocolates and tug idly at the ribbon, but it's glued in place and I can't be bothered to try any harder. I lean my head on my bag, feeling the sharp corner of my special box pressing against my neck. Water flashes and glitters through the air as Oliver splashes his way across the pond.

I told him I was in love with him. Oh, God, I told him I was in love with him . . .

I close my eyes and look at the bright orange of my eyelids. For a moment, out of habit, I start to imagine I'm with my real mother, in a foreign country under a hot Middle Eastern sky . . . But I don't want to be anywhere but here, right now.

When I wake up, he's gone.

It's a little bit cooler than it was, but the air is still warm and heavy, sticking to me like honey. The stream is chirruping, singing to itself, and I can smell hot earth and grass. I don't want to open my eyes, but I do. And Oliver's gone.

For a second I feel more bereft, more alone, than I've ever felt in my life.

I sit up. The remains of the food are still spread out around me, but shadows have grown over them like

90

moss. The bottles of champagne and elderflower stuff are still in the stream, rocking gently in the current. I look round, squinting through the trees to see where the sun is. I don't know how long I've been asleep.

I put my hand down on something soft and warm. It's Oliver's T-shirt, neatly folded but still dented from where my head was resting on it. He must have put it there for me to use as a pillow, after I went to sleep – carefully, without waking me. I pick it up and put it to my face, breathing in the scent of summer soil and grass, my own shampoo, cigarette smoke and, under-neath all that, the clean laundry smell that was the first thing I noticed about Oliver when he hustled me out of Tyme's End like a bouncer. That was only yes-terday. It feels like years ago.

I stand up, still clutching the T-shirt, and look round. His bag is still here, and I feel a wave of relief. If his bag's here, he's coming back – although *my* bag isn't where I left it. For a moment I wonder whether he's stolen my special box, but it's not like he would want it. He probably moved it to stop me rolling over on top of it and squashing everything when I was asleep.

Anyway, if he's coming back, I don't care about anything else.

I walk over to the nearest tree and sit down against the trunk, facing towards Tyme's End and the sun, the way we came. I watch and watch, narrowing my eyes against the low green glow of the sunlight on the grass, waiting for Oliver. And it's not long before I see him, materialising through the dazzle like a mirage, becoming more and more solid as he gets closer. In this light he could be anyone: he could be a ghost, except that he throws a long shadow. It points to me, like a finger. He raises his hand when he sees me, but I don't move. I savour the feeling of staying still while he walks towards me.

He's wearing jeans and trainers but nothing else, and he puts his hands into his pockets and hunches his shoulders when he gets close. His skin is paler than mine, and greenish spots of shade slide over his chest. I want to stare at him, but from the way he's standing I know I shouldn't.

'Hello,' he says. 'Did you have a nice nap?'

'Where did you go? I woke up and you weren't here.' I sound like a little girl, but it's too late to take it back.

'I went to check on the lawnmower situation.' He twists and looks over his shoulder at Tyme's End, shading his eyes. 'Which is non-existent, unfortunately, so I stuck the petrol in the study, just behind the secret door to the cellar, because I thought we shouldn't leave it lying around. Oh, and –' He glances at me quickly. 'I put your bag in there too, your papers, because I thought it was probably safer, in case it rained or something.'

I look up at the sky and then back at him, raising my eyebrows.

'Yeah, well, you can't be too careful.' He holds out his hand to help me up. 'You don't mind, do you?'

'No,' I say. ''Course not. Thanks.' I take his hand and pull myself upright, too suddenly, so that I reel into him and have to put my hand on his bare chest to get my balance back. He flinches. 'Sorry – sorry.'

'It's OK. Just – no, really, it's OK. Your hands are cold.' He walks through the trees, a few paces ahead of me. Then he stops and we stand side by side, looking at the water, the stream pouring itself over the rocks, the smooth trembling of the reflected trees. 'Did you swim?'

'No,' I say. 'Not yet.'

He smiles. 'You should. It's nice.'

'Only if it won't traumatise you to see me in my underwear,' I say, and instantly want to bite my tongue.

He laughs, without looking at me, and walks away to the side of the stream, kneeling to fish the bottles out of the water. 'It's all right, I won't watch you.'

'I don't mind if you do.'

He still won't look at me. He's fiddling with the wire on the champagne bottle, untwisting it.

'When I said –' I wish he'd look at me. I want to go and kneel next to him. 'Oliver, what I said – I wasn't joking. I meant it, really, I –'

'I thought you probably did.' Suddenly he jerks his hand away from the bottle and puts his index finger in his mouth. He says, indistinctly, 'Bugger.'

'Are you OK?'

'Yes, I – stupid, jabbed myself on the – I didn't mean I believed you because it didn't surprise me – just from the way you said it. I'm not that arrogant.'

'You could –' I drag my foot through the grass, pushing a plastic bag aside. 'You could say something about it. If you wanted. You could tell me you're really embarrassed and let's forget I ever said anything and I'm not old enough to know what love is anyway.'

Then he does look at me. He grins. I don't know if he's laughing at me or himself.

'Bibi, I'm twenty-seven. You're *sixteen*. Words can't express how bad an idea it would be. Trust me, OK?'

'You think I'm a kid.'

'I think –' He stops, and his smile fades. 'Yes. Because you *are* a kid.'

'I'm not. I'm over the age of consent.'

He puts his hands over his face and laughs through his fingers, shaking his head. Then he looks up and smiles at me. 'Yes, but the fact that you even need to *say* that . . .' He picks the bottles up, comes towards me and sits down at my feet. He doesn't say anything else until I sit down next to him.

'Bibi, in my experience, the love affairs you remember most kindly are the ones that never happened.'

'That's really profound. Is that Confucius?'

'Do you want champagne now or after your swim?'

'Both, please.'

'OK,' he says. He pushes at the cork with his thumbs, frowning, until it comes out with a discreet, tactful pop.

'Impressive,' I say.

'My grandfather used to have champagne every Sunday night. When I got old enough he made me do the corks because his hands got stiff, and he said it would be a useful skill for later life.' He inclines his head towards me. 'He obviously had a point.'

'Why Sundays?'

'Because they were dreary. Apparently.'

'Oh.' I watch him. He's smiling down at the neck of the bottle, an odd, loving, bitter expression on his face. I say, 'He sounds nice.'

'He was. He was the nicest man I've ever known. To me.'

I realise, suddenly, that the sun's almost set. I'm not cold, but my skin prickles.

I say, 'We don't have any glasses. We'll have to drink straight from the bottle.'

'OK,' he says, and takes a gulp. A drop of champagne rolls down from the corner of his mouth, fizzing. 'Wait – you probably shouldn't swim if you've been drinking. Swim first. I'll save you half a bottle.' He gives me a wide, untrustworthy grin, and I laugh.

'Yeah, right.'

'No, I'm serious. Afterwards. I don't know how I'd break it to your parents that I let you drown.'

I open my mouth and shut it again. Then I turn away and undress down to my bra and knickers. I don't think he's watching but my nerves tingle as if he is. I'm not exactly embarrassed – I told him he could watch, after all – but I sidle towards the pond because I can't bring myself to look in his direction. I jump in, and it's icy. I hear myself yelp, and when I've wiped the water out of my eyes and found my feet in the mud Oliver's laughing at me, holding the bottle of champagne in both hands so that he doesn't spill it.

I roll over on to my back and tread water, looking up at the trees. Now that the sun's set the light is green-grey-blue, the sky high and clear. I love the feeling of weightlessness, like I'm not real. Oliver's stopped laughing now and all I can hear is the click-rattle-chirrup of the stream and my own heartbeat. I hold my breath and put my face underwater, but it's too dark to see anything. The water seems warmer now, just cooler than my body. It's lovely. I float in silence.

After a while the water is lighter than the sky. It ripples round me, opalescent. I pick it up in my hands, half expecting it to be opaque and silvery against my skin.

It's almost completely dark before I stand up and wade back towards the bank. Oliver's watching me, his hands round his knees. There's a breeze, and suddenly I'm freezing. My teeth start to chatter.

'Sorry, I don't have a towel. You'd better use this.' He holds out something dark to me, and when I take it I realise it's his T-shirt. I wipe the water off my face and when I look up again he's standing up with my clothes in his arms. He passes my T-shirt to me, then my jeans, and I lean on him while I drag them on. The denim sticks to my damp legs. I'm a little bit warmer but I'm still shivering. He stands in front of me, his hands in his pockets. Then, suddenly, he reaches out, pulls me towards him and starts to rub my back in a brisk older-brother kind of way. He's put on a jumper, and I press my face against it, taking in the clean-laundry warmth, feeling his arms round me. 'You'll warm up in a sec,' he says. 'I've got another sweater in my bag. You can borrow that if you want.'

'I'm OK.'

Somehow we sit down, so that I'm cross-legged, leaning back against him. He dries my hair for me, very carefully, like he's scared of breaking it. I'm still shaking, and he puts his arms round me and squeezes, so that I feel the warmth of his whole body. 'Better?'

No would be a lie, and I don't want to say *yes*. So I stay quiet.

'You should go home. It's getting late.'

'I haven't had my champagne yet,' I say, and I hear him laugh. The vibration goes through my back and straight to my heart.

96

He shifts, and reaches backwards. I'm leaning on him, so I move too, until we're lying down, my head on his chest. He grunts, and then makes a satisfied noise. 'Got it. Here we go.' He passes the bottle to me. I have to tilt my head forward to drink. The champagne's warmish and flat, but it tastes great.

I prop it in the crook of my elbow and look up at the patch of clear sky above the pond. The stars are starting to come out.

I say, 'Do you want me to move?'

'It's fine.'

'Because – I know you don't want to –'

There's a pause, and I hear him swallow. 'I never said I didn't *want* to.'

There's another pause. The undergrowth rustles as the dark things start to wake up. I open my mouth, but I'm smiling so hard I'm not sure I'll be able to make words.

'Bibi,' he says, very softly, into my hair, 'if you laugh, or say anything, or make so much as a joke I swear I'll –' He hesitates. Then he puts on a theatrical, reading-aloud kind of voice, parodying himself. 'I'll break your neck in one swift practised movement like a stick of sugar candy.'

'Rock,' I say. 'Not "sugar candy". *Rock.*'

'God, teenagers,' he says. 'You have to have the last word.'

'Yes,' I say.

He shakes his head and we both laugh quietly, as if neither of us wants to break the silence. And we lie and look up at the stars.

VII

It's starting to get light. I lift my head a little and the sky above the trees is so blue and clear I want to touch it.

I say, 'Are you asleep?'

Oliver yawns and I feel him shake his head. 'No. Are you?'

'Definitely. Can't you tell?' I lie back down, resting my head in the hollow between his shoulder and his chest. He got his spare sweater out of his bag for me – fumbling around by the light of his cigarette lighter – when I woke up at midnight, freezing and not sure where I was, but even so I'm cold. The warmth of his body is comforting, and his sweater is like another pair of his arms, hugging me. I breathe in his smell. I'm knackered and covered in midge bites, and my neck aches from leaning on him all night, but I don't want to go home.

'It'll be morning soon.'

I don't answer. If I pretend we can stay like this for ever, maybe we can.

'Bibi? You should go home. Your parents – won't your parents be –'

'Not yet,' I say. 'I want to watch the sun come up. Forget my parents.'

'Oh. OK,' he says, and yawns again. 'I wonder what time the first train is.'

'To Gatwick?' I raise my head again to look at him, but there's not enough light yet to see his expression.

'Yeah. Well, to Tonbridge.'

'Have you booked your flight?'

'I'll get the first one I can, when I get to the airport.'

I feel sick. I sit up. My hair's sticking to my cheek where I was leaning on him, and I brush it away. 'When are you coming back?'

'Probably never.'

'OK.'

'Bibi, you knew – I said, all along. I told you –'

'I said it's *OK*.' I look up at the sky. It looks fragile. If you hit it with a hammer it would shatter, with a huge musical smash. 'What about Tyme's End? I thought you weren't going to sell Tyme's End?'

'I'm not. I'll get my solicitors to give it to you. Miss Habibah Hope of 19, Marks Cross Road, Falconhurst.'

'Very funny.'

'I'm not joking.'

I look round at him. He shrugs and smiles. In the half-light his face is pale, eaten away by shadows like an old man's. I wonder suddenly what his grandfather looked like. 'But – I thought –'

'You want it, don't you? This.' He gestures to the smooth, blue-grey water and the trees. 'I don't mean the hou— not just the house. I'd like you to have *this*.'

'I thought you . . .' I don't know what to say.

'As an apology,' he says, and runs his hand over my hair and down my back.

It makes me shiver. 'You don't have anything to apologise for.' I turn my head so that his cheek is only a few centimetres from my mouth. He's still smiling, but not at me. 'Really – Oliver, you don't have anything – I promise, there's nothing to apologise *for*.'

'That's what you think,' he says. Then he turns and kisses me, very lightly, on the mouth. It's so quick and gentle it's like something brushing past me: a ghost, a memory, a premonition of a kiss.

I go to kiss him back, but he's already getting to his feet.

'Come on,' he says. 'Let's get this trash cleared up before the sun rises.'

The dawn is beautiful. I'm not sure I've ever seen the sun come up before – not watched it rise, like this, concentrating on every second as the sky goes green and lemon-green and amber and rose. We stand a little way apart, and even though we can't see the sun through the trees the sky is so lovely I want to pause it, like a TV, and keep it like that for the rest of my life. It makes me sad to know I'll only see it once, and then it'll be gone. I feel like I'll never see anything as good ever again.

I say, 'What's the time?' because if he says how beautiful it is I'll start to cry.

'Five past five.'

'What time's your train?'

'First one's about quarter to six, I think.'

'And that's the one you're getting.'

'Yes,' he says.

'Then you should go,' I say. 'It'll take half an hour to walk there, probably.'

He glances at me and nods. 'Will you come to see me off?'

'If you want me to.'

Suddenly he pulls me sideways, so I stumble into him, and he puts his arms round me and squeezes me so tightly it's hard to breathe. 'Yes,' he says. His mouth is next to my ear, and it tickles. 'Yes, I'd like you to.'

I clench my jaw, because I'm not going to cry until he's safely on the train to the airport.

'I'm really glad I met you, Bibi.' He pulls back, his hands on my shoulders, and smiles. 'I can't tell you how glad. If I hadn't – I don't know what I would've done.'

'Good,' I say. 'Great. That's excellent.'

He watches me for a second, and then laughs. 'Yeah, OK. I'm getting sentimental. Sorry. Forget it.'

'Yeah,' I say, although I know I won't forget it, ever.

'Let's go,' he says. And we start to walk up through the trees towards the house and the bit of broken wall that I know better than my own front door by now.

I thought it would be quiet – it *feels* quiet – but actually there's birdsong and things rustling and there's already the occasional swish of a car from the road. I hear a motorcycle drone past, cutting out at the loudest point, and an aeroplane goes overhead, leaving a double trail on the blue like a scar. Everything's wet, shining with dew, and it smells of fresh air.

Then Oliver stops dead, and points. 'Bibi. Look.'

For a moment I don't know what I'm seeing. Tyme's

End, with reddish copper light blazing through the windows, the panes glaring the colour of fire. For an odd second my heart jumps into my throat. But the light's too even, too still, to be a real fire: it's only the dawn reflected in the glass. I breathe out slowly, half wanting to laugh. It's as beautiful as the sunrise, but in a different way. I can feel goose pimples prickling on my arms. Everything goes very still, as if we've walked into a photo.

There's something wrong. I don't know what it is, but –

'I think it remembers,' Oliver says. His voice is funny, quiet and focused, as if he's talking to someone hidden, just within earshot. 'I think – especially now, at dawn, in summer . . . I think Tyme's End knows what happened there, all the things that happened, the things that people don't know and can't ever know. I think the past leaves traces that we can't see. And sometimes . . . We think things have gone, when they haven't.'

I don't want him to go on. I *really* don't want him to go on. I close my eyes and dig my nails into my palms, because there's something – I don't want him to say any more. I wasn't scared last night, but now – in this glorious, chirping, dazzling morning – I am.

'I think . . . we look at the past. And sometimes it looks back at us.'

I squeeze his hand, pressing it against my leg. 'Oliver –'

He looks down at me, his eyes narrowing as if he's trying to remember who I am. Then he shakes his head. 'Sorry.'

'You're freaking me out. I don't know why. You looked – like someone else.'

'Someone better-looking, I hope.' He grins, but that other expression – the trace of unfamiliarity – is still just visible.

I shrug and pull him forward. 'Let's go. Your train.'

'Wait. I –' He doesn't move. He's still got hold of my hand. 'There's something I . . . Will you give me a minute?'

'What?'

'I want to go and – say goodbye. I know it sounds stupid. Just go and have a last cigarette and . . . look round.'

'It's not stupid.'

He nods, the corners of his mouth turning up, but his eyes are distant, staring over my shoulder at the house. He says, 'My grandfather died there. I was upstairs when he – I came downstairs, at dawn, and found him.'

I haven't got a clue what to say. I still feel a dragging, dull pain in my gut. It takes me a moment to realise it's fear.

He pulls his hand out of mine. 'Stay here.' He takes his rucksack off his shoulder and slings it into the grass at my feet. 'I won't be long. One cigarette.'

'OK.'

'Actually, why don't you wait for me at the wall? Then I won't have to retrace my steps. It'll save time. If I want to catch this train –' His tone is brisk and businesslike, as if this is just an ordinary day, as if we'll see each other again tomorrow.

I say, 'Sure. Fine. I'll wait for you at the wall.'

'Great.'

He strides off towards the house, breaking into an irregular run. The windows have started to fade now. But the unease stays with me, even though the flat fire on the glass has died.

I remember suddenly that my special box is inside – but it's safe there. I'll get it later, when he's gone. I watch him until he slides in through the back door. Then I pick up his rucksack and make my way diagonally through the trees, turning my back on Tyme's End.

I wait for him at the wall. He doesn't take that long – fifteen minutes, maybe – and then he's walking towards me, hurrying, with his hands in his pockets and his head down, as if he's making an effort not to look back. He smiles when he sees me, and reaches out to take his rucksack. I can smell the smoke on his clothes, but in the fresh air it's not as bitter as normal; it's more like woodsmoke or a bonfire. He pushes me forward, so I almost trip and have to brace myself against the wall. It's cold and wet under my hands, like damp sand. 'Come on. Let's go. I'll miss the train.'

'OK, OK,' I say. 'If you make me break an ankle there'll be all sorts of complications and it'll take even longer.' It's meant to be a joke, but it just sounds petulant. I can't help it; I don't want him to go. I hope he *does* miss the train.

We walk down the High Street. I want him to take my hand, but he doesn't. There's hardly any traffic, but I can smell petrol. It makes me feel queasy.

He's biting his lip, frowning. When he glances sideways he sees me looking at him and looks away.

We don't say anything until we get to the station. The ticket office is closed, but the gate on to the platform is open, and the boards are flashing up the train to London. He says, 'That's the one. I have to change at Tonbridge.'

We've only got seven minutes. I feel my throat tightening and tightening. I want to turn round and walk away. I want to go with him.

'Bibi,' he says. He's talking very softly, as if he doesn't want to be overheard, but there's no one else around. 'Listen to me. I wanted to say . . . You belong here, OK? Even if you don't always live here, in England, you've got as much right to be here as anyone else.'

'OK.'

'And I meant it, about Tyme's End. The land, the river – it'll be yours. It'll be *really* yours. As much yours as it was mine, or my grandfather's, or H. J. Martin's. Don't keep telling yourself you belong somewhere else, because you don't. Inheritances don't always go through bloodlines.'

I'm not completely sure what he means with that last sentence; but he's talking so earnestly, carefully, looking straight into my eyes, that I think I understand what he's trying to tell me.

'And – the things you don't know . . .' He pauses, and, without quite knowing how, I realise he's talking about my mum, my real mum. 'Don't let them haunt you. Don't let anything haunt you.'

'Right.'

'But – don't forget, either. The past does matter. But not as much as the present.'

'OK.'

He stares at me. There's a pause; then, suddenly, it's like he can see my expression. He rubs his forehead with his hand, laughing. He's got a smear of something dark on his hand, like mould. 'All right. I just needed to give you the benefit of my superior wisdom.'

'Was that all of it? Eleven years' worth?'

'Don't be a smart-arse.' He shakes his head. 'I did mean it, though.'

'Yeah, it was really . . . interesting.'

We look at each other, and we both grin.

'OK,' he says. 'I'd better go.'

'Go on then.'

'OK, I will.' But he doesn't move. Then he grimaces and digs quickly in the back pocket of his jeans. 'Shit. Sorry, I –'

He's holding something out to me: familiar glossy rectangles, the top one shiny ochre and brown.

My photos. I meet his gaze and I don't know what my face is doing.

'I'm so sorry. I took them out of the box to have a look, and – I must've forgotten to put them back. Do you mind?'

'No,' I say. 'I'm glad.'

He smiles at me. I take the photos and hold them gently, making sure I don't make fingerprints on them. He says, 'Thanks. Sorry. Was that out of order?'

'Oliver,' I say. 'I'm *glad*.' And I don't know why, but I am. It's as if he's given them to me, like a gift. I think of him flipping through them – no, *staring*, holding them up to his eyes as if he could get closer than the camera was, the way I do – and it makes me feel odd and surprised and *free*.

'My train,' he says. 'I don't want to miss it.'

'Do you – wait –' I feel panicky, like I've forgotten something. 'Your email or something – mobile number –'

'Give me yours,' he says. 'I'll text you. But I had to borrow a cellphone from a friend – damn, that reminds me, I'll have to post it back to him – so don't save the number.'

I give him my mobile number, and by the time he's put it into his phone the recorded announcement is saying, 'The train now approaching platform one . . .' I can't see the train yet, but the rails are hissing and singing.

'Promise you'll text me.'

'I promise. From the train, I expect.'

I laugh, but not for very long. The train's going to come, any second now.

He says, 'Goodbye, beloved.'

Then he kisses me.

And this time it's a proper kiss.

The train comes. I feel it rumbling under my feet, and Oliver pushes me away. I hold on to him for as long as I can, and then I stand with my arms at my sides, my hands empty, watching him run through the gate on to the platform. He smacks the button next to the train door with the flat of his hand and steps through it as soon as it opens. Then he stands looking out, his hand raised in a kind of frozen wave. I can feel myself smiling and crying, both at once, because I don't want him to leave but I'm ridiculously, impossibly happy. I wave back.

Then, before the train goes, I turn around and walk away.

My heart's racing. I can still taste Oliver's mouth – the bitterness of smoke, and the staleness of neither of us having slept properly, and champagne, river-water, strawberries.

It's already getting warm. The long sideways shadows are starting to recede. I turn my head towards the light. I want to spin and jump and shout, and there's no one around, so I do.

I'm in a kind of daze, light-headed and thirsty. I don't know where I'm going, but I bounce and jump and tap-step-ball-change all the way down the High Street. Where I could turn right to go home I carry on walking, because once I have a shower and go to bed this feeling will go and never come back. I want to hang on to it for as long as I can. I try to remember what the kiss was like, but it's already slipping away, and last night is a blur of champagne and silver water. All I know is that it happened.

But right now that's enough.

I stop, squeeze my eyes shut, and try to see Oliver's face. I can still smell him: the bonfire scent of smoke, the sourness of petrol fumes . . . I try to hear his voice, the way his American accent came and went. I play our conversation over in my head, the last few seconds before he kissed me. I gave him my mobile number, and then he said goodbye, and then . . .

After a while I open my eyes. I'm still standing on the pavement, on my own.

I get my phone out of my pocket and turn it on, just in case. There are three voicemail messages, a text from Sam (*WHERE R U? M AND D NOT HAPPY!*) and another one from Mum (*PLEASE CALL HOME, WE WANT TO KNOW YOU'RE OK*). Oh, bugger. I grit my teeth and dial our landline number, but I can't bring myself to press the call button. Anyway, it's only ten past six. They'll be asleep.

I walk along the High Street, holding my mobile in my hand so that if Oliver does call I'll be able to answer right away. He *said* he'd text me from the train. I thought he was joking, but maybe he wasn't. I hope he wasn't. I really hope –

The phone beeps. It makes me jump. I almost drop it in the gutter.

A text message. It has to be Oliver. I hear myself make a noise like a sob, but I'm laughing, not crying. I take a deep breath and try to steady myself, because it might only say *AM SAFELY ON TRAIN* or *HAVE BOOKED FLIGHT SUCCESSFULLY*. I feel shaky, like I'm getting exam results.

I'M SORRY. GO STRAIGHT HOME.

I read it again.

It still says, *I'M SORRY. GO STRAIGHT HOME.*

What the hell –? I don't get it. I want to call him back, but he's withheld his number. Why would he withhold the number? I know he said it was his mate's phone, but . . . Maybe he didn't mean to. Or maybe it isn't Oliver at all; maybe it's someone from school winding me up, or just a wrong number.

I'M SORRY. GO STRAIGHT HOME.

All of a sudden I feel strange, as if the hangover and sleepless night have finally caught up with me. The sun's too bright, and my mouth is dry, and there's a bitter, itchy smell in the air that makes me want to cough. I put my phone back in my pocket. *I'M SORRY.* Oliver's regretting everything – having kissed me, having stayed out all night . . . I feel a sharp edge in my throat, like dust. I look into the sun until my eyes start to water. It's starting to cloud over; there's a thin haze in the air, spreading out over the sky. Further down the High Street, to the left, behind the trees, someone's having a bonfire. The column of smoke is grey in the sunlight, billowing upwards. He's *sorry.* He's sorry he kissed me. He probably wishes he'd never met me. It's the worst thing he could have said. I blink the tears out of my eyes and turn round to go home.

But something niggles at me, making me twist and look over my shoulder at the smoke. I stare at it, shading my eyes, because there's something –

I start to run.

A moment ago I was weightless, skimming the surface of the pavement like someone had turned gravity off; but now it's like I'm running on sand. *GO STRAIGHT HOME.* He couldn't have. He couldn't have –

I can smell the fire from here. I keep running, my head bent, concentrating on keeping my feet going, and when I look up again the smoke has thickened and darkened. *I'M SORRY.*

I get to the gates of Tyme's End and stop, breathing so hard my lungs hurt. Through the gates I can see the smoke pouring upwards in a high grey cloud, so wide and blurred I can't believe I thought it was a bonfire. The stink of it is unmistakable. Beyond the trees there are flickers of gold, glints of copper and red, so that if it wasn't for the smoke and the noise you'd almost think it was the sunrise reflected in the windows. The building rumbles. I lean forward through the bars, trying to get a better view, but the trees are in the way. Oh my God.

Tyme's End is on fire. Tyme's End, that Oliver said he'd give to me.

I reach for my phone. I've never made a 999 call before, and my hands are shaking. The first time I try I press the 8 instead of the 9. I have to stop and take a deep breath.

I look down at my hand, clenched and pale round my phone. Something stops me trying again.

He set it alight on purpose. He planned it. He already knew, yesterday, when he bought the petrol, when he said it was for the lawnmower . . . This morning, when he said he was going for a last cigarette, to say goodbye to the place . . . I can see him in my mind's eye, getting the petrol out from behind the secret door, splashing it carefully over the furniture, flicking his cigarette lighter open, the silver glinting in the light of the sunrise – and him standing in the doorway, dropping the lighter, watching a line of flame slide over the floor. And then he'd have run, ducking swiftly out of the side door, hurrying to catch me up, trying not to look back.

This is what he's sorry for. Nothing else.

Goodbye, beloved.

I can taste woodsmoke. I lean my forehead against the bars of the gate and start to laugh.

I hear the siren coming down the road but I don't turn to look. The smoke haemorrhages into the sky, spreading out and over me like a ceiling. I'm clutching the bars of the gate with my hands, like a prisoner looking out of a window, but I'm still laughing. I can't help it. Even when I hear the fire engine right behind me, the siren blaring through my head, I can't stop. It's only when I hear it brake that I realise I have to leave, before someone decides I'm drunk and makes me call my parents. I take one last look at Tyme's End, and then I turn and run past the fire engine.

Oh, God. When I get home I'm going to get bollocked for staying out all night. There'll probably be a fight. And this time I won't be able to run away to Tyme's End, because it's on fire.

And I remember, with a funny kind of jolt, that my papers – my special box – are in there too. Oliver must have left them there on purpose. He kept my photos for me, and burnt the rest. It's gone, my I-don't-belong-here box, my you're-not-my-real-parents box. It's turning to ash at this very moment, along with Tyme's End.

What was it he said? *Don't let anything haunt you.*

I can still hear Tyme's End burning. As I make my way home I tilt my chin up and look at the sky. There are tears running down my face and dripping on to my T-shirt, but I'm smiling.

1996

I

The last time I saw my dad, I was thirteen.

We were supposed to have a week together – actually,
just under a week, because he'd got the cheapest ticket
he could – and it was Wednesday. He'd taken me out,
the same as he had the day before and the day before
that. It was raining, and we were in the special exhibition at the Imperial War Museum, and I wanted to
go home.

I stood in front of a perspex-covered picture, letting
my eyes blur until it was just a mess of black and
white, with my reflection behind it looking back at
me. Dad was somewhere over the other side of the
room. He'd moaned about the weather while we
were waiting for the bus, but ever since we got to the
museum he'd hovered at my shoulder silently, not
meeting my eyes when I looked at him. Now he
wasn't even doing that. I glanced over, and he was
staring blankly at a display case. He'd been the one to
suggest the special exhibition, but he looked like he
was hating every moment. I felt my throat tighten.

Three more days and then he'd go back to Sydney, and he hadn't even said he was glad to see me.

He sauntered over. 'Enjoying yourself, mate?'

I looked round, then back at the poster, willing my voice to stay steady. 'It's OK.'

'You know who he was, right?'

I didn't know what he was talking about. Then I followed his gaze to the photo and the plaque next to it. *H. J. Martin was seconded to the Arab Intelligence Bureau.* I said, 'Yeah, wasn't he that guy who got seconded to the Arab Intelligence Bureau in Cairo in 1914, where he swiftly made both enemies and staunch allies?'

Granddad would have laughed, but my dad just said, 'Yeah. That's the one,' without even letting on that he realised I was reading it off the wall.

'Including Morgan Astley, of course,' I said, in my best smarmy-private-schoolboy voice, 'who later wrote the introduction to *The Owl of the Desert*.' I pointed at the photo and added, 'Second from left.' But he still didn't get it.

He glanced at me. 'You're a bit of an expert, aren't you?' There was a gleam of something like malice in his eyes. 'Bet your grandfather loves that.'

'What?'

'Your grandfather. I bet he thinks it's great, you knowing all about H. J. Martin. Reminds him of me, maybe.'

'I –' I stared at him. It was weird, the way he said *your grandfather*, not *my father*. And there was a triumphant, aggressive sort of note in his voice, like he'd won a fight. I said, 'I don't know anything about him, really, I was only – it's on the plaque.'

A second's silence. Then he laughed, but it was like I'd let him down. 'Oh. Right. Clever.'

I put my hands in my pockets and dug the toe of my trainer into the floor. 'Why wouldn't Granddad want me to know?' I said. 'I mean, he's a historian. He really likes it when I know things.'

'No reason,' he said. 'Got a bit of a thing about H. J. Martin, that's all. He – Martin was a hero of mine when I was your age, and your grandfather . . .'

It didn't sound like he'd finished his sentence, but he didn't say anything else. I looked up at him, feeling lost. Who cared about H. J. Martin? I just wanted Dad to care about *me*. I heard his voice again – *reminds him of me, maybe* – and wished I'd pretended I did know about Martin.

'Old hypocrite,' Dad said, suddenly. There was a hard, venomous edge to his voice that made me feel cold and lost, as if he'd forgotten who I was. 'Get's so uptight about a bit of hero worship, and all the time he's living off the inheritance, living off the same bloody money that –' He cut himself off, staring at a picture on the far wall. 'And Tyme's End is *sitting* there, just –'

I had no idea what he was talking about. I wanted to reach for his hand – or touch his arm, just to remind him I was there – but I didn't. I waited.

And after a long moment, Dad seemed to relax. He looked down at me, and his expression was smoother, more neutral. But there was still a strange emphasis in his voice, as if he was giving me the clue to a puzzle. 'He knew him, you know,' he said. 'Your grandfather knew Martin. He's probably in some of the pictures.'

'He knew loads of people,' I said. 'People are

always coming round to interview him. Granddad knew *Churchill*.'

I'd got it wrong. Whatever Dad wanted, I hadn't done it. His expression changed, hardening. 'Jesus. He's got you thinking the sun shines out of his arse, hasn't he?'

'No – I only meant –'

'Forget it.' He turned away. 'Just don't kid yourself he's perfect, OK?'

I opened my mouth but my nose was prickling and I didn't trust my voice. I thought, *I know Granddad's not perfect. If he was perfect, you'd never have had to go away. You'd never have left me behind.* But I couldn't say it.

I moved sideways, pushing blindly through a knot of people, until I was looking at another photograph, trying to swallow the lump in my throat.

After a while he came and stood next to me. 'You finished?'

'Yeah.' I wished, too late, that I'd said no.

'Fine. Me too. Let's go.' He put his hand on my shoulder and steered me through the last room, walking quickly so I didn't even have time to glance at the display cases. His fingers dug into the tendons over my collarbone.

'If Granddad –' I said. 'Would he mind you bringing me here? I mean, what you said, about it reminding him of you – do you want me, you know, not to mention it? I don't mind. I don't have to tell him. I can say we went to the Natural History Museum if you want. We went there with school, so I can lie –'

He stopped walking suddenly, so I lurched into

him. It was almost like he'd put his arm round me. I felt my face going red.

There was a pause. I heard a little sticky sort of sound as Dad opened his mouth. He said, 'No. No, Olly, you don't have to lie for my sake.'

'I don't mind – I mean, I can keep a secret –'

'No.' He smiled at me. 'Your granddad won't be angry with *you*. And you're my son. Why shouldn't I take you wherever you want to go?'

My cheeks blazed again. *You're my son.* It was the first nice thing he'd said to me.

'Come on, Olly,' he said, and went down the steps ahead of me, clicking his fingers behind his back to make me follow. 'You've been a good lad today. Didn't complain about the rain or anything. I want to buy you a present.'

'But –' *But you can't even afford the Tube*, I wanted to say. *I don't want a present. I'm fine. All I want is for you to come and live in London.* But he was already striding round the corner, into the gift shop. He glanced round, then made a beeline for the table in front of him. There were piles of books, all with a black-and-white photo on the front, the same photo that I'd been staring at before. I stood and watched as he picked one up, turned it over to check the price, and then took it to the till.

I said, 'Um . . . I'd rather have –' and stopped, because it didn't matter. He was buying me a present. I didn't care what it was. Even if it was a big adult book about someone I'd never heard of before today.

The woman at the till gave Dad his change and put the book into a plastic bag. He smiled over his shoulder and held it out to me with one hand, putting his wallet away with the other. I smiled back and took it from him, tilting the bag so I could see the front cover. *H. J. Martin: A Biography*. It was huge. It looked serious and thoughtful, the kind of book Granddad wrote. The face in the picture was already familiar, like someone I'd known when I was too small to remember. But I couldn't imagine ever actually reading it. I said, 'Great. Thanks.'

'You could sound a bit grateful.'

'I am. Honestly. Thanks. I'll try to – it looks good.'

'It ought to impress your granddad anyway,' Dad said. He had a gleam of enjoyment in his eyes, and I told myself it was because he liked giving me something. 'I'd've loved it, at your age.'

I squeezed my tongue against my teeth and swung the plastic bag from my fingers. *In that case I'll read it,* I thought. It was funny though, because Dad didn't seem like someone who liked books at all. He didn't even have a proper job. And Granddad talked to him like he was stupid.

'I'd better take you home.'

'OK,' I said. I swung the bag hard against my leg, so that the corner of the book bashed into my knee. That was it for today, then. And then there was tomorrow, and Friday and Saturday, and then he was flying back to Sydney.

He didn't say anything, even while we were waiting for the bus. I watched the rain spatter against the sides of the bus shelter and tried not to feel miserable. He'd bought me a book. That was good, wasn't it? He liked me enough to buy me a book. And when we got on the bus he gave me the seat next to the window and leant over me to rub the condensation off the glass. I sat very still and breathed carefully, hoping he'd put his arm round me. But he didn't.

The front door was double-locked, which meant that Granddad wasn't in. My dad was already going back down the steps, his hand raised in a kind of wave. I ran halfway down to catch up with him and managed to stop myself before I grabbed his arm. 'Do you want to – Granddad's not here. Do you want to come in? I'll make you a cup of tea or something. Please?'

He turned round and looked at me, grimacing. 'I'd better not, Olly. See you tomorrow, OK?'

'But he's not *here*,' I said. 'Are you hungry? We've got crisps and things. Rosina went shopping yesterday.'

'Thanks, son, but I'd better scarper. Really.'

'*Please*. Just for a bit. If Granddad comes back I'll say I invited you.'

'Well . . .' He tugged at his nose, staring at me like I was a maths question he was trying to solve. 'Not for long, OK? Just a quick cuppa. Then I'd better go.'

'Yeah, 'course,' I said, trying to sound cool. 'That's fine.'

It was funny though. Making tea and getting the biscuit tin out and trying to find the crisps, and all the time thinking, *I'm making tea for my dad, I'm getting biscuits out for my dad*. I felt all warm and floppy. He *did* like me. He wouldn't be here unless he liked me. I dug around in the cupboard looking for the sea salt and balsamic vinegar crisps that Rosina bought and took it all up to the drawing room on a tray. He grinned when he saw me. 'Bloody hell, Olly, you've got enough food to float a battleship.'

123

'I'm hungry.' But I wasn't. I watched him pour the tea – he took three sugars – and it was like the drawing room was glowing.

He glanced up and saw me looking at him. For a moment I thought he was going to say something like, *I'm not a bloody circus, mate*, but then he blinked and gave me a sort of uncertain smile. He picked up his tea, holding the cup in both hands like it was a mug, and tilted his head towards the bag on the sofa. 'You left your book downstairs. I brought it up for you.'

'Thanks.' I picked it up and slid the book out. It still didn't look like the sort of thing I'd ever read, but . . . 'Thank you.' I put it down on the arm of my chair.

I heard the front door squeak and bang and click, the way it always did. My dad heard it too; he stopped before the teacup got to his mouth and said, 'Is that –?'

'Don't worry, it's probably Rosina.' But it wasn't Rosina's day. My heart was banging. It was Granddad. He'd popped out for cigarettes or matches or something and now he was back and he'd know I was in because of the front door not being double-locked and he might come to say hello and then he'd see –

My dad half-rose to his feet; then he sat down again. 'It's your grandfather, isn't it?'

'I dunno. But, look, it's not your fault you're here, I made you –'

'You didn't make me do anything, mate.' He squared his shoulders, like Granddad was already there in front of him, threatening to call the police. 'Who does he think he is, anyway? How am I supposed to get to know you properly if I can't even come into the house? It's ridiculous.'

'How could you possibly *get to know him properly* in a week? An equally ridiculous suggestion, I'd say.'

Granddad. He was there in the doorway, peeling the plastic film off a packet of cigarettes.

I said, 'Granddad, he was only having a cup of tea, and I asked him, because you weren't in, and we were hungry, and –'

'Thank you, Olly.' He held up a hand to stop me. 'Please, sit down, both of you.' He came into the room and put a hand on the teapot, checking how hot it was. 'May I?' He didn't wait for me to answer, just poured some tea into the cup I'd brought up for myself. He was casual and deliberate at the same time, like he was doing it on purpose. He stirred it and tapped the spoon on the edge of the saucer. 'Philip, I thought I made my preferences on this point perfectly clear. You're not welcome in this house.'

My dad's face did something strange. He said, 'Look, I'm only here because – come on, Father –'

Granddad turned to me. 'Olly, did you pour your father's tea? There appear to be tea leaves floating in it.' There was an edge to his voice; someone was in big trouble. I just didn't know if it was me.

'I don't know,' I said.

'Well, perhaps you should –'

He stopped, because he'd caught sight of the book on the arm of my chair. It was almost a double take; it would have been funny except for the look on his face. Like – I didn't know what it was like. Like meeting your worst enemy in heaven. Like seeing a ghost.

'Whose is that?' He raised his hand and pointed with the spoon. It *should* have been funny. But it wasn't, somehow.

'Mine,' I said, scared to speak but more scared of not answering him. 'Dad gave it to me.'

He lowered the spoon, very, very slowly. 'Did he,' he said, but it wasn't a question. 'Give it to me, please, Oliver.'

I picked it up and held it out for him to take. He reached out –

But I didn't let him take it. I snatched it away, just as his fingers touched it, before his grip could tighten. I jumped back, my heart pounding, and ducked out of his way, but I couldn't hold on to the book. It dropped on to the floor. Granddad's cup of tea fell and smashed next to it, splattering tea all over the cover.

For a moment we stared at each other. His face looked bleak, foreign. I didn't recognise it.

My dad said, 'It's none of your business. He's my son.'

Granddad's gaze faltered and he glanced down at the wreckage on the floor, but when he looked back his face was his own again. 'Go to your room, Olly. I need to speak to your father alone.'

I looked down at the book, and then at him. 'But –'

'*Go to your room.*'

I went. Granddad stood in the doorway of the drawing room, watched me go up the stairs to my room, and shut the door with a sharp, decisive click. I stood on the landing, counted to twenty, and then crept back down to sit on the lowest step, my arms wrapped round my knees. I felt sick and cold. My stomach was sinking slowly, like a battleship.

At first their voices weren't loud enough for me to hear what they were saying. I leant forward, watching the shadow under the door. Then I heard my dad say,

'For God's sake, it's just a book!'

The shadow moved suddenly, as if Granddad had walked towards him, away from the door. He replied quietly, precisely, so all I could hear was the rumble of his voice and the consonants.

Dad said, loudly, 'I thought Olly would like it, that's all! Jesus, you are so arrogant. This is about me and *my son*. Why the hell would it be about *you*?'

I felt a little flash of warmth because of the way he'd said *my son*, but it died immediately, leaving me colder than ever. My face felt funny, like the skin was sticking to my skull.

Granddad said something else, indistinctly, in that low, dispassionate tone.

'Well, what if I *do*? You've got him wrapped round your little finger – he bloody worships you! Do you have any idea how hard this is for me? I've come all this way, and all I find is that he's a spoilt little brat who thinks you're the bee's knees because you buy him everything he wants –'

And then the noise of something breaking. My dad must have broken something, because Granddad wouldn't – I'd never seen him break anything, even by accident. I could feel the tears building up again in my throat, inexorably, like when you put your thumb over a dripping tap.

I heard Granddad's voice again, still quiet, but suddenly so clear it was as if he knew I was there and wanted me to hear. 'Don't you *dare* call Oliver a spoilt brat!'

Then, unbelievably, there were two voices shouting at once, blurring, wiping each other out so I couldn't hear the words. I'd never heard Granddad shout, not in thirteen years. His voice rose above Dad's, making my teeth vibrate.

'You know nothing whatsoever about him! You reckless, selfish, predatory idiot – you come over here and think you can play at being his father. You appal me. It's contemptible. Who do you think you are? Have you even noticed how upset he is? Or did you imagine that it was perfectly normal for him to be constantly on the edge of tears? He was fine before you got here. It would have been better if you'd never come. Have you any conception at all of the damage you've done? If you had any decency you'd leave him alone –'

And it went on. On and on and on, a tight, furious, *wounded* voice I'd never heard Granddad use before, telling my father I'd be better off without him. I wanted to go down and shout at him to shut up. I wanted to say, *I don't care if he does damage me, I'd still rather he was here, I'd still rather . . . He's my dad.*

'And I cannot express my – Philip, you bought him that book because you knew how I'd react. You let the boy think you wanted to buy him a gift, when you were simply using him to get at me. You haven't changed, have you? It's despicable. I suppose you still think that somehow *I* am responsible for what *you* –'

'Don't lecture me, you pompous bastard! As if *you* knew anything about being a decent father – as if you cared what I did, as if you'd *ever* –'

'All right. I don't propose to discuss the past. I am only, and absolutely, concerned with Oliver. And I *will not let you* do this to him.'

'Oh, yeah, of course, you want to turn him against me –'

'I hardly think I need to bother. Oliver is quite intelligent enough to understand the situation.'

Silence.

Then my father's voice again, only this time it was low and sibilant, spitting the consonants, and for the first time he sounded like Granddad. It made my back feel shivery, like I had a temperature.

He said, 'All right. You want to keep on punishing me. You want to keep me away from my son. You win.'

I opened my mouth. There was a tiny noise, barely audible, as my vocal cords opened and closed. *No.* He'd go away and never come back, and he was my *dad* . . .

The drawing-room door opened and Dad was standing there, his face blotched and red over the cheekbones. He stared at me, and his mouth moved, but he didn't say anything. I looked at him, scared that he could see how I felt, but glad too, because if he could see how I felt he might not leave.

He met my eyes. And I think – even now, I think he *could* see how I felt.

Then he shoved his hands into his pockets, walked straight past me and down the stairs. I heard the front door bang.

There was a pause, and footsteps. Then Granddad was leaning in the doorway, lighting a cigarette. I was looking at the carpet, but I could see his shoes, and hear the clink of his lighter. A second later I smelt the smoke. I was used to it, but it still made me want to gag.

He said, 'Olly . . .'

There was silence; just the sound of him smoking.

'Oliver. How much of that did you hear?'

'Quite a lot.'

'I'm sorry.'

I clenched my jaw, pushing my tongue against my lower teeth. I couldn't help listening for a knock at the door, because Dad had to come back any second now. He couldn't have left without even saying goodbye. Any second now . . .

'Olly, I'm afraid your father has – I'd be very surprised if he comes back.'

I said, 'He's taking me to the Tower of London tomorrow.'

'No,' Granddad said, 'I'm rather afraid he isn't.' A pause. 'Would you still like to go? Shall I take you?'

'No,' I said.

'Very well.' He looked around for an ashtray. His eyes seemed to flicker, as if he was somewhere he didn't recognise. 'I'm truly very sorry, Olly. I know how hard it's been for you. I promise you that I didn't want your father to leave like this.'

'I'm fine.'

I wasn't looking at him, but I could still feel his gaze on my face. I knew he didn't believe me, but he didn't say so.

There was a pause. He sighed and lowered himself slowly down until he was sitting next to me on the stairs. His right hand rested on his leg, the smoke streaming up between his fingers. The skin over his veins was crumpled and shiny, like paper. His other hand was still holding his lighter, turning it over and over so that the silver caught the light.

'Olly, the book he bought you . . .'

It wasn't like Granddad not to finish a sentence. I

couldn't help glancing at him. He was watching the drawing-room door as if it was . . . I recognised the expression on his face, but I wasn't sure why.

'That book – I'm going to keep it for you until . . . I don't think you'll enjoy it. It's somewhat too . . .'

I waited. Granddad didn't turn his head. I realised, with a strange, distant shock, that his face looked the way mine had when I looked at Dad. As if he could see someone standing in front of him, someone older than he was.

'Granddad,' I said, 'please let me have it. It's only a book. Please give it back. *Please.*'

'I'll find you something you'll enjoy more.'

'No – Granddad, I want *that* book. Dad bought it for me. *Please –*'

He stood up, making a brief painful noise as he braced himself against the wall. Tiny flecks of ash drifted down on to the carpet. I got to my feet too, holding on to the banister because I wanted to touch something solid. I said again, 'Granddad –'

'No.' He didn't look at me. 'I'm your grandfather, Olly, and I know better. You'll have to trust me on this.'

'Well, I *don't*,' I shouted, and heard my voice crack. 'You *made* him go away – you won't let him in the house – you stole my book –'

'Oliver –'

'I hate you! Why couldn't you just let him –' I was choking. I could feel the tears running down my cheeks. I forced the words out, although I could hardly speak through the sobs. 'I *don't* trust you! You don't care about me – you just want him to go away. And he's your *son*! Why couldn't you just be nice to him?'

'What happened between your father and me is over. Do you understand, Olly? I am not going to discuss it with you. I'm sorry about what happened tod—'

'No, you're *not*! This is what you wanted, all the time! For him to go and never come back and –' I wanted to keep talking – wanted it desperately, because it was working, I could see Granddad struggling to control his anger – but I ran out of breath and leant over, crying too hard to make the right shapes with my mouth.

'Olly . . .'

He put his hand on my back. I spun round and lashed out at him, not caring how hard. My hand knocked his arm away. He drew his breath in and there was a thunk as his lighter dropped against the skirting board.

I looked straight into his eyes and said, 'I *hate* you.'

He didn't answer. For a moment I thought he was going to hit me.

I waited, glaring at him, until he turned away and bent, wincing, to pick up his lighter. Then I ran up the stairs to my room and lay face down on my bed.

II

I knew Dad was going to come back. I knew it. He'd come back and apologise for letting Granddad wind him up. He'd tell me I should go and live with him in Australia. Or he might even decide not to go back to Sydney at all.

The next day I got dressed and put my coat and shoes on, so I'd be ready to go when Dad came to pick me up. At eleven o'clock Granddad came up to see me. He brought me tea and toast on a tray like I was ill, and three or four books that he said he thought I might like. He put them down carefully on my desk, and sat on the edge of my bed. He asked me if I was all right, and if I wanted Rosina to buy anything special at the supermarket, and what did I want for dinner, and was I sure I didn't want to go to the Tower of London, because he could take the day off and he knew I'd enjoy it. I didn't answer. I didn't even look at him.

In the end he went away again. He was meant to be working but when I crept past his study on my way to the loo I couldn't hear any typing. I imagined him staring at the engraving of Napoleon on his wall and feeling the way I did, and I thought, *He deserves it. He made Dad leave me here. It's all his fault.*

On the day after that I made Granddad phone up and tell the coach I wasn't coming to football practice that evening because I was ill. I didn't dare to leave the house in case Dad came round and I missed him.

On the third day I still thought Dad might turn up. Dad's flight was Sunday afternoon.

The day after that I had to go back to school.

I didn't tell anyone about what had happened, not even Adeel, my best mate. But I couldn't get it out of my head. When I got home from school that Monday I went straight upstairs and stood outside Granddad's study. He was typing, but the door was ajar, which meant I could go in and talk to him if I wanted to. I shifted from foot to foot, imagining what I'd say. *You made Dad go away.* Or, *I want my book back. It's mine, you've got no right . . . Please . . . I don't understand why . . .* I took a deep breath, shuffling back and forth, making the floorboards creak.

The typing stopped. Granddad said, 'Olly? Is there something I can help you with?'

Weren't old people meant to go *deaf*? I swallowed. 'Um, yes please.' I peered round the door. 'I wanted to ask you – to talk to you about – um . . .'

Granddad leant back in his chair and smiled at me. The air in the room was grey and rippling with smoke. He pushed his typewriter to one side and reached for his cigarettes. He was still looking at me but his hand went straight to the right place. 'The Roman legions again, is it?'

'No, it's –' I stopped. 'About – Dad.'

'Ah.' He took a cigarette out of the packet and fumbled with his lighter. It took four goes before he got a flame, and he flipped the lighter shut and clenched his fist over it, staring at his knuckles.

'I – Granddad, please can I have the book he gave me? He's never given me anything before, not even for birthdays or Christmas, and –' I swallowed.

'No. I said no, and I meant no.'

'But –'

'Oliver.' He looked at me for what seemed like ages. Then he sighed and got up, put a hand on my shoulder and pulled me gently into the room. 'Sit.'

I sat down in his chair. The seat was warm. I bent my head and frowned at the typewriter as if this was my study and Granddad was disturbing me.

'Olly, old chap. Listen to me. I –' He leant against the bookshelves, flicking the ash from his cigarette into the ashtray at my elbow. 'I'm not going to give you that book. Not until you're much older. Possibly never.' I started to say something and he raised his voice a little, so that his words cut through mine. 'You have every right to be angry. I myself, in your situation, would be furious. But you must understand that I have only your best interests at heart.'

'You told me I should read more. You said –'

'Yes. And you *should*. How are you getting on with those books I found for you?'

'I want the one Dad gave me.' I twisted to look at him, wishing that I could trust myself not to cry. 'Granddad, *why* won't you –'

'Because –' He tilted his head back against the shelves, blowing smoke at the ceiling. 'Your father . . .

I suppose you've gathered by now that he was – we were something of a disappointment to each other. He made us both – Marian, your grandmother, and me – very unhappy. He got in with a bad crowd, and . . . We weren't on good terms for some time before he married your mother, and then . . . Marian died, and when – he had to go away, and your mother needed my help . . .'

I sat very still.

'I don't want to speak ill of your father, Olly. I know you – you were very excited to see him, and that does you credit. But I've lived almost sixty-seven years longer than you, and I want you to trust that I *do* know what's best for y—'

'How can a book be bad for me? He's *gone*, Granddad! He's not coming back! Why won't you –?'

'What?' His voice was sharp all of a sudden, as if he was talking to someone else, not me.

'You shouted at him until he left!'

'Oh.' He breathed out in a tight, uneven way; it was like a laugh, but it wasn't one. 'Very well. The book.'

I hooked my feet behind the rung of the chair and stared up at him.

'The truth is, Oliver,' he said, 'your father – when he was your age, or perhaps a little older – discovered a great liking for – an obsession with, one might even say – H. J. Martin, the subject of the biography he bought you. Your father knew that I had met Martin once or twice, and that I'd disliked him, and it seemed – to amuse him, I suppose, to develop this – hero worship. It was an act of rebellion against me, I think. An attack. And when he took you to that exhibition, and bought you the book, it was not only in spite of the fact that he knew I would see it, it was *because* he knew I would see it. It was nothing more nor less than an attempt to remind me of the tensions of his own adolescence.'

'You mean he doesn't care about me at all.'

'I –' Granddad paused, took a last drag on his cigarette, then leant towards me to stub it out. 'It is entirely possible that he does care about you, Oliver, very deeply. I'm simply afraid that it wasn't uppermost in his mind when he chose that particular gift for you.'

I looked down at my hands, spread out flat on Granddad's desk. I didn't want to believe him, but it was *Granddad*. He didn't tell lies, not even when everyone else would, to be kind, or to make his life easier. He always told me when something would hurt. Even when I was small, when I'd asked he'd told me that my mother had got ill and died, and that God didn't exist, and what *gay* meant.

'Olly?' He bent his knees and put his arm round me, so that our faces were on the same level. 'Oliver, old chap. There's no need to be ashamed –'

'I'm not,' I said. 'And I'm *not crying*.' I pulled away. Granddad watched me for a few seconds, and then stood up. He reached for his cigarettes, glanced at me, and put them in his pocket without lighting one. He didn't say anything. I swallowed over and over, trying to breathe normally, trying not to blink, because my eyes were full of water and I was *not crying*. I said, 'I hate you,' but only my mouth moved, and the cowardly bit of me was relieved that I hadn't said it out loud this time.

I heard Granddad take a deep breath. 'I don't – I

honestly can't imagine that you would *enjoy* the book, at your age.'

I felt something odd squirming in my stomach. I didn't look up.

'It isn't – Oliver, I don't want your father to . . . You were terribly miserable all the time he was here, and I don't want . . .'

It had started to rain again. I could hear it against the windows.

'Oliver. Suppose we make a bargain?'

I turned my head. Granddad was leaning against the mantelpiece, gazing into his own eyes in the mirror. He reached out and straightened a photo frame, touching the glass gently. My grandmother beamed at the camera, cradling me in her arms, and my mum touched my hair with one hand, as if she couldn't bear to let go of me completely. That was taken when I was tiny, before my grandmother died and Mum got ill. I couldn't remember either of them.

Granddad cleared his throat. 'If I were to give it to you, Olly, would you be willing to make me a promise?'

'Yes,' I said.

His reflection smiled at me. 'You don't know what it is yet.'

'Whatever. I don't care.'

'Very well. Suppose I ask you to promise that, if I give you this book, you won't read any other books about H. J. Martin; that you won't let him become – an obsession, the way your father did.'

I stared at him. I don't know what I'd been expecting, but it wasn't that. I opened my mouth to ask why, but there was something about Granddad's face that made me stop.

'Will you, Olly?'

'Yes,' I said. 'Yes.'

His reflection searched my face with his eyes. 'You won't seek to know more about him? Once you've read that book, you'll stop? You give me your word?'

'Yes,' I said. 'But why? I thought you were worried about *Dad*.'

'I – yes. Yes, I am.' But he didn't look at me, and if I hadn't known that Granddad didn't lie . . . 'You can be a much, much better man than your father, Oliver. I don't want you to end up like him. Neither do I want to be reminded of him. And as for H. J. Martin, I hardly knew him, but he was –' For a second his voice seemed to hang in the air, but then he started speaking again and I thought I'd imagined that silence, that fractional pause. 'He was simply a rather good-looking upper-class dilettante, who happened to be in a particular place at a particular time. He took in many people, but then we – they were like children: eager for myths, for heroes, for easy answers. He was . . . not a good man.'

'Oh,' I said. 'Right.'

He caught my eye and smiled, but he looked more tired than I'd ever seen him, even more tired than he had on Wednesday afternoon when Dad walked out. His face was all creased and baggy, like the framework underneath was rusting away. 'All right, then, Olly,' he said. 'We have a bargain. Now . . .' He got his keys out of his pocket, unlocked one of the low cupboards and took out the book. He held it for a moment, looking down at the photo, and then passed it to me without a word.

'Thank you,' I said.

139

'You're right,' Granddad said. 'What harm can it do?'

I opened my mouth, but he wasn't expecting an answer. I wanted him to pat my shoulder, or kiss me goodnight, or say something so that I knew I wasn't in trouble, but he turned away and propped himself against the desk, watching the rain spray the window. It was getting dark.

I waited until I knew he wasn't going to look at me, and then I left.

As I shut the door behind me, I heard Granddad say quietly, 'Stop being stupid, Oliver. What harm can it do? The man's been *dead* for nigh on sixty years.'

I turned round, confused, but he wasn't talking to me. He was still looking out of the window, staring into his own reflected eyes.

I went upstairs, trembling, holding the book in my arms like it was alive. I was filled with an odd mixture of shame and triumph – because Granddad had given in and I'd *won*.

I sat on my bed, opened the book, and started to read.

On June 21st 1936, at half past five in the morning, a motorcycle and its rider hurtled along the long, straight road that still runs from Falconhurst in East Sussex north-east towards Tunbridge Wells. It was already a clear, sunny day. In that era the traffic along the quiet country roads was minimal, and it would have been unusual – even startling – to meet another vehicle, especially so early in the morning, on a Sunday. The road holds no other surprises or hazards for the driver, stretching as it does for several miles without unexpected changes in direction or gradient. It was also well-known to the motorcyclist who rode along it that morning: his familiar, habitual route to the nearest town. We know, from evidence I will examine later, that he was travelling at no more than 38 mph; we also know that he was ordinarily a careful driver, averse to taking unnecessary risks.

Why, in the early hours of that glorious summer morning, H. J. Martin should have crashed his motorcycle – in such a violent impact that he was apparently flung several metres from the machine – and been killed instantly, we simply do not know.

There are other, secondary, questions that surround his death. We do not know, for example, where he was going; indeed, we do not know the direction in which he was travelling. We do not know why he was travelling so early in the morning, or where he had been. We do not know whether he met another vehicle on the road, or whether the boy who discovered his body under a tree next to the road and alerted the police was the first person to learn of the accident. We cannot even be sure that he was travelling alone.

These are not questions which I can answer. They are not, perhaps, questions that will ever be answered. But to me, and to all the other biographers of H. J. Martin, they are an incisive reminder of the enigmas which make him both a fascinating and an elusive subject. The ease with which Martin's life has achieved the status of myth – to the extent that the contemporary military historian S. S. Hamley remembers being told by his father that 'H. J. Martin would come back, if we needed him, like King Arthur' – has in part been increased by the circumstances of his fatal accident. But there is an element of the reverse: that while the mystery of Martin's death satisfied a collective desire for intrigue, it was the interest aroused by his life that created that desire in the first place; that a solitary, violent, perplexing death was felt to be a fitting end for the hero who had so inhabited the imagination of the British public.

What died that morning was not simply a celebrity, a man who had made a name for himself first on the vast battlefield of the Middle East and then in the smaller, more intricate spheres of politics, academia and literature. Neither was he merely, as the politician Dominick Medina said, 'a piece of the old England'. H. J. Martin was indeed an icon – a living metaphor, as it were, for 'the old England', the last avatar of Victorian Boy's Own heroism – but he was also an extraordinarily complex figure, a man who told and retold his own story so inconsistently and ambiguously that he seemed to occupy a no-man's-land between truth and fiction. Martin was not only a magnetic, charismatic, seductive personality, but a man whose life seems to embody the spirit of empire, of danger, of history itself . . .

I wasn't a very quick reader in those days. By the time I got to the end of that first section it was late and I'd missed dinner. I knew Granddad would've kept some for me, but I wasn't hungry. I had a hot, sick feeling in my stomach. I couldn't believe it. All this fuss, for *this*! It was just history. It was the kind of book Granddad wrote. I reread the last sentence. *Martin was not only . . . whose life seems to embody . . . history itself . . .*

Then I threw the book across the room as hard as I could. It hit the wall with a thump and dropped into the corner behind my laundry basket.

A few days later Rosina picked it up when she was cleaning and put it on my bookshelf. But I never opened it again.

III

Dear Dad,
thank you for the book you bought me, it was very good. Granddad gave it back to me because I asked. ~~I read it~~ I have just finished reading it. I hope your flight ~~home~~ back to Sydney was good. I like aeroplanes.

I am doing well at school, we had a test in history and I got 89% which was good. I got a commendation because I knew when the 1st World War was.

~~When are you coming~~ I really liked meeting you, I hope you did too. ~~I am sorry it would be nice~~ My Christmas holidays start on Wednesday and I have until the 6th of January.

How are you? I hope you are well. How is your job? It sounded very fun when you told me about it. My best friend Adeel says you can go scuba diving in Cornwall.

Love from Oliver

Dear Dad,
I hope you are well, and had a good Christmas. Me and Granddad had a good Christmas. I got a new

games console and some games. My favourite is called DARK CLOUD: ENIGMA. Rosina gave me some money and a box of chocolates. What did you get? Do you have lots of friends in Sydney?

I am still doing alright at school. I am not very good at French because we drop things out of windows. Me and Adeel dropped everyone's textbooks out of the window the last day of term. Adeel says its more French and educational if we say ooh la la! while we do it. Granddad told me off. ~~but he said de Gaulle would be proud of us.~~

How are you? Is it good weather there? I expect it is much nicer than England at the moment because it is summer. ~~Maybe you could~~ I hope you are well.

Love from Oliver

Dear Dad,
Happy Easter! I hope you are well. I've just broken up for Easter and Granddad is taking me to Italy but I have two weeks holiday and I am spending the second week ~~at home~~ in London. How are you? I hope you are okay.

~~I hope you don't mind me writing to you.~~ I don't have very much to say but I am fine. Please write soon.

Love from Oliver

~~Dear Dad,~~
~~Could you tell me if this is the right address for you?~~

~~Dear Dad,~~
~~Please will you answer my letters because I want to know if you're dead.~~

Dear Dad,

I know it's been a while since I last wrote. I'm hoping this is the right address for you, because, as you know, you never wrote back. But all I can do is hope that you'd have the decency to tell me if you'd moved, or if you wanted me to stop writing, so here we go, I'm writing to you anyway. If you've managed to earn enough money to buy a phone, then you could even ring on +44 208 779 6454. I'm still at the same address. You know, the one where Granddad shouted at you and you walked out without saying goodbye. Remember?

I don't have much to tell you. I did OK in my GCSEs (mainly A's and B's. I expect Granddad told you, because he at least takes your paternal responsibilities seriously). I'm taking a couple of A-level modules this summer, but my main exams aren't until the end of sixth form.

Sixth form is OK, although the girl I was going out with last year left to go to another school, and we've kind of drifted apart. I liked her, but we don't see each other much, and I think she's seeing someone else now. It's fine, though. (My mate Adeel was really jealous when I asked her out and she said yes. He said that she'd gone for style over substance, although when I told her that she said it was more like mind over matter. I couldn't tell whether that was meant to be an insult.)

Oh, by the way, you remember that book you bought me? The only thing you've ever given me, in sixteen years? (Did I mention that my birthday is the 3rd of July? Not that you'd care.) I told you I'd read it and it was really good. Well, actually, I didn't read it at all. It was really boring. I don't know why you even bothered to buy it for me. Let me know if this is the right address and you can have it back.

Anyway. I won't bore you any longer. I don't know why I'm writing this, really, as I know you won't reply. Maybe you're dead. Or maybe you want me to think you are. Whatever.

Your son, Oliver

It was all wrong, but I sent it anyway.

That was the day I got home from school and found Granddad celebrating. You could hear the music – some classical thing, Mozart or someone – playing from halfway down the street. That day we'd had a school trip to the British Museum and I was in a strange mood; I didn't feel like talking to anyone, even Granddad. I was going to go straight upstairs to change my clothes but Granddad flung the kitchen door open and called, 'Olly! How are you? Duly edified by our national treasures, I trust?' He'd turned the music down a bit, but he still had to raise his voice. He looked flushed and excited.

I paused on the bottom stair. 'Shouldn't you be working, Granddad?'

'Good news. I'm celebrating. Come and have a drink.'

He grinned at me and my bad mood receded. How many of my friends got home to their legal guardian playing music too loud and plying them with drink? I said, 'OK,' and followed him back into the kitchen. There were piles of CDs on the kitchen table, an overflowing ashtray, and a half-empty glass of something fizzy. 'What's the occasion?'

He pulled the fridge door open just slightly too enthusiastically; the jars rattled and clinked ominously. 'Champagne, my boy?'

He only ever called me that when he was drunk. Or *tight*, as he'd say – *I'm a trifle tight this evening, my boy*. I'd told him once that tight didn't mean that any more but he was still sober enough to get the *Oxford English Dictionary* out and teach me the error of my ways.

'Thanks.' I watched him pour it; it looked like it wasn't the first bottle. 'I thought we only had champagne on Sundays.'

'High days and holy days. They're going to publish *Arthur*.' Granddad handed the glass to me with a flourish.

'Who's Arthur?'

'My book on King Arthur, Oliver. The one I've been working on. And talking about, every evening, for a year or so. The pinnacle of my life's work. The one –'

'Oh, yeah, *that* one. Congratulations.' I raised my glass to him and took a mouthful of champagne. It was cold and slightly sour, like fizzy water.

For a second Granddad carried on smiling at me: the huge, unlikely, lighthouse-beam grin that seemed to extend beyond the actual edge of his face. It was irresistible; I couldn't help smiling back. He lit a cigarette, sauntered over to the CD player, and turned the volume down so we could talk without having to shout.

He still had his back to me when he said, 'Oh, and there's a book tour for it in the summer. In the United States and Canada.'

'Fantastic,' I said. 'How long for?'

'Hopefully a month or so, Robin said. Starting in New York, then moving west. The details aren't fixed yet.'

'Great.' I'd never been to America. I took another swig of champagne. 'When's it start?'

'June.' Granddad reached over and plucked an olive from a plastic tub balanced on the nearest pile of CDs.

'What about my exams?'

Granddad paused, the olive poised between finger and thumb a few centimetres from his mouth. 'Well, you don't need me to be here, do you?'

I took the largest gulp of champagne that I could, and felt a trickle of something wet slide down from the corner of my mouth. After I'd swallowed I said, 'No. 'Course not.'

'I'll send you an appropriate present.'

'Right.' I watched him eat his olive. It was one of the ones Rosina liked, the ones that came in a tub with bits of soggy garlic and lemon peel. I hated them but Rosina bought them anyway.

'You're not bothered, are you, Olly?' He wiped his fingers on the tablecloth.

'No. Of course not. I'm fine. I'm pleased for you.'

'I've been away before. And you are, after all, an exceptionally independent and resourceful young man.'

I wanted to say, *Yeah, and it's just as well, don't you think?* I wanted to say, *Only because I have to be, because everyone keeps going away, or dying – if they're not dead already.* I wanted to say, *No, I'm not, Granddad. Stay, please stay – I know it's babyish . . .*

149

I shrugged and made myself smile.

He frowned and peered at me, absently tapping the ash off his cigarette on to the table. I watched a few dark grey flecks drift down into the tub of olives. 'Rosina will be here, of course –'

'I said I'm fine. It's not a big deal.' And the funny thing was, it *shouldn't* have been a big deal. It was only a month. And I was sixteen, for God's sake, it wasn't like I needed someone to hold my hand.

Granddad picked another olive out of the tub. It had grey speckles of cigarette ash on it, but I didn't say anything, just watched him put it in his mouth. As he was chewing he said, 'Good lad. I knew I could rely on you to be a man about it.'

''Course,' I said. 'I like being on my own.' *Don't go*, I thought, *please, Granddad*, and for a sickening moment I wasn't sure if I'd said it aloud.

'Excellent. We can work out the details with Rosina later. About meals and – and laundry and so on.' He beamed again, but impersonally, as if he was suddenly very fond of the kitchen wall.

I drained my champagne. It couldn't have gone flat in that time, but that's how I remember it: tasteless and still, like tap water. I put the glass down on the table. 'Great. Well. Congratulations. Again. Right. I'm going upstairs.'

'Oh – I thought I might open another bottle.'

'I've got school tomorrow.'

'Bugger that.' Granddad lit another cigarette off the end of the last one. 'You're sure?'

'Yeah.' I thought, *Just once, just once I'd like someone to tell me to go to bed. Not ask me, not suggest, not treat me like a responsible adult – just* tell *me.* I said, 'Goodnight, then. Don't set the house on fire.'

He looked at the clock above the bookshelf. 'It's five o'clock, Olly. You're not ill, are you?'

'I didn't mean goodnight *now*, I just meant – I'm going upstairs.'

'What time would you like dinner?'

'I'm not hungry.'

As I walked out I heard him start to say, 'Very well, shall I save some?' but I carried on up the stairs without answering. I thought, *I should be glad he's going. I should be glad he's well enough to go. I mean, bloody hell, he's nearly eighty, and all excited about getting his book published, and all I can think is,* Please don't leave me on my own, *like some pathetic kid.* I said aloud, 'Jesus Christ, for God's sake, get a *grip*,' and tried to whistle the music from Granddad's CD.

When I got to my room I sat down at my desk and leant my face on my hands. I wasn't crying; just breathing deeply, trying to ease the ache in my throat. I said silently, *It's not that I can't live on my own for a month. It's just that everyone* goes. *Everyone goes, and I'm sick of it.*

I got out my mobile to phone Adeel, then put it on my desk, stared at it for a couple of seconds, and turned it off. *Hi, Adeel,* I'd say. *My grandfather's going away for a month when we do our exams.* And he'd say, *Great! Let's have a party. We can do anything we want. You're so lucky not having any parents.*

The pain in my throat swelled again and I swallowed, trying to force it away. Then I got my notebook out and started scribbling before I even thought about it. *Dear Dad.*

I knew – even as I was writing it – I knew the letter was all wrong. *I'm still at the same address. You know, the one where Granddad shouted at you and you walked out without saying goodbye. Remember?* But I carried on writing anyway, not rereading, not letting myself cross it out. *I don't know why you even bothered to buy it for me. Let me know if this is the right address and you can have it back.* That made me wince, but I left it as it was.

Anyway. I won't bore you any longer. I don't know why I'm writing this, really, as I know you won't reply. Maybe you're dead. Or maybe you want me to think you are. Whatever.

After I'd signed it I folded it up into a little thick square and shoved it into one of the posh envelopes I'd nicked off Granddad ages ago. I sealed it and scrawled the address on it and then put it in my bag, where I wouldn't stare at it and change my mind. I knew I shouldn't send it. But I was scared that if I didn't, sooner or later I'd write something even worse.

I hate you. You bastard, I wish you were dead. I hate you.

Even what I'd written was better than that.

For weeks after that I waited for a reply, half hoping, half dreading it. Dad hadn't answered my other letters – but this one was different. He had to answer this one, surely. But I'd come down to breakfast every morning and there'd be nothing, or just a postcard from Auntie Jo in America, or a bank statement

152

addressed to Granddad that he'd left for me because the money was invested in my name. But there wasn't anything from Dad. He didn't care enough to answer. And by the time Granddad went on his book tour I'd almost forgotten I'd sent it.

Granddad left a couple of weeks before the end of term, just before our exams started. He'd been excited all week – like a kid about to go on holiday – rushing around leaving piles of things everywhere (books, socks, and teabags, for some reason) and making copious notes for Rosina (in Spanish, *por supuesto*) every time he thought of something else I'd need while he was away.

But the morning when he left was different. It was ridiculously early – about four in the morning – but I hadn't slept well and in the end I got up to see him off. He was sitting in the kitchen waiting for the taxi, with a big cafetière of coffee and what looked like his tenth cigarette. I gave him a kind of salute and went over to open the window. It was already light-ish, but rainy, and water spattered in over the windowsill.

I said, 'Morning.'

Granddad didn't smile. He ground the end of his cigarette into the ashtray and immediately lit another. 'You're up early. Revision?'

I rolled my eyes, like, *Yeah, right, revision at four in the morning.* 'No, Granddad, I got up to see you off. You're going to America, remember?'

'How kind.'

I shot a look at him to see if he was being sarcastic, but he was just staring blank-faced at the wall. 'Well, I thought so.'

A silence.

Eventually, against my better judgement, I said, 'Are you OK?'

'I'm not sure . . . yes, yes, of course, Olly. I'm perfectly – indeed. I was simply – would you like some coffee?' His voice was slack, skating over the consonants. For a horrible second I thought he was drunk.

'Thanks.' It was all I could think of to say. I poured myself a cup of coffee, staring at him sideways. Jesus, was he *ill*? 'Is it – I mean, how long's the flight?'

'Eight hours or so.'

I knew it wasn't that, anyway; Granddad loved flying. I swallowed and coughed: the coffee was so strong I could hardly drink it. I said, 'What's up?'

He looked at me then. 'I . . .' He tailed off. For a moment I was sure he was going to say more; then he shrugged and carried on smoking his cigarette as if that was his highest priority.

'Is it about leaving me? I'll be fine. You can't just – I'll be fine. I don't – ' I stopped. 'Seriously, what's the matter, Granddad?'

'Oh – nightmare,' he said, and gave a little laugh. 'Absurd, at my age. Nothing of any import.' But his eyes slid away from mine.

'About going to America?'

'About leaving you on your own.' A beat, then he tapped his ash into the ashtray. 'But, as you say, Olly, you will be fine. As, I hope, will I. So there is no need to discuss it further.'

'Are you scared I'll make Rosina let me live on chips and ice cream?'

Granddad shook his head. 'I can't say that was my main preoccupation.'

'Ah well,' I said, 'maybe you *should* be scared. Of that, I mean.'

'Believe me, young Oliver, you couldn't stand up to Rosina any more than I can. That woman is formidable. In fact I have a sneaking suspicion that she's descended from the Borgias – an illegitimate branch, of course.' It wasn't quite as casual as it should have been; but it stopped me saying anything else.

By the time the taxi came he looked better: less grey, less drawn. He stubbed his cigarette out carefully in the ashtray on the hall table, gave me a brisk kiss on my forehead, and picked up his case. 'Goodbye then, Olly. Look after yourself.'

'Yep.'

'Any problems, contact me or Robin at Reid Hartley –'

'At Reid Hartley. Yes, I know, Granddad, the number's in the black book –'

'And –' He stopped suddenly, and the pause got longer and longer. I'd never seen him at such a loss for words: as if he'd suddenly been transplanted into a foreign country, where he didn't speak the language. It was strange to watch.

'Granddad.' I tried to laugh. 'Get into the taxi. I'll be fine.'

He put his bag down.

'*Granddad*. The taxi's waiting.' More silence. 'Call me from New York, OK?' *Just go,* I thought. *Just go.* 'I thought you said you were perfectly –'

'So I did.' Granddad nodded. 'Very well.' He ruffled my hair, then turned away. 'See you in July, then. Goodbye.'

'Goodbye,' I said. He glanced back at me as the taxi

155

driver slung his case into the boot of the car, then beamed, unexpectedly, like a light coming on. It made everything all right. I grinned back, waved, thumbed my nose, and then waved with both hands, widely, as the taxi went down the street. Granddad waved back, flapping his travelling hat at me through the back window. He was still smiling his wide, warming, unfakeable smile.

That wasn't the last time I saw Granddad. But I wish it had been.

'All right, ladies and gentlemen,' Mr Fletcher said, 'put down your pens – *now*. You know the drill: papers on your desks –'

Possibly he carried on speaking, but the noise of twenty chairs being pushed noisily away from twenty desks drowned him out. I got up and fought my way to the door, through clusters of people, then stood outside in the corridor, waiting for Adeel. I heard him say, 'What do you mean, the *Allies* won the Second World War? Oh my *God*, Eithne, you're joking, right?' before he sauntered over to me, still laughing. 'Hey, Olly, how was it for you?'

'Fine.'

'Looking forward to the *partay*?'

'Yeah. Gotta go home and change first.'

'Yeah.' Adeel grinned at me. 'Good idea. And bring some decent drink, OK? I'm really skint, and –'

'I'll see what I can do.'

'No, really, something decent. Hey, Sarah's smiling at me, see you later.'

When I got home I was so tired I could have gone to sleep on my bed. After I'd showered I pulled on jeans and an old T-shirt – no point in changing into my nice shirt until later – and had lunch, fighting to keep my eyes open as I forked my way through the olive-and-anchovy pasta Rosina had left for me. It was about a quarter past one, which meant I could have a nap before I went to the party. Then I'd be fresh and alert, ready to drink heavily and stay up all night. I thought, *I'll go and look in the cellar first, work out which wine to take.*

But the cellar door was locked. I tried the door twice, incredulous, then rummaged through the drawer in the dresser for the key. It was never kept locked. And where the hell was the key? It was supposed to be in here, with the string and brown paper and packs of playing cards. Where –?

I thought, *Rosina.* She'd obviously decided I wasn't allowed free run of Granddad's wine. Who did she think she was, for God's sake? I pounded on the cellar door with my fists, but it was too sturdy to give way. Damn. I didn't have any fake ID, and it was the last day of exams, they'd ask *everyone*. And I couldn't turn up without anything, because Adeel was relying on me.

Wait –

I stopped hitting the cellar door and stood still for a second. Granddad had a decanter in his study. And it was proper Scottish malt, I knew – something decent if ever I saw it. I wasn't allowed to go in there while he was away – the penalty would be death, or possibly something worse, if he found out – but the study key definitely *was* in the dresser drawer, for Rosina, in case of emergencies.

It didn't even occur to me to feel guilty. Not even

once I'd opened the door and gone in. It felt – well, pretty normal, really. As if I'd gone in to ask Granddad a question, and he'd just popped out for a moment.

I should have gone straight to the decanter, picked it up and walked out. I should have taken it into the kitchen, poured the whisky into a bottle, come back, put the decanter down, left, closed the door behind me, locked it again. But I didn't.

Of course I didn't.

I was curious, I suppose. I could look at all Granddad's stuff properly, without him breathing down my neck, making suggestions about which books I might like. I had time to stare at the pictures on the wall, go through the drawers in the sideboard. I could get out the old photo album from Granddad's desk, the one with all the photos of Mum and Dad from before I was born, before Dad left. There was even the long row of Granddad's diaries in the glass-fronted cabinet.

Jesus, *no*. What was I thinking? I'd half sunk into the nearest chair, one hand already reaching for the handle of the cabinet. *No way, Olly, that would be seriously out of order. Definitely not.* I stood up again and picked up the decanter. It was half full.

One of the cupboard doors in the sideboard was ajar. The key wasn't in the lock, but you could see it'd been turned – like someone had tried to lock it in a hurry, pocketing the key and walking off without realising the door wasn't properly closed. But I didn't notice that until a few seconds later, when I was kneeling in front of it. What I noticed first of all was the gleam of glass through the gap. Bottles.

Wow. Who would have thought he'd have so *much*? I rocked back on my heels, and then started to get the bottles out one by one, lining them up on the Turkish rug. And all nearly full. Rum and brandy and cassis, and something with a label in German, and something in Russian, which had to be vodka. For a nasty dizzying moment I thought, *Oh, Christ, he's an alcoholic*. Then I thought, *No. It's just because he doesn't want me to get at them*. No wonder he never kept any spirits in the cellar. So he didn't trust me after all.

I leant forward. There was another bottle right at the back of the cupboard, lurking in the shadows, shining dark green. I reached for it, my forehead pressed against the wood above the cupboard door, my fingers touching cardboard or paper or something before they found the neck of the bottle. I grabbed it and brought it out into the daylight. Absinthe.

I couldn't. Could I? I put it at the head of the little squadron of bottles and narrowed my eyes at it. Absinthe could *kill* you. I really, really shouldn't. Oh, but I could imagine Adeel's face. It would be a night to remember.

I shook my head, feeling the dust from the cupboard in my nose, and slid down on to the rug, propping myself on one elbow. Granddad would know I'd taken it and he'd kill me. It would be worse than when I'd borrowed his lighter without asking, or when Adeel and I had been suspended, but . . .

I was staring right into the cupboard. There was an old shoebox at the back, giving at the corners, held together with an elastic band. It was too small to hold any more bottles, of course, but I pulled it out and

took the lid off idly. I was still thinking, *Absinthe.*
Granddad's not due back for a week or so . . .

Then I glanced down at the papers in the box.

Dear Olly,
Good to meet you too. I have lived in Australia so
long it is always nice to come back to old England, as
they say. I am sorry that your grandfather and I had
a fight, it was not to do with you, I mean it was not
your fault and I am sorry.

Oh God. Oh my God.

Dear Olly,
Thank you, I had a very nice Christmas, of course
here it is summer, it is a bit hard to get used to when
you're English. I do not 'do' presents very much but I
am pleased that your grandfather gave you something
nice. I have got a girlfriend now, her name is Kathleen,
and she says I should have sent you something from
Oz. But I thought you probably would not like a
boomerang or a surfboard, I thought you are not that
sort of boy! I mean you're very English, like your
granddad . . .

Dear Olly,
I had a very nice Easter, it is autumn here. Kathleen
and me went to Adelaide, which was very nice, it is a
long way though.

Dear Olly,
Yes, this is the right address, are you not getting my
letters? I am sorry to here about your girlfriend, it is

a pity she had to change schools.

I was going to write to you anyway because I wanted to tell you that me and Kathleen are getting married next year. She is in the family way so I will be in Australia for good now. We are both very pleased, I hope you will be happy for us. Kathleen would love to meet you, she is very interested and says you sound very English! But at the moment we are very busy doing up a new house and making arangements for the wedding. We would love to invite you but we cannot really 'put you up' because the house is quite small. The baby is due in May.

We have just got a computer so if you would like to email me my address is keithandkath@hotmail.com. It will be good not to have to write letters any more!

I hope you are well and so is your grandfather.

Yours sincerely –

Yours *sincerely?* Yours *sincerely?*

The baby was due in May. Now it was July. *So,* I thought – *my father's baby –*

Then I wasn't thinking any more.

IV

I have no idea how long I sat there. It could have been forty seconds; it could have been forty minutes. The sun moved round until it was shining straight into my eyes. That was the first thing that made me remember where I was. I put my hands over my face. Suddenly I started to shake. The thoughts all kicked back in at once.

My father was getting married again. He had another kid. He was staying in Australia. And my grandfather –

Granddad had kept Dad's letters. He hadn't even told me about them.

I folded my arms across my chest to try and stop them trembling, but it made my whole body shudder. I forced myself to take deep breaths. Why would he do that? Lying to me, making sure he was the first to get to the letterbox in the morning. *Yes,* my mind added, *and why* keep *them? He should have burnt them while he had the chance. Because now I've found them, and now . . .*

I scrabbled for the letters and started to stuff them back into the box, not caring whether I crumpled them up or tore them by mistake. My hands were still trembling. I put the lid shakily back on the box, hearing my heart pounding in my ears. The elastic band was just next to my foot, where I'd flicked it aside. I picked it up and started to pull it over the top of the box, but my fingers wouldn't work properly. The box slid out of my hands and fell on to the floor, spilling bits of paper everywhere – old photos, an exercise book or something, envelopes . . . I looked at the mess, knelt back down, started to gather it in my hands and drop it untidily back into the shoebox. Then, in spite of myself, I started to cry.

I kept sniffing and wiping my face on my arm, still scooping up bits of paper and dropping them into the shoebox, not giving myself time to think. I grabbed the old exercise book without looking at it, the tiny black-and-white photos, the flimsy yellow newspaper clippings. A couple of spots of water appeared on the topmost bit of paper – an envelope, *O. Gardner Esq.*, *Sidney Sussex* – and I pulled back, scrubbing at my eyes. *Stop crying*, I thought. *Stop it. Stop it now*. It didn't work. I leant over to one side so I wouldn't drip on anything else, and dabbed at the envelope with the edge of my T-shirt. I didn't know why I was bothering – I didn't care if Granddad saw, I didn't give a damn about him any more – but I did it anyway. It left a smudge: *O. Gardner . . .* I looked at it for a moment. It must be important, if Granddad had kept it. He was always throwing stuff away and then regretting it. If he'd kept this since he was at Cambridge . . . I ran my thumb over the name, obliterating it. Now it wasn't addressed to anyone. It gave me a nauseous, triumphant feeling.

I reached for the lighter on the mantelpiece, the spare one he kept there to light the fire. I put the shoebox in the hearth, picked up the last few papers in handfuls and piled them on top. They quivered slightly in the draught.

Wait. *Wait* –

What if there were more letters from Dad? What if there was one to say, *Don't worry, Kathleen wasn't really pregnant, we're not getting married after all*? What if there was one saying, *Sorry about the misunderstanding, why don't you come and live with us in the new house*? And what if I burnt it along with everything else?

I pulled the box out of the hearth again and started to rummage through it.

Olly Gardner, Sidney Sussex. OK, not that one. *Olly Gardner, The Old Vicarage, Church Street, Peltenshall.* No, not that one either. *Oliver Gardner, Sidney Sussex* – no. *Oliver Gardner* . . .

It took a long time. And there wasn't anything else for me. Or at least . . .

Just one lumpy envelope, right at the bottom of the box. A heavy, yellowing envelope, with a key-shaped bulge that I could feel with my fingers. It said: *Oliver*. Not my father's writing, but I'd seen it before somewhere. Or – I was *almost* sure I'd seen it before, as if it was someone I'd known when I was too young to remember, or – I shook my head, trying to get rid of the feeling.

Tyme's End, May 1936

My dear Oliver,
Splendid news – so glad you can come! You can take

a direct train to Falconhurst from Charing Cross via Tunbridge Wells Central, or change at Tunbridge Wells West from Victoria. Once you're at the station, Tyme's End is a ten or twenty-minute walk. Simply follow the road, turning right out of the station, and walk for about half a mile along the High Street until you see a pair of wrought-iron gates on your left. This is the entrance to Tyme's End. Go through the gates and follow the drive: the house is another quarter of a mile or so from the road. I have drawn a small map for you – see below. (I hope your knowledge of hiero-glyphics is sufficient to decipher it.)

I do hope your exams go well, and I'm sorry that I didn't have a chance to see you last week. I'm very much looking forward to your visit – there'll be a couple of other people here, whom I'm sure you'll like.
Yours,
Jack

And there was an old, heavy, rusting key, which was almost as long as my middle finger, making the envelope bulge. It had a neat little paper label tied to it with a fraying scrap of string, that said *Front Door*. It wasn't the same handwriting as the letter; it was more familiar, and the ink was blacker, as if it had been written more recently. It took me a second to realise it was Granddad's writing – but untidier than it was now, more like mine. Granddad's writing from a long time ago.

The other side of the label said, *TYME'S END*.

I looked at it, and my hands stopped shaking, and everything was solid again.

I knew – of course I knew – that Granddad's name

was the same as mine. The other letters, the ones to Cambridge and Peltenshall, were for him. And this one was just as old; it was falling apart along the creases, as if it had been read and reread. I didn't even know where Falconhurst was, or who Jack was. I'd never heard of Tyme's End.

But . . . I squeezed the key in my fist, until the edges dug into my palm.

I knew that the letter wasn't for me. I knew that the invitation had been for Granddad, years and years ago. Jack, whoever he was, was probably dead. But none of that made any difference.

I was going to go to Tyme's End. I didn't care about the party, or what Adeel or Rosina would think. I wanted to run away, and Tyme's End was there, waiting for me.

It was mad. I knew it was a stupid, crazy idea. But the rational part of me wasn't strong enough to override the calm, quiet certainty that I was doing the right thing, something I *needed* to do. The key was meant for me. Granddad had hidden it but I'd found it. It was just as much mine as Dad's letters were. I put it in my pocket. Then I paused and decided to take the papers, too.

I packed my stuff. I took my sleeping bag and two changes of underpants and another T-shirt and my mobile phone and wallet and my toothbrush and a bar of soap and a towel. I took the emergency cash from the spaghetti jar. And then, because I had space in my rucksack, I took a carrier bag of food.

And I left Granddad's study door open, with the empty shoebox still sitting in front of the fireplace, so that when he got back he'd know why I'd gone.

It was like a dream. I got the train from Charing Cross, and although there wasn't a Tunbridge Wells West any more the Tunbridge Wells train still went to Falconhurst. I sat on the wall outside Falconhurst station with the letter in my hand, squinting along the road into the sunlight. I could feel the sweat on the back of my neck starting to trickle down my spine, but it was cooler here than in London – pleasant, not like the train, where everyone had been beetroot-red and pissed off, flapping newspapers and sighing.

And the little hand-drawn map on the other side of the letter was easy to follow – too easy, easier than it should have been. A couple of years ago I'd navigated in Italy while Granddad drove, working from a map a few years old, and we'd ended up on a brand-new motorway that apparently didn't exist. But this was different. Falconhurst hadn't changed. The landmarks were in the same places. There was the one-armed stone cross at the crossroads. There was the signpost to Tunbridge Wells. And the church was there, on my left, set back behind a shady churchyard, only the tower rising above treetops. The High Street was quiet, as if everyone was drowsing indoors, away from the heat. A couple of times I stopped and stood still. It wasn't like London; it was another country.

And when I'd walked down the High Street for a quarter of a mile, the gates were there, exactly where the letter said they'd be.

I stood in front of them and heard myself laugh, because they were padlocked, and there was a sign saying TRESPASSERS WILL BE PROSECUTED. What had I expected? Someone to welcome me in?

I rubbed the key in my pocket with my fingers, feeling the rust crumble against my skin. Someone else owned this house now. The locks would have been changed. Trespassers would be prosecuted.

My dear Oliver . . .

I don't know why I didn't turn round and go back to the station. Maybe it was because I'd come this far; or because of the letter in my pocket, or because it was so quiet, so green, so hot . . . But somehow I couldn't bear the thought of giving up now, of leaving without even seeing what Tyme's End looked like.

I followed the wall, keeping an eye open for a gap or a tree growing close enough to help me climb over. It curved away from the road, until there was only the occasional swish of a car or the dull drone of a motorbike coming from a long way away. And I saw there *was* somewhere to climb over the wall, where the railings had been knocked out like teeth. I felt a great electric surge of triumph. I pulled myself up and over, dropped into a bed of bracken, and stumbled through a thin band of trees on to a ragged-edged lawn.

And there was the house, pale in the sunlight, windows glinting.

It was quiet, even quieter than the road; as if the world had swung slowly to a stop, and the moment went on and on. I felt like I'd stepped into the past. All I could do was stand there and stare, forgetting to think, forgetting to breathe. The place, the sunlight, the way the shadows fell . . . I'd been here before, seen it before – not just the house, but the summer afternoon, the exact position of the sun, even the heat. At least – I *hadn't*, of course. But déjà vu swirled round me like water, filling my ears, silencing everything.

Tyme's End looked back at me, waiting.

And I knew then, somehow, that there was no one there.

The house hadn't been forgotten exactly. It wasn't derelict. It hadn't gone to rack and ruin – but it wasn't lived-in any more. The grass must have been mown and the roof hadn't fallen in and the windowpanes were intact, but all the same I could tell it'd been left to itself. I felt a kind of strange tension in my gut that I thought, then, was excitement. I'd be able to have a look after all.

And I was happy. Even now, I can remember how that felt. It was like I'd come home.

And when the door key actually *opened* the front door, it seemed like . . . it didn't surprise me, somehow. It was like being in a dream, where you know everything's going to happen the way you want it, smoothly, easily, without any fuss. The lock was stiff and the door was swollen, and it took all my strength to push it open; but it seemed inevitable that sooner or later I'd stumble through the gap and stand in the porch, my arms trembling from the effort. I walked into the hall, watching the dust billow up into a narrow blade of sunlight. There was a massive fireplace with white-shrouded chairs hunched in front of it, and more doors. My heart was beating hard. I heard the front door scrape shut behind me, and I jumped and swung round, but there was no one there.

I took a few steps into the room, hearing the small sounds of the floor under my feet so clearly it was as if they were amplified. There was a smell of cigarette smoke. For a second it made my skin prickle, until I realised it was only my clothes, because of being in the same house as Granddad. I was too hot, and breathing too fast. I tried to take a deep breath but it only made me feel dizzy.

I went to the door beside the fireplace and opened it. It opened easily, almost before I'd touched it, as if there were someone on the other side pushing it open just as I put my hand on the handle.

It was the drawing room. There was another fireplace, more white-cloaked furniture, a wall of bookshelves that had been curtained with more dust sheets. The sun streamed in, throwing a lattice of shadow over the floor. And –

My heart leapt. Suddenly I couldn't breathe.

Someone had been in here just a moment ago.

I didn't know how I knew. There was nothing moving – no dust swirling or cobweb drifting to the floor, no footprints, not even the tiny noise of the floorboards settling – but I *knew*. Someone had been there. I'd only just missed him. If I'd been a second quicker . . .

But there was only one door: the one I'd come in through.

And no one lived here. There was no one here.

I stood still, frozen to the spot. I could smell fresh air, dry grass and flowers, and still that bitter trace of tobacco smoke. It should have smelt musty, a room that had been closed up for years, but it didn't. The silence settled like dust.

There was the sound of someone tapping on the window.

I jumped violently and stumbled backwards. My back smacked into something hard, and something dropped palely over my eyes, wrapping itself round me. I panicked, fighting to get free, until I was panting and sweating. Oh, God, there was someone trying to get in, someone – I stood still, shaking, with a dust sheet still draped over me like a toga. I clung on to the bookshelf behind me and stared at the window.

The casement was slightly open. There were tendrils of ivy moving in the breeze, beating gently against the glass. That was what had made the noise.

I started to laugh. My voice hit a high note and stuck there. I pulled the dust sheet off my shoulder and bundled it up, still shaking with laughter. The tension went out of my body and I sagged over one of the hooded chairs, limp with relief and embarrassment. *Honestly, Olly*. An empty house with an open window could reduce me to hysterics. I coughed and shook my head, dragging the air into my lungs. Of course there was no one here.

When I stood up again it was as if the room was bigger than before, as if the walls had all taken a step backwards. The breeze from the open window played on the back of my neck and in my hair. I could smell flowers.

I shrugged my rucksack off and leant it against the nearest chair. The huddled, bulky shapes underneath the sheets seemed to inhale slowly, like sleeping animals. I felt floppy and hot, holiday-ish, half tired, half excited. I didn't know what I was doing here, but it felt . . . right.

There were more windows in the opposite wall, and I went over absently and opened them, pushing against the friction of rust and damp-swollen wood. More outside smells flooded in, and the warm air billowed round me. The loose corners of the dust sheets fluttered and moved, as if the furniture underneath was waking up. I turned my back to the windows and looked at my shadow falling across the dusty, bright floorboards. I felt as if I was waiting for someone; as if the owner of the house had just popped out for a second to get something. Without really thinking about it, I wandered back to the bookcase and stared at the spines of the books. There was a thin veneer of dust, but the sheet had kept the worst of it off and the titles stared back at me. There were gold-lettered leather books – Dickens, two volumes of *Middlemarch*, a lot of Shakespeare – but there were mouldy-looking canvas hardbacks too, that looked as if they'd been read over and over. The *Odyssey*, *Le Morte d'Arthur*, *Treasure Island* . . . I slid *Le Morte d'Arthur* out and held it gently in my hands. Then I let it fall open on the first page and brought it up to my face, smelling the old-book tobacco-and-dust fragrance. *Le Morte d'Arthur* was one of Granddad's favourites, and for a second, in spite of myself, I could hear his voice reading it aloud to me years ago, when I couldn't sleep. I squeezed my eyes shut and opened them again, clearing my mind. It hurt to think about Granddad. If I didn't concentrate hard I'd be back in his study, kneeling over his shoebox of papers, reading the letters from my dad over and over again.

I thought, *Stop it. You're here, now. You're miles away from all that*. I took a deep breath, tasting the pollen in the air. This wasn't London, this was another country. It was as if none of that had happened yet.

I glanced down at the flyleaf of the book in my

hand before I put it back. There was a line of dark brown handwriting, thin and clear.

H. J. Martin, August 1923.

The book missed the shelf and fell on the floor.

The noise was so loud that I stood frozen. What if someone heard? What if the owner was coming down the stairs at this very moment, to see who was in his house? What if –? Even though I knew the house was empty, I felt my whole body prickling.

But there was nothing. Nothing happened. No one came; the dust rippled round my feet and came to rest again. The book lay face down, its covers spread like wings.

I picked it up. It felt heavier in my hands than it had done, warmer, like something alive.

H. J. Martin, August 1923.

I put it back on the shelf and slid the next one out. *Treasure Island.* This one was older, but sturdier too, covered in thick ash-coloured fabric that might have been another colour once. I flipped it open to the fly leaf. *Hugo JoHn MArtin. His Book. The Year of Anno Domini, 1899.*

My stomach felt funny, and my knees. I reached out and leant on a dust sheet-covered chair. It seemed to rock gently, pressing itself into my palm and then pulling away. I thought, *I'm dehydrated. I need to sit down.*

But my body wouldn't obey me. I watched my hand – pale skinned, smudged with dust – reach for another book. The *Odyssey.* But this time the handwriting was different.

It was –

To Jack, from Oliver, Cambridge, 1936.

I stared down at it. Oh, God. The familiar-unfamiliar shapes, the words that were taller, untidier, *younger* than they should have been but were still, unmistakably, Granddad's. *To Jack . . .*

I didn't understand. The house shifted around me, creaking almost silently.

Jack. Hugo John Martin. H. J. Martin.

This was his house. Had been his house. But –

I shut the book and held it to my chest, bending my head to breathe in the old-book smell. It was only a coincidence. H. J. Martin wasn't *relevant*. He didn't matter. I was here because of Dad and Granddad, and H. J. Martin was just someone from long ago, from the book that Dad had bought me. He was just someone Granddad had met, and disliked, and made me promise not to read about . . .

I lifted my head. I wasn't sure how I felt, except sick. But there was something . . . A coincidence. Yes. Maybe. But of all the places I could have run away to, I ended up *here*.

And the door was damp and swollen, and it had taken all my strength to get open. But it had closed behind me of its own accord.

I nearly panicked then. I nearly dropped the book, grabbed my rucksack and made a dash for the front door; and if it hadn't opened I'd have smashed a window, broken the door down – anything, just to get out. I'd have sprinted to the station and caught the next train back to London, and maybe I'd have got there in time to go to the party and get plastered on Granddad's absinthe. That's what I nearly did.

There was a cool gust of perfume from the open

window, and somewhere, distantly, the faint bitter fragrance of a cigarette.

And it was as if Tyme's End said to me, *Don't go*.

I turned my head, as if I expected to see someone behind me. But I wasn't scared. I felt . . . curious, detached and safe, like I wasn't really there. None of this was to do with me. I was an observer, that's all.

I opened the book and looked again at Granddad's writing. *To Jack, from Oliver* . . . And that clear, emotionless part of me noted coldly that Granddad must have lied about this as well. He'd said he hardly knew H. J. Martin, and that he'd disliked him. But he'd given him this book. And what about the letter in my rucksack, that he'd kept for years? And –

Why did Granddad have the key to Tyme's End? Why hadn't he given it back to whoever owned it these days? Granddad was conscientious about things like that, always orderly, methodical.

And somehow I knew then that it *wasn't* a coincidence that I was here. Not exactly. I knew that out of everywhere in the world, this house was the one place that Granddad had tried to keep me away from. And that filled me with a kind of burning gladness, like acid. It served him right for all those lies, those betrayals, those days when he must have watched me praying that Dad would answer my letters, when all the time he knew about that little cache of envelopes.

Stay, Tyme's End whispered. *You're welcome.*

I slotted the *Odyssey* on to the bookshelf. My hand was steady, and for a moment I looked at it and thought it was someone else's.

Then I bent down and swept the sheets away from the furniture, pulling armful after armful of pale cotton off chairs and little tables and a gramophone, loitering in the shadows, that I didn't notice until the ivy tapped on the window again, drawing my attention to that corner of the room. And then I was coughing on the dust and there was a pile of sheets at my feet like laundry, and the room was *awake*.

Something was strange, though. I stared round at the room, trying to put my finger on it. It looked lived-in, as if someone had just walked out and never come back, like a photo. And there was something odd about that.

I took a step backwards into a table and heard it rock, and a clink as the stopper rattled in a decanter. I looked round, and then I knew what was bothering me.

There was a dark stain round the middle of the decanter, as if there'd still been something in it when the dustsheets were thrown over it. And there were other things on the tables – a photo in a frame, a box of cigarettes, the paper sleeve for a gramophone record. There was even a folded newspaper on the sofa, yellowed and densely printed. No one had even bothered to pack any of it away before they covered everything up. That was odd. Wasn't it?

As if someone had done it as quickly as possible. As if they hadn't cared about any of it, as if all they'd wanted was to leave. Or as if they'd been told to do it, but whoever had told them to do it didn't care, didn't want to think about it, never wanted to come here again.

I leant over and picked up the newspaper. It ripped as I pulled it, and the last page stayed stuck to the leather of the sofa. I didn't unfold the rest in case it fell apart in my hands. A phrase in the dense print caught my eye: *Italy's disregard of her obligations under the Covenant of the League of Nations* . . . The date was 15 June, 1936.

I thought, *No one's been here since 1936.* But it wasn't true. It couldn't be true. It felt as if someone had only just left. And, anyway, it wouldn't happen. Why would someone cover everything up and leave it for sixty years? A house like this would be worth – well, millions, surely? No one would just leave it to rot.

But they had. I looked down again at the newspaper. *AGGRESSION AND ECONOMICS. THE WARPATH IN CHINA* . . .

1936. Slowly, gently, I laid the paper back on the sofa, lining it up so that it covered the page that was still clinging to the leather. I stood back and looked round the room, taking it in. I couldn't shake the feeling that someone was about to walk in and pick up the conversation where he left off, sixty years ago. H. J. Martin. Jack.

And out of a deep, forgotten part of my mind, something surfaced from the biography Dad had bought me. It was strange how clearly I could see it, the one page I'd managed to get through, that I hadn't looked at since. *On June 21st 1936, at half past five in the morning, a motorcycle and its rider hurtled along the long, straight road that still runs from Falconhurst in East Sussex north-east towards Tunbridge Wells* . . . The house must have been closed up immediately after his death and never lived in again. Whoever owned it never came here; and Granddad kept the key . . .

I walked back to the door and slipped through it quietly. I wasn't scared, but all the same I trod carefully as I walked past the cowled chairs in the entrance hall. There was another door on my right and I opened it. There were more dust sheets in here, but I could see the shape of a chair and bookshelves and a lumpy desk. I tugged gently on the sheet, and the desk was exactly as someone must have left it: a notebook, a half-addressed envelope, one of those brass-and-green-lampshade lamps. A fountain pen rolled on to the floor, and an open bottle of ink tilted and toppled as the sheet caught it. I swore and reached out for it, but it was empty. There was a photo in a silver frame: two men, grinning, in a stone archway. The older one had a face that I thought I'd seen somewhere before: he had to be Martin. He had his arm around the other man, who –

Was *me*.

No. I laughed aloud, although it sounded strange, as if I was out of practice. Of course not me.

It was Granddad. Granddad sixty years ago, a few years older than I was now. He was leaning towards Martin, and beaming – his familiar wide, unfakeable smile – at the camera. He was wearing a tweed jacket and tie, but his top button was undone and the tie-knot was sloppy and crooked. It gave me a pang to see him like that, not just because he'd hidden Dad's letters and I was furious with him, but for some other reason. He looked so happy.

I picked the frame up and tilted it this way and that, watching the reflected sunlight blank them out. The way they were smiling; that easy, paternal arm draped over Granddad's shoulders . . .

He really *had* lied to me. Not an exaggeration or a little white lie, but proper, deliberate lies. Granddad, who wouldn't even say it was all right, the injection wouldn't hurt a bit. About Dad, yes, but about this too – and why, why would he lie about *this*? It was so pointless. As if I'd care about H. J. Martin. Somehow it made me even angrier than the other lies.

But I was here now. He'd lost. Whatever he was trying to do, he'd failed.

I dragged the last corner of the dust sheet off the desk, then put the picture back. I narrowed my eyes at it, imagining that it *was* me. I could almost remember being there, in an archway in Cambridge on a summer's day, Martin's arm over my shoulder, making jokes at the person behind the camera. Martin would have liked me, I knew that.

I took all the dust sheets off so the room looked lived-in again, ready for the owner to come back.

Then I made my way through the rest of the house, taking all the sheets off the furniture, until it was as if I'd gone back in time, right back to the moment sixty years ago when Martin closed the door behind him and started up his motorbike. There were musty, moth-eaten clothes in the bedrooms, beds still made up and stinking of mildew, enamel baths centimetres deep in crumbly, gritty dust; but even so, Tyme's End was awake. I felt reckless. I whistled as I worked through the rooms one by one, half dancing in the sunlight that streamed in. None of the windows were broken, the water from the taps ran clear after an initial spurt of red, and some of the lights worked. Nothing was quite as bad as you'd expect, after sixty years of neglect. It was as if someone *had* been here, quietly fighting the worst of the decay, keeping everything going, just in case.

But all the same, every room in the house was fiercely, hungrily happy to be uncovered again. Tyme's End had been starving to death, only just clinging to life as it stifled under dust sheets. And now I was here. And I thought of Granddad, oblivious across the Atlantic, and that made me feel even better.

At last I came down the back staircase and into the drawing room. I'd left my rucksack there beside the pile of dust sheets, and I sat down, dug out an apple and started to eat it.

Then I stretched out, put my hands behind my head and shut my eyes. I could feel the sunlight on my face, and smell the breeze and the scent of smoke that must have been clinging to the furniture. I remembered the first time I'd walked into the room, as if it was a long time ago. I'd been *scared*. But I couldn't remember what that felt like. I didn't believe in it, somehow. There was nothing to be frightened of here. I was welcome; I *belonged*.

I heard myself say drowsily, 'Thanks for inviting me.'

But if there was an answer, I was asleep before I heard it.

V

When I woke up it was dark. Something jolted me out of sleep so suddenly that it felt as if my brain hit the front of my skull. For a while I looked blankly at the darkness in front of my face, bewildered. I didn't know where I was, or my name, or the year.

Then I felt the sticky leather of the sofa against my face and remembered. My arm was trapped underneath me and I had pins and needles down the side of my body. I was cold, too. There was a draught playing round my neck, making my scalp prickle. And it was so dark – darker than London, where there was always light coming through my curtains – and so still.

Then I knew what had woken me.

Quietly but clearly, I could hear something: a soft, regular sound coming from the other side of the room. It was so faint I could only just make it out. But I wasn't afraid. It was something I'd heard before, something familiar, but I couldn't place it.

I stared up at the shadowy ceiling, not moving. I felt disorientated, heavy-eyed, as though I had been dreaming. That intriguing, gentle sound went on and on, tantalising me. What was it? I strained my ears in the silence, wishing my heartbeat would quieten down. It wasn't the breeze: it was too rhythmic, too repetitive. I closed my eyes again, puzzled. I held my breath until I ran out of oxygen and had to inhale; then, suddenly, I realised.

It was someone breathing.

There was someone there, standing by the window. I knew that if I rolled over to look I'd see him, outlined dimly against the glass. But I didn't move; I listened to the soft sigh of air: in, out, in . . . Perhaps I was wrong – perhaps it was the wind, or an animal outside the window, or cars going past on the road – but I didn't believe it. There was someone else in the room. I gazed at the smooth leather blackness in front of my face and wondered how he'd got there, and who he was. What was going on? I eased my arm out from underneath me, ready to roll over as quietly as I could.

Then there was a kind of rustling, a brief papery noise and a clink.

I recognised that sound too; I knew what it was. My mind fumbled, moving too slowly for me to put a name to it. Something I'd heard hundreds, thousands of times at home. Then I heard the breathing resume more deeply, and a creak, a half-footstep, as he shifted his weight.

He'd lit a cigarette.

I could smell the smoke instantly; the same scent that had been in the air when I first came into the room. I'd thought it was on my clothes, from Granddad – but how could it have been when

Granddad hadn't been at home for weeks? No, it was here, in the room. Maybe there really *was* someone there – a real person, a burglar. Maybe someone sneaked in every night to stand there and smoke. Maybe it was the caretaker, who got a kick out of breaking the rules.

But there should have been a spark.

I'd have seen it. If there'd been a light, I'd have seen it – a flicker reflected in the leather in front of my eyes, or just a golden tinge to the darkness. There'd been the clink of a cigarette lighter. He'd lit his cigarette; I could hear him smoking it. But there hadn't been a flame.

I took a deep breath, thinking how strange it was; very strange. But I still wasn't scared. There was nothing threatening about it: I knew nothing could hurt me. It was like a dream, like it was happening to someone else.

The breathing paused, and resumed. There was a footstep: someone turning to look over his shoulder at the sofa, where I was lying.

And a voice said, 'Oliver?'

The voice was . . . old. It was a skeleton of a voice, dusty, brittle, but it had a kind of friendliness to it. It didn't sound quite *right*; but it wasn't frightening.

I didn't answer, because I didn't know what to say.

It coughed. 'Oliver,' it said. 'I knew you'd come back.'

The floorboards creaked. I heard the tap of shoes on the wood, moving in my direction. The voice – whoever that voice belonged to – was coming towards me.

I thought, *I don't understand. What's going on?*

I sat up. There was no one there.

There was no one in the room except me. There was silence and dim blue light from the windows, and the only thing I could smell was damp leather and my own sweat. There was a gentle, fragrant gust of wind, and the rattle of ivy against the window.

Had I dreamt it? Maybe I had. If it had been real I would have been terrified, surely? And I wasn't; I wasn't even uneasy.

A wave of tiredness hit me. I shifted slowly until I was lying down. The leather sucked at my skin, making a farting noise, and I felt myself smiling. I was safe here – safer here than in London, probably. There was nothing to be afraid of.

I shut my eyes, and the darkness and silence were comforting, luxurious. They rose round me like a sea until I was asleep again.

I woke up in a haze of orange, half blinded by the sun shining through my eyelids. My T-shirt had got rucked up around my shoulders, and the skin of my lower back was stuck to the leather of the sofa. It made a ripping noise as I pulled away and sat up, rubbing my eyes. The light from the window was green-tinged, flooding flatly through the ivy. It showed up the dust on everything, but it made the room look beautiful, like something from a museum, all leather and books and old wood. I thought, *I'm staying here*, and smiled. My night's sleep left me with a clean, serene feeling, as though I'd recovered from an illness. And it was the first day of the summer holidays.

I laughed aloud. I couldn't think of anywhere else I wanted to be. Far better to be here than in London, or in LA with Granddad, or even Casablanca or Paris or Sydney . . . I glanced at my rucksack, remembering my letters from Dad, but now the pain was dulled, as if Tyme's End was an anaesthetic, surrounding me with warmth and welcome-ness. I thought, deliberately, about the other papers – Granddad's letters and photos and exercise book – but all I felt was curiosity and anticipation. On an impulse I bent forward and pulled them out of my backpack, and put them in a precarious, yellowing pile on the nearest table. They fitted in; I'd enjoy going through them later, discovering all Granddad's secrets.

But first things first. I needed breakfast and a shower. Well, maybe a wash would have to do if there wasn't hot water, but breakfast was important. There was food in my rucksack – but there was Granddad's emergency stash of money too, and I was ravenous. I stood up, stretched, and shoved my wallet into the back pocket of my jeans. I'd get breakfast in the village – and anything else I felt like, because Granddad's idea of an emergency was something that cost five hundred quid.

The drawing-room door groaned when I opened it, scraping along the floor as if it had swollen in the night, and the front door was worse, refusing to open. I braced myself to pull at it, laughing. The sun was throwing a thin grating of shadow on to the floor. Something rustled outside the window.

I said, 'Oh, come on. For God's sake.' The floor-boards creaked again, as if there was someone watching me, listening. 'I'm coming back – I only want to get breakfast – I'm *coming b*—'

The door burst open, almost knocking me off my feet. I hung on to the edge of it, still laughing. Bloody hell. It hadn't even rained in the night. Nothing had changed, to make the door stick, but it had stuck.

Not that it mattered now it was open. I took a great breath of early-summer-morning air and puffed it out. My lungs felt double their normal size. I thought, *I have never been this happy*.

Then I took off towards the break in the wall, running for the sheer hell of it.

I went to the bakery first, then wandered down Falconhurst High Street, eating a bun out of a paper napkin. It was still early, and there weren't any people around. Once I'd had something to eat I felt more solid, as if someone had turned the volume knob back up.

I finished the bun, chucked the rubbish in a bin and paused, wondering whether to go straight back to Tyme's End. I could feel it tugging at me like an anchor, wanting me back. It was telling me there wasn't anything else worth looking at here – nothing that compared to Tyme's End. There were Granddad's letters to look through, and the rest of the house to explore, the gardens, the woods . . .

Granddad . . .

For a moment, standing there in the sunlight, I just wanted him to be here. If only he'd been at home when I found those letters. I could imagine how he'd have sat me down, and it would have been too serious for champagne – serious enough for brandy, or a tiny glass of absinthe. He'd have looked at me like I was the same age as him and explained why, exactly, he'd hidden all the stuff from my father.

I was staring absently into the window of a bookshop. There was a display of hardbacks. *The Owl of the Desert*, *Walks in East Sussex*, *H. J. Martin: A Biography*.

I swallowed. It was the same book that Dad had bought me, that Granddad had stolen.

I looked over my shoulder, down the High Street, towards the station. I could go back to London. Or – I checked my pocket – or I could just phone Granddad right now, wherever he was. I imagined his voice, saying my name: *Olly, old chap, how delightful to hear from you.*

No. For a moment I was there, in his study again, staring down at Dad's letters, frozen. *No.* Whatever he said, however he said it, *nothing* could make me forgive him that.

I said to him, in my head, *I don't owe you anything. Screw you.*

Watch.

I walked into the bookshop, leant my elbows on the counter, and said, 'Could you give me a copy of every book you've got about H. J. Martin?'

The bloke glanced up from his newspaper and took a swig of his tea. He didn't smile until after he'd swallowed. Then he said, 'You sure? All eight biographies? That'll be about hundred and sixty quid, boyo.'

'Oh,' I said. 'OK. Just two or three, then.'

In the end I left with a hefty plastic bag of books. I went into a little grocery shop and bought a couple of bottles of water and some other stuff, and then I made my way back to Tyme's End, loaded down with bags.

I'd only been away an hour or so, but I felt like I was coming home after a long journey. The front door opened almost smoothly, giving at my touch as if it was trying to make up for sticking before.

I went back into the drawing room, dumped everything beside the sofa and stretched out on it, putting my feet up on the arm. I rummaged in the bag of books for my new copy of *H. J. Martin: A Biography*. It felt strange to be holding it in my hands again, knowing that the face on the cover was the man who had lived here, the man that Granddad knew. He'd probably sat here, sixty years ago; everything that was in front of me had been in front of him. It made me feel giddy for a moment, as if I was as close to him in time as I was in space.

Then I reached for one of the eclairs I'd bought from the bakery, and started to read.

I read for hours, eating my way through an eclair and an apple turnover and another eclair, until when I looked up it was hot in the room and the light had narrowed and brightened as the sun went overhead. I felt like I'd been miles away, and I stretched, surfacing slowly. I couldn't believe I'd never got further than the first few pages. How could I have thought it was boring? Right now it felt like – it was amazing. H. J. Martin was . . . I grinned up at the ceiling. He was . . . great. I felt as if he was in the room with me, making jokes, talking me through his adventures, making me hang on his every word. I was hardly even *reading*; it was going straight into my ears, as if I was there, living it, falling in love with the desert and the war and – I could almost hear his voice: clipped and upper-class, like Granddad's, but warmer, deeper, nearly-but-not-quite familiar, as if I'd heard it before.

I let the book fall gently on to the floor and lay down. The back of my neck stuck to the leather of the sofa. I shut my eyes and imagined that Martin was here, smoking at the open window, tapping the ash absent-mindedly into the ivy. God, I wished he *was* here. When I'd been reading it was like I knew him already, as if the book was just reminding me. I *knew* him, as well as I knew Granddad – better than I knew my father. And Martin wasn't like them – he was . . . special. My stomach twisted and my throat tightened. Why had I got stuck with Dad and Granddad? Why hadn't I been born sixty years ago? If only . . .

I wanted to stay here for ever.

Well, I thought, *that's tough, because I can't.* I sat up and rubbed my eyes. I grabbed an apple and reached for the book again.

When I turned the next page, I was looking at Tyme's End.

It was a photo – black-and-white, of course – and the caption said it had been taken in 1902, but the house looked the same as it did now. Then there were a couple of pictures of Martin's parents, one of him as a child, two whole pages of desert scenery, another page of other faces I didn't know. I turned the page again, and I saw the same photo that I'd seen in Martin's study: him and Granddad, laughing. *HJM and Oliver Gardner, May 1936.* It was strange, seeing my own name there, even though I was used to it. I slid my finger over the glossy paper. So Granddad was important enough to be in the biography. On impulse, I flipped to the index.

I glanced down, running my finger over the entries. *Fortescue . . . Fraser, James, 32-33; suicide note, 408 . . . Frobisher . . .*

He was there.

Gardner, Oliver, 393-5, 402; and HJM's will, 405-7; Tyme's End, 409.

Something made me pause then – a flash of unease or guilt or . . . It felt like spying. And I could remember my thirteen-year-old self giving Granddad my word of honour that I wouldn't try to find out more about Martin.

But he'd forfeited any right to expect me to keep that promise when he took all Dad's letters and hid them, and I didn't pause for very long.

On the same evening Martin made the acquaintance of Oliver Gardner, then a student of Philip Langdon-Down at Sidney Sussex College, Cambridge. Gardner, now a popular historian of some standing, has been somewhat taciturn on the subject of his relationship with Martin (understandably, perhaps, given the amount of attention he received after Martin's will became public knowledge) and has commented that 'while I was, as most people would have been, impressed by Martin's celebrity and charisma, it was – as far as I was concerned – an unemotional, social, superficial friendship.'[2] While this may be slightly disingenuous, it seems clear that Martin, uncharacteristically, was the more emotionally involved of the two; although, if we are to believe Gardner's statement, Martin seems – more characteristically – to have hidden his feelings extremely effectively. Apparently the extent of his attraction was only revealed, even to Gardner himself, after Martin's death.

However, that evening in the Lent Term of 1936, Gardner's reaction when he was introduced to Martin was no doubt flattering enough, and Langdon-Down noted in his diary that the evening had been a success. A few days later, after he returned to Tyme's End, Martin sent Gardner a copy of The Owl of the Desert, *which he mentioned in a letter to Langdon-Down: 'Sent your young protégé a 1st Ed of the Ood [i.e.* The Owl of the Desert] *. . . should really have sent him something better, but I didn't like him that much . . .'[3]*

There was more, on the next page, but I was already flicking back to the index . . . *and HJM's will, 405-7* . . .

Given that Martin had no immediate family, there was no question of his will being contested; nevertheless, the mere facts were enough to raise the spectre of scandal in the popular press and among some of Martin's less charitable friends. For him to leave his entire fortune – including Tyme's End, the house that had been in his family for generations – to a young man, not yet twenty-one, whom he had known for only a few months, seemed at best extraordinarily capricious, generosity raised to rather histrionic level. At worst – as Edie Quincey pointed out, in rather more robust terms – it implied an unsavoury element to their relationship. Gardner himself denied all suggestions that Martin had been infatuated with him. When the will was made public, he commented: 'Martin was notoriously unpredictable. I'm naturally very glad of the money, but I really can't say what his motives were for leaving it all to me.' On the rare occasions in recent years when he has been questioned further on the subject, Gardner has shown the same reluctance to speculate, and has restricted himself to pointing out the current laws regarding libel . . .

I stopped reading because I couldn't take it in. Part of me wanted to laugh, because – well, I could imagine Granddad answering impertinent questions with a courteous, point-by-point summary of the libel laws. But the rest of it was . . .

I looked down at the page again and the room seemed to shift and slide around me. Granddad had been left all Martin's money when he wasn't even twenty-one, only a few years older than me . . . *denied all suggestions that Martin had been infatuated with him* . . . I couldn't get hold of the idea; it kept slipping away, like a bead of mercury. The *spectre of scandal*? It couldn't be the same Oliver Gardner . . . But I knew it was.

So Granddad *owned* Tyme's End.

It made sense, now I thought about it. Of course. Why else would he have the key? But to have kept it all that time, for sixty years, not living here but not selling it either – why would he do that? He must have had to employ someone to do the repairs, to mow the lawn, to make sure no one broke in. He must have gone on paying the electricity bills, and the water, and . . . Why would he *bother*? It didn't make sense, any more than it made sense that someone had chucked the dust sheets over everything without even emptying out the sherry decanter first.

And there was something else. I could hear Granddad's voice, talking about Martin, the afternoon when he'd given me my book back: *He was . . . not a good man . . .* It was a strange thing to say about someone who'd left you his entire fortune.

Not that it mattered now. I shut the book. The breeze from the window ruffled my hair, smelling of warm grass, and I suddenly realised how thirsty I was. I thought, *So I* can *stay here. No one's coming to chuck me out.*

And – I hated myself for thinking it, but I couldn't help it – *one day Tyme's End will be mine.* My heart gave a great joyous thump at the thought. I wanted it so much – even more than before, now I knew that one day it could be, *would* be mine. It was as if nothing mattered – not home or school or Adeel, not Dad, not Granddad – except being here. As if my whole life had been leading up to this moment.

Yes, the house said to me. *Yes.*

I carried on reading and reading. I didn't remember eating lunch, but when I got up to go to the loo, hours later, there were crisp packets and banana skins scattered around, and the water bottle I'd opened was empty. The sun had dropped out of sight behind the trees, and there was only just enough light to read. It was hard to stand up, and I was aching from being in the same position all that time. I had to keep blinking to stop the world spinning.

But I still felt that elation, that wonderful sense of being in the right place, doing the right thing. My heartbeat was fluttering in the roof of my mouth. It was extraordinary, like the barrier between then and now had worn thin, almost to nothing.

I felt someone's eyes on the back of my neck. I swung round and for a fraction of a second I thought I saw a movement near the window, but it was only the ivy leaves fluttering in the breeze. Nothing. Just my brain playing tricks.

There was that smell of cigarette smoke again, and a gust of air ruffled the pages of the biography I'd left on its back on the floor. The pages turned slowly and then stopped, open on the photo of Granddad and H. J. Martin. I crouched down and looked at it again. *HJM and Oliver Gardner, May 1936*. It must have been taken in Cambridge, a few months after they met, almost exactly sixty years ago. I stared down at them, standing together, laughing at the camera, and I felt an odd twist of hatred in my stomach. How could Granddad have lied about that? How *could* he? Even after Martin had left him all his money – left him Tyme's End, for God's sake! – Granddad couldn't say what a great man he was, couldn't even be grateful.

I thought, *If I knew someone like Martin I'd* – But I didn't know what I'd do, except that I wouldn't let him leave, like Dad or Granddad. And I wouldn't let him get killed, stupidly, for no reason, on a flat, straight country road.

I stared so hard at the picture, narrowing my eyes, that I half believed it was me. I could almost remember the photo being taken, the smell of hot stone and the flash of the sun on the camera lens. It was what I wanted more than anything in the world: to be there, in Granddad's place.

And suddenly it was as if something clicked inside me.

I stood up and took a quick look round at the mess I'd made; then I picked up the rubbish and gathered my rucksack into my arms so that the room was back to how it had been before, except for the papers on the table. I went upstairs and put my stuff in one of the bedrooms – not the biggest, that was Martin's – and if I ignored the musty smell, I could pretend I was here by invitation and this was where I was supposed to be sleeping. The garden below was shadowy and dim, the last fingers of shade creeping past the house. I turned the light on and the room leapt into stage-set brightness. It was amazing that the bulb still worked, but maybe the caretaker had replaced it – if there was a caretaker.

I went from room to room, turning the lights on. I worked my way round the bedrooms until I was back where I'd started, standing outside Martin's room, my heart hammering. Then I knocked, feeling stupid, and slowly opened the door.

There was a movement by the window that made me jump, but it was only a curtain swaying in the draught.

I said, 'I'm here. If you want me, I'm here.'

And then I laughed, because I was talking to myself, and switched the light on, and went back downstairs.

And the house felt different. There was a new scent in the air – a sweet, musty smell that I couldn't identify – and the floorboards creaked as if there was someone moving around upstairs. But it wasn't creepy. If anything, it felt friendly, comforting, like having someone I trusted around.

I went back into the drawing room and started to

look through Granddad's papers, while the darkness got bluer and thicker and the reflections in the windows solidified. Most of the stuff wasn't important – letters from his mother, my great-grandmother, letters he'd written to her from his boarding school, a couple of brief notes from Martin – *Am in town, lunch today? Porters' lodge, 1 o'clock, J* – that I didn't know why he'd kept. I tossed them aside, picked up the exercise book, and opened it at random. There were loads of blank pages. I flipped to the beginning.

It was a diary; which was strange, because Granddad's other diaries were hardback notebooks that he kept in a glass-fronted cabinet in his study.

12th June, Cambridge. Last day of full term – lunch with Marian – wonderful as always, but couldn't concentrate for thinking about seeing J tomorrow. She was talking about the Crusades . . .

15th June, Tyme's End. Got train down here, must bathe before dinner so more later, only trying to capture moment of seeing Tyme's End: gorgeous weather, house like a picture postcard, J coming out to meet me, smiling . . . Others here, Tony Morton-Smith, Edith Quincey, Dr Langdon-Down . . .

There was a noise overhead like a door opening, and I half rose to my feet, automatically, as if I didn't want to be found reading Granddad's diary when someone walked in on me. Then I caught myself, and sat down again. There was silence, as though I'd imagined the noise, but the diary had fallen to the floor, its covers spread out like wings. I picked it up and paused, looking down at it.

Part of it had been ripped out: neatly, methodically, each page torn away separately, close to the margin. I ran my thumb along the rough edges. Twenty pages? Fewer, possibly. I checked the dates. Every entry from 17th June to –

To 21st June.

The breeze brushed my face like a hand, pushing my hair off my forehead. I could smell the fresh evening air coming in from the window – cooler now, damper – and hear the cars coming and going along the road. The wind sighed in the trees and I heard a motorcycle drone past and cut off. I took a deep breath. Something was nagging at me. There was something wrong. Something I'd read . . .

21st June, Tyme's End.

I stared at the entry without seeing it. Then I blinked, and saw what I was looking at.

The date was written at the top of the page, and below it there was nothing but blank space, except for one word. It was in pencil, dug so heavily into the paper that it had almost gone through the page, and it was big, in block capitals, hardly recognisable as Granddad's handwriting.

It said, *REMEMBER*.

I ran my finger over the word, and even though he'd written it sixty years ago my fingertip came away grey with graphite.

And suddenly – although he hadn't written it for me – I did remember. A paragraph from the biography I'd been reading came into my head so clearly, word-perfect, that it was uncanny. I closed my eyes.

*

*Anthony Morton-Smith, the last person to see Martin
alive, had left only the day before. He reported that he
had left Martin in 'the best of spirits, with a glint in
his eye, as if he were planning something'.[9] As several
biographers have commented, Morton-Smith was
clearly not intending to imply that Martin's death was
not only suicide, but premeditated; however, his
remarks were taken as such by . . .*

But Anthony Morton-Smith hadn't been the last
person to see Martin alive. Not if Granddad had been
at Tyme's End on the 21st of June.

And when I opened my eyes again Granddad's
writing was still there, dark and deep as the carving
on a gravestone.

REMEMBER.

VI

There was someone moving around upstairs. I noticed the noise without paying much attention to it, in a quiet, still part of my mind, while I stared at Granddad's writing. *REMEMBER* . . .

And then, slowly, gradually, like the feeling coming back into a frozen limb, I started to be afraid.

It was hard to move. But in the end I looked up, feeling the tension in my neck, the skin on my hairline prickling. It was dark outside, but the breeze from the window was hot and heavy, not as fresh as it had been. The air smelt bitter. I thought, *I shouldn't be here. What am I doing here? I shouldn't be here* . . .

I stood up. I took a deep breath, trying to control my heartbeat. If I didn't make any noise, if I didn't draw attention to myself . . . But I knew it was too late for that. Tyme's End had pulled me in, opening itself to me like a trap, and now –

I had to get out.

I thought for a second about my rucksack. I'd left it upstairs and it had everything in it – my wallet, my phone, even my jumper. But I couldn't go up there. I had to get out *now*. My skin was aching and itching with cold, even though the air was warm. *I shouldn't be here.*

I moved to the door, treading as quietly as I could, but the floorboards creaked under my feet, and the door groaned as I pushed it open. I stood for a moment in the hall, and the ceiling above me settled and grumbled. The light in here was dim and there were shadows collecting in the corners of the room like dust. In front of me were the windows that looked out on to the lawn, and the front door, and somehow I knew that once I was outside I'd be safe, that whatever I was scared of was here, in the house with me.

I swallowed and walked towards the door. I made myself do it casually, as if someone was watching and I didn't want them to know anything was wrong.

When I reached out for the handle there was a patter on the window, and I jumped. But it was only a few drops of rain. I could feel the heaviness in the air that comes before a storm, as if the world was waiting for something. I thought, *Great, I'll be out in the rain in just a T-shirt and jeans*, but I didn't care. I could feel my body shaking with tension, half wanting to run, half wanting to turn round. I was sure there was someone behind me: at the bottom of the stairs, watching. I took hold of the door handle and pulled.

The door didn't move. A wave of nausea rose in my throat and I swallowed. I thought, *Don't panic. It did this before, remember? Just pull hard enough and it'll open*. More rain spat against the window.

I dragged at the door handle until my feet slid on the floor and I almost lost my balance. I could hear myself gasping for breath, the air catching in my larynx like a hook.

A low sound rumbled overhead, as if someone was dragging something over the floor. Thunder. For a second I felt a mad rush of relief. There wasn't anyone upstairs after all . . . But I kept pulling at the door handle, my hands cold and clammy on the metal. *Come on, come on!* It would open sooner or later. I had to keep trying, that was all.

Then I heard footsteps behind me. They crossed the hall from the stairs to the drawing room, making a clear, precise sound.

The space between my shoulder blades flared with cold. I turned round, a kind of dread unravelling in my stomach, too cowardly not to look. But there was only the drawing-room door swinging slowly shut and I'd gone through that door a few seconds ago – it might have been closing behind me or moving in the damp draught from the window. There was nothing to make me afraid. There was nothing to tell me I hadn't imagined the footsteps, the way I might have imagined that sense of being watched, the sense of a malicious, amused gaze on my back as I struggled to get the door open. The way I might have imagined the sweetish, rottenish scent in the air, and the tang of tobacco smoke.

I pulled at the door. I was hissing under my breath: prayers, swear words, and then just *please, please, please*. The wind was rising outside and the rain splattered the window, tapping on it like fingernails. Behind me the lights buzzed and flickered and for a second I saw my reflection in the window disappear and blackness press against the glass. When my face came back it shone white, even in the dirty yellow light from the lamps. My eyes looked desperately back at me from the other side of the glass. My expression scared me as much as the footsteps had.

And then the lights went out completely.

I froze. The wind was rushing in the trees, but inside the air was stagnant and still and every sound I made seemed to echo. I could hear my teeth chattering and my breath rasping in my throat. It was dark, but there was enough light from the window to see denser shadows around the hearth and in the doorways: shadows that I was scared to look at, in case they moved.

I took my hands away from the door handle, very slowly, even though I wasn't sure that I could find it again in the blackness.

I don't know how long I stood there, half blinded by the dark, waiting for something to happen. But nothing did, and after a while the terror that had taken me over subsided and something else grew in its place. I wasn't sure whether it was curiosity or anger, but it swelled until the fear had to give way, and the darkness took a step back, giving me room to breathe.

I wanted to go into the drawing room. I wanted to see him face to face. I wanted to be sure. In a distant, steady part of my head, I was starting to understand how he'd tricked me: setting me up, reeling me in, as if my whole life were nothing but a mechanism to draw me here. But whatever had happened here was between Martin and Granddad, not me. I clung to the thought, as if it were the only solid thing in the world. *I don't belong here. This is nothing to do with me. It can't touch me, not really.*

I kept saying it over and over to myself, and the little spark of bravery grew inside me until I could move back into the hall, keeping away from the hunched shadows in case something reached out for me. There was a knot of deeper dark in the hearth, like a nest. I half wanted to close my eyes, like a child trying to be invisible, but the thought of stumbling over something filled me with blank, irrational horror. Another few steps and I'd be at the door to the drawing room. And that door, I knew, *would* open.

It did. It swung open with the same oily smoothness as before, as if someone was pushing it from the other side at exactly the same moment. I stood motionless, straining my ears in the silence. But there was no sound except my own heartbeat and breath, and the tiny reluctant creak of the hinges. There was more light in the drawing room: an unhealthy, livid light that wasn't moonlight, but enough to see that the room was empty. It was just as I'd left it, with Granddad's exercise book still open on the sofa. *REMEMBER*.

The rain was harder, now, splashing against the windows like spray, and tendrils of ivy were whipping to and fro in the wind. It made me feel calmer. I could keep telling myself that the noises I'd heard in the rooms above might have been thunder, after all.

I sat down on the sofa. The fear was still there – a solid, cold core that ran from my larynx to my gut – but now at least there was room to think.

I knew – of course I knew – that the sounds I'd heard hadn't been the wind, or the rain, or the house creaking.

Something had happened to Granddad here: something so terrible that he'd ripped the pages out of his diary, something so terrible he didn't dare to forget it. And it hadn't been forgotten; it was still here, still bleeding through, like a wound that had gone rotten. Something had made the house welcome me in, wrap itself round me like a web and not let me go.

I started to shake again. I pressed my hands together to keep them still and the skin felt sore, flayed, as if they were frostbitten.

Something wanted to keep me here: something that knew who I was. Something old, and hungry.

For a moment I felt nothing but bewilderment, and a sense of betrayal so acute I could have cried. This wasn't *fair*. No one had told me, no one had warned me. *This isn't how the world works. This just doesn't happen.*

But it was happening. And in spite of myself I thought, *Granddad* did *warn me. He knew, and he did warn me. I should have listened.*

And it was too late for that anyway. I was here now and I didn't know what to do.

I bent my head and put my hands over my face. The dread weighed down my stomach like sickness. I wanted to give up; I wanted to surrender. But I didn't even know how to do that. I opened my mouth, because I'd spoken to Martin before, hadn't I? *If you want me, I'm here.* He'd heard me then, hadn't he? I knew, with a horrible pang of helplessness, that if I hadn't said that, hadn't *offered* . . .

I took a deep breath. I heard myself say, 'I haven't done anything to you.' For a moment I felt a lurch of horror at my own voice. It was creaky and dry, like the voice I'd heard, that brittle, graveyard voice . . . but I swallowed, and when I spoke again it was steadier, clearer, more human. 'I don't owe you anything. Please leave me alone.'

Then I knew that I shouldn't have spoken to him.

I felt the house suck the words into itself, feeding on them. The air filled with an impossible scent of sunlight and heat, a summer fragrance that wafted towards me from the window, as if it wasn't nighttime or raining. It made me feel sick. I shut my eyes.

And there was the smell of cigarette smoke. And that was impossible too.

I drew my knees up and hugged them into my chest, hiding my face.

There was a rumble of thunder, a distant roar that cut off and skidded dully away behind me, like something crashing. Then it was silent. Dead silent. Even the wind died, and the warm air stagnated around me, making my skin creep. I felt sweat crawling on my scalp like lice. My heart was thumping so hard I thought I might black out.

I heard footsteps. There was no point, now, pretending that they were anything else. He went past me to the window, and paused there. There was the rustle of clothing, the clink of a lighter, the quiet, close sounds of someone smoking. I stayed where I was, not looking up. I didn't want to see him.

There was a pause that seemed to go on for ever. I waited.

Quietly, in that terrible desiccated voice, he said, 'Oliver?'

I only knew then that I'd been expecting it. I flinched and started to shake more than ever, but

I didn't feel any shock or surprise, only misery. The darkness pressed on my eyes like a blindfold.

'Oliver. I knew you'd come back.'

The voice was clearer than before, no longer just the bare bones of a voice, but it wasn't any less horrible for that. It had an edge of malice, of triumph, that filled the air and made it hard to breathe.

I swallowed. I was afraid to try to speak in case I couldn't do it. But I had to; and I clung to my anger, trying to balance the fear. 'Leave me alone. I don't owe you anything. I'm not my grandfather. Whatever he did –' I stopped.

He laughed.

It made a nasty, crackling noise, like someone treading on an insect, or a fire just starting to take hold. It wasn't loud, but somehow the quietness made it worse. It was . . . inevitable. Merciless. There was no amusement in it, only mockery. It made me feel tiny, as if it were the past itself laughing at me, the whole weight of sixty years.

My teeth were rattling. I clenched them, biting down to stop the vibration. Then, mustering all my courage, I looked up.

There was no one there.

I heard myself make a noise like a sob. For a second I felt nothing but blazing, wordless fury. I knew he was there. Even in the dark I should have been able to see him. If he was there, I could be angry with him, I could *fight*.

But now I was on my own, and the flame of fury died. I could almost see it gutter and disappear; I could almost feel the cold settling on my skin again, relentless. *No hope*, I thought. *No escape*. The terror rose again, formless, seeping into my mind like fog. I was shaking so hard my body felt blurred at the edges.

A sudden fan of water hit the window, and the rain hissed and widened into a roar. I felt a fine spray of rainwater hit my face, and I licked the moisture off my lips. If only I couldn't still smell daylight, sunshine . . . I said, 'Please, please,' and I didn't know if I wanted mercy or just for it to be over quickly.

Nothing answered. There was a pause while I waited, just long enough to feel an absurd prickle of hope. I thought, *He isn't here. He isn't –*

And the room flashed into being, filled with dazzling white light. It leapt out of the shadows, bleached and unreal, clear as a photo. For a split second it hung like an apparition in front of my eyes, branding itself into my retina, so bright it hurt.

I heard myself scream.

Not because of the blinding, unearthly light; and not because of the black darkness, thick as tar, that followed it. Not because of the crack of thunder that broke over the house like a bomb, so loud it drowned out my voice.

In the flash of lightning, I'd seen a figure by the window.

A man, still as ice, who stared straight back at me. A man I'd never seen before – not face to face, not in real life. But I knew him.

A man who'd been dead for sixty years.

And in his gaze a blind vicious malevolence that took my breath away, and a hunger that rooted me to the spot.

I squeezed my eyes shut. In the darkness it made no difference, but I stayed like that for what seemed like hours, shaking. The thunder faded and the rain gulped and spat at the windows. I was holding my breath. He was still there, in the dark, still with those eyes turned on me. There was nothing in my head except the unbearable press of fear. I fought it, trying to steady myself against the wordless, freezing rush of it. I held on. I held on until words began to float to the surface like wreckage after a storm. *I can't move. I'm too frightened to move.* And then, rising through the panic, came a smaller, steadier voice.

This is 1996. Whatever happened here has nothing to do with me. This is not my past. This is NOT MY PAST.

I opened my eyes. The darkness was thinner, like worn fabric. There was something by the window that could have been a figure. But it could have been something else too: a curve in the curtain, a shadow.

It wasn't much courage, but it was enough to make me move.

I ran, stumbling and shaking. For the first few seconds I was sure I would feel a hand catch hold of me, dragging me back. As I went through the doorway something clung and stuck to my face, and I dragged it away frantically, on the edge of hysteria. I swerved towards the front door, and then away again, because I knew that if I tried the door and it still didn't open . . . Nothing could be as terrible as that. I turned the other way, up the stairs, keeping a step ahead of the fear. The drawing room was the heart of the house. Anywhere but there.

I went into the bedroom that I'd thought of as mine a few hours ago. *Mine.* There were tears running down my face now, although I wasn't sure exactly why. I slammed the door and then spun round, horribly certain that he'd be waiting for me, smiling at my panic. But I was on my own, and there was enough light from the windows to see that everything was as I'd left it. I knelt down beside my rucksack and put my arms round it, burying my head in the jumper spilling out of the top. I inhaled the smell of home, the floral laundry powder Rosina insisted on using. It drowned out the odour of damp that came off the walls and the bed, and pushed the fear a little further away. London existed. 1996 existed. Rosina, and Adeel, and Granddad existed.

Granddad.

I knelt up, suddenly feeling a draught of cold air on my face. My mobile was digging into my hip. With trembling, clammy hands, I dug it out of my pocket and turned it on. The display lit up, throwing a dim green light over my hands. It was after midnight. The phone battery was down to its last bar, and the reception was flickering on and off. I fumbled at it, trying to call up the text message Granddad had sent me with the numbers of all his hotels.

The phone beeped loudly. **1 New message From: Voicemail. You have 9 New messages, call 901 to retrieve.**

I paused, struggling to think. I just wanted to talk to Granddad – I didn't care about anyone else. But what if he'd phoned to tell me he'd changed his plans, or –? I dialled 901. The phone made a noise like something skittering across a polished floor – the battery failing – but it connected me.

'Olly, my boy, good morning, or rather good evening, congratulations on finishing your exams, I hope the History paper went well. Give me a call when you can, room 267 at the Los Angeles Hilton, I should get there tomo—'

I laughed shakily, because I wanted to cry. I skipped to the next message.

'Olly, I expect after an evening carousing with your comrades the very mention of alcohol will be anathema for at least the next day or so, but I forgot to say that I put some bottles of champagne aside for you. They're in the cupboard under the stairs. Unless of course you've already discovered them –'

'Olly, Heaven forbid that I should add onerous duties to what is no doubt a hefty hangover, but according to my calculations you should be surfacing in the next couple of hours and I should be grateful if you could contact me. It's the same number as before –'

'Oliver, I have tried the landline several times, and I am beginning to be really rather concerned for your well-being. I'm sure I'm being foolish, but if you could possibly put my mind at rest by phoning me –'

'Oliver. Please phone me. The number is the same as the one I gave you –'

'Oliver, please –'

'Oliver. Are you all right? Call me as soon –'

'Oliver. *Are you all right?* Phone me.'

'*Phone me.*'

His voice got harsher, terser, every time, but I was almost crying with thankfulness just to hear it. It would be OK. I should have phoned him before. He'd know what to do, he'd understand. *To return the call, press five.* I pressed five. As the phone rang at the other end I heard the low-battery tone again.

Someone said, 'Good afternoon, Los Angeles Hilton. How may I help you?'

I said, 'Could you connect me to room 267, please? Mr Gardner?'

'Just one second, sir . . . Yes, I'm afraid Mr Gardner's reservation has been cancelled. I'm sorry about that. Is there anything else I can –'

There was a noise like a marble spinning across stone tiles: the noise of the battery dying.

I said, 'Please – he's there – I think you've made a mistake. I need to talk to him, please, *please*.'

'I'm sorry, sir, his reservation was definitely cancelled. Can I help you with anyth—'

And then the phone cut out.

I stared at the screen, waiting for it to light up again. I wanted to be angry with myself for letting the battery run down; I wanted to feel disappointed, or irritated, or afraid. But all I could feel was a kind of numb disbelief, as if I was watching something die. The storm rumbled outside, a long way away. I heard a gurgle of water as a gutter overflowed, and then the steady tick of drips falling from the ceiling on to the floor. I thought, without urgency, *I shouldn't be here. I need to leave.*

I pressed the power button on my phone, holding it down until the pad of my thumb started to hurt. Nothing. It made me think of the door downstairs that wouldn't let me out. It was no good. Nothing would be any good.

I closed my eyes and I could see the drawing room lit up by the lightning, and Martin standing by the window. I was frightened again, and I was so *tired* of being frightened. I wanted to go home; and I knew, helplessly, hopelessly, that I couldn't. Maybe not ever. I was trapped.

And I wanted Granddad.

I put my arms round my rucksack again and hugged it, like a little kid. I was knackered, but I was too scared to go to sleep. It seemed important, somehow, to stay awake. If – when – I fell asleep, that would be the end. I knew I wasn't going to get away; whatever the debt was, I was going to pay it. It was like being on a sinking ship: the past was leaking in, swirling icily round me like seawater. But there was nowhere to go. If I'd been able to talk to Granddad . . . but I couldn't. Now there was nothing to do but wait.

And after a while I started to cry weakly. I cried because I was afraid, but for other things too: for Dad and my little half-brother or sister; for Mum, although I'd never known her properly; for Granddad. I cried because I was reduced to this, crying alone in someone else's house, and because it was my own fault. And I cried because I was giving up, because I was letting the past win.

I curled up, blind and deaf with misery and fear, like an animal. And the rotten, flowery smell of the past rose around me, until the air seemed to be thick with it. I noticed it, but there was nothing I could do except breathe it in. I went into a kind of trance, hardly knowing where I was, or who. I waited, determined to hold on for as long as I could, but only just remembering what I was holding on to.

The storm slackened until the rain was soft, blowing against the windows like a curtain. Moisture slid down my face like a hand, and I didn't move.

After a long, long time I thought I heard someone saying my name. It was loud, demanding, like someone was calling me. I froze but nothing happened.

There were footsteps downstairs. The drawing-room door opened and the steps paused, then started again. I heard my name again. It seemed to echo, so that I thought there were two voices saying it: the old, sepulchre voice that made my skin crawl, and – another one. But I was too tired and cold to raise my head to listen. I kept my eyes closed and heard the silence swallow both voices.

Then, very faintly, I heard music.

It was scratchy and distorted, and it only played for a few seconds before it deepened and slowed grotesquely to a stop. But I thought I knew it, although I couldn't think of the name of the piece. It was classical – we'd done it at school. It made me feel uneasy, as if there was something I should have remembered. It was a sharp, nagging feeling, so unlike the dull weight of fear that I sat up straight and stared into the dark, wondering.

I stood up, wincing at the pain as the blood came back into my hands and feet. I didn't know why, but I needed to go downstairs again. There was something . . .

I opened the door and I heard voices. A voice. Or two voices; I wasn't sure. I drew in my breath slowly, listening.

The world reeled, fizzing and boiling with black, so that I swayed in the doorway, reaching out for something – anything – to steady myself. The nausea rose in my throat as if I was drowning in it. I felt the floor shifting under my feet, as if I were in two places at once. The dark sucked at me, pounding in my head like a heartbeat, beating at me like wings.

And from the room below, I felt something evil seeping up through the floorboards like mould or poisonous gas. It was worse than the malevolence I'd seen in Martin's eyes, worse than anything – and it was mixed with a kind of triumph that wasn't aimed at me.

For a moment I stood there disorientated, clinging to the door jamb. Such *evil*. I couldn't bear it. I dropped to my knees and curled over, covering my head with my arms as if I was bracing myself for a crash. I thought, *No, no, no* –

And then it was gone.

It went suddenly, cleanly. It left nothing behind except a kind of emptiness and peace.

And the darkness was nothing but darkness.

It was a cool, bright morning. I opened my eyes, and I was curled up on the floor outside the bedroom. I sat up. My body ached all over, as if I'd been beaten up. It was hard to straighten my fingers, and it took me two attempts to get to my feet.

But . . . something was different.

I could feel it in the air around me: the peace that had come so suddenly last night. The peace of a paid debt, of finished business. What Granddad would call the *quietus*: quits. I walked slowly down the stairs, wondering at the emptiness in the air, the way Tyme's End was . . . only a house.

The front door was open, wedged on a clump of

weeds on the doorstep, and the rain had blown in and soaked the floor. The air was fresh and clean, and I stood for a moment, breathing in the moist smell. I could have gone outside then, but I knew the door would stay open; that it would never close of its own accord. I turned and opened the drawing-room door.

And maybe I already knew what I'd see.

Granddad was sitting on the sofa, looking towards the window where Martin would have been standing. He didn't move, or say anything, or even glance at me. He carried on staring across the room. He'd taken his hat off and left it on the back of a chair, and his jacket was sagging and creased from the plane journey. His lighter and cigarettes were arranged on the table next to him, as if he'd been having a conversation with a friend. And in the ashtray beside them were the last blackened margins of his exercise book.

I wanted to sit down next to him, but I couldn't. I moved to the window and looked out. My footsteps on the floorboards jerked the gramophone into a split second of life and it sputtered into a bar of the music I'd heard the night before. I glanced at it, waiting for it to grind to a halt again, and it did.

Then, slowly, I turned and looked at Granddad. He seemed to meet my eyes, but he didn't speak or blink. I waited until I was sure. Then I knelt down in front of him and touched his jacket. It was rough and dry; I'd expected it to be cold. I could smell the tobacco smoke on his clothes. I leant forward, very gently, and felt the hard solidity of his chest against my forehead.

I said, 'Granddad . . .' and heard my voice crack.

I looked down at my hand, clutching his lapel, and I couldn't remember how to make my fingers let go.

I stood up finally. I didn't know what to do. I picked up Granddad's packet of cigarettes, put them in my pocket and then picked up his lighter. I turned it over and over in my hands, watching my reflection slide across it in fragments. My mobile was in my other pocket but the battery was dead, and anyway I didn't know who to call.

I went outside and stood on the lawn where the drive curved. I thought, *Tyme's End must be mine now*. It made me laugh, but it hurt. It was what I'd wanted, wasn't it? I looked back at the blank windows. Granddad . . . I didn't even know if he'd gone home, before he came here. I hoped, desperately, that he hadn't – that he hadn't known why I'd run away, that he hadn't seen that I'd taken those letters.

I walked away, not looking where I was going. I think I was trying to find the gap in the wall, but my mind wasn't working properly. I walked and walked, pushing through undergrowth and raising my arms to protect my face from brambles. When I looked over my shoulder Tyme's End was still behind me. I'd walked in a circle. I didn't care. I kept on going, down a slope, through trees, until I had to stop on the edge of a river. It was peaceful here: not the dead, used-up calm that had filled the house, but a clean, impersonal peace full of running water. There were midges dancing in the cool air and I could hear the swish of cars on the road.

I sat down on the riverbank and smoked a cigarette, and then another. I didn't smoke, but they were Granddad's, and I knew he wouldn't want them to go to waste. I couldn't think straight. I kept fiddling with his lighter, holding it tightly, not letting the warmth go out of the metal. After a while I felt sick, but the smell of nicotine was comforting.

I thought, *I'm safe. Nothing's going to hurt me. It's over.*

And after a while I felt something inside me thaw, and I put my head down on my knees, and cried.

1936

I

Someone said, 'Falconhurst!' and I jerked out of a sweltering half-doze, reached hurriedly for my suitcase and staggered out of the train on to the station platform. I heard someone grumble and the door slam behind me; then the rumble and hiss as the train gathered its strength to leave again. There was a whistle and the smell of steam, and the little train drew away, filling the air with a grimy fog that shimmered in the sunlight and dispersed.

I stood blinking and disorientated on the platform, and looked about me. There were the customary embraces and greetings, not to mention a young girl waving her handkerchief until long after the train had gone out of sight; but I was alone, and no one gave me a second glance. It was a hot, quiet afternoon, but a breeze was already beginning to cool the sweat that had trickled down my face and soaked my collar. I was thankful for it; in Cambridge, when I left, the heat had been unbearable, an oppressive, un-English heat that reflected off the pavements and old stone, and in the railway carriage it had been no better.

Here, though, the air was softer and newer, as though it had been freshly brewed, and I felt my heart lift as I breathed it in.

'It's heavenly, isn't it?'

I didn't look round at once, presuming that whoever had spoken was addressing someone else; but when, after a few moments, I did turn my head, I found my gaze returned by an auburn-haired woman who seemed not to notice my confusion. She said, 'You can simply *smell* the countryside. Isn't it gorgeous? London is so dreary in this heat.'

'Yes, I'm sure you're right,' I said. She was standing in front of me, and I hesitated, wondering whether she had mistaken me for someone else.

Her eyes narrowed, and it was as if she had read my thoughts. She said, 'I suppose you *are* Mr Gardner? Only it would be too typical of me to fasten on to a perfect stranger. You mustn't be too polite to tell me, you know.'

'Yes, I am, but I –' I hesitated. 'I wasn't expecting –'

'I know. Jack said there was absolutely no need for anyone to lame-duck you. But I thought it was such a lovely afternoon for a walk. And to tell you the truth I was rather curious to meet you.' She gave me a frank, direct gaze that made me suddenly conscious of my sweaty collar and rumpled hair.

'Oh, I see,' I said, and ignored a jab of disappointment that Jack hadn't come to meet me himself. 'Well. Thank you.'

She smiled, revealing straight, shiny teeth, and held out her hand. 'Edie Quincey. How do you do?'

'How do you do?' I said. 'Oliver Gardner.' Both our palms were wet; when she released her grip I had to check an impulse to wipe my hand on my trousers.

'Let's go, then. Have you all your luggage?' She glanced at my suitcase.

'Yes, thank you. This is all I have. That is . . .' I followed her gaze and wished abruptly that my case were not quite so shabby, and that I had had more belongings with which to fill it. I straightened my arm, imperceptibly, so as to give the impression that it was heavier than it was. 'Most of my things are in my trunk. Jack said there was no need to bring very much – only clothes, and so on.'

'Of course,' she said, and gave me a bright, undeceived smile. 'You must be a man after his own heart, travelling so light.'

'I hope so.'

She looked away thoughtfully. Then, without a word, she jerked her head, like someone summoning a dog, and walked off. I followed her through the fuggy warmth of the ticket office and out of the station. We made our way down the High Street, past several shops and a public house, and although I had never been here before I knew, with a flicker of irritation, that I could have found my way perfectly well from Jack's instructions. I had read his letter so many times I had it practically by heart, and I had imagined myself arriving alone, cool and collected, greeting him with a casual handshake; but now I could see that I would be shepherded into his presence like a child. I glanced sideways at Edie, trying to stifle my resentment. I noticed, for the first time, that she was dressed in an eccentric, boyish fashion, and was walking with her hands pushed deeply into the pockets of her slacks. Her hair was in a dishevelled marcel wave, but strands were blowing across her face in the breeze, and the general effect was incongruously masculine. As I looked, she caught my eye and smiled; but it was a smile which made it clear that she had noticed – and thought the worse of me for – my curiosity.

She said, suddenly, 'Your first time here, is it?'

'At Tyme's End? Yes. I've only known Jack a few months.'

'He thinks very well of you.'

I looked aside so that she wouldn't see me smile, and said, 'I hoped I could deduce as much from his invitation.'

'And you think well of him.'

'Naturally,' I said. 'If I didn't, I should hardly have accepted it.'

She opened her mouth as though to question me further, but seemed to think better of it. Instead she inhaled deeply, flinging her arms out in a clumsy, histrionic gesture. '*I* should have come anyway,' she said. 'I don't have your scruples. Isn't it divine?'

To my relief, she didn't seem to expect a response. She took a few more loud breaths, her bosom heaving, then dug in her pockets, producing a box of cigarettes with one hand and a box of matches with the other. 'Cigarette?'

'No, thank you. I don't smoke.'

'Oh, you will. Jack makes everyone smoke. It's his particular form of tyranny. One of them, at least.' She paused, cupping her hand around the match to protect the little flame. 'Who was it said that a cigarette is a perfect type of a perfect pleasure, it is exquisite and it leaves one unsatisfied?'

I said, 'St Paul, wasn't it?'

She grinned unexpectedly, as if I'd finally said something that met with her approval. 'Actually, it was Oscar Wilde.'

'Well, I was close, then.'

Her grin faded, and she gave me a sideways look, blowing the smoke upwards from the corner of her mouth like a street urchin. 'How old are you?'

'Nineteen.'

'Ah.' She frowned, as if it were an intriguing and rather disquieting answer, and went on, in a thoughtful tone, 'You're too polite to ask, naturally, but I'm thirty-two. Anthony – I think Jack said you hadn't met Anthony Morton-Smith before – is forty. Philip – but of course you know him, he's your tutor at Cambridge, isn't he? – is fifty-three. Jack is nearly forty-five.'

I had the disconcerting sensation that she was speaking another language. I said, 'I'm sorry, I – I'm not sure I see your point.'

'Oh . . . I'm afraid you might find us a little fogeyish.'

'As you're not my host,' I said, 'I don't see that you need concern yourself on my account.'

She caught my eye. Her face was serious, with something in her eyes that I couldn't identify; under different circumstances I might have thought it was anxiety, but the idea seemed absurd. She held my look, and then nodded, as though with reluctant approval. The corners of her mouth quirked up. 'Fair enough.' We walked in silence for a few moments. Then, in a softer tone than she had used so far, she added, 'What did you say your people did?'

'My father was a clerk in a factory.'

She turned to look at me, eyebrows raised. 'Golly,' she said, and then seemed to recollect herself. 'I mean, Jack didn't say . . . *Was?*'

'He's dead.'

'The War, I suppose,' she said, glancing away.

'Arras, 1917.'

She nodded again, as if it was unfortunate but only to be expected. Her eyes slid down to my suitcase, and lingered on the initials that were still just visible on the scuffed leather. I felt the blood rising in my cheeks.

She had finished her cigarette; she flipped it carelessly into the roadway and dug her hands into her pockets. Then, as if on a sudden impulse, she stopped in her tracks and took a firm hold on my arm. I halted, thinking for a moment that she had stumbled, but she was standing quite still, looking up at my face.

'Oliver – if I may call you Oliver –'

I said automatically, 'Of course.'

'Oliver,' she repeated, as if I hadn't spoken. 'Listen to me. Jack . . .' Her voice died and she cleared her throat. 'Jack would be a very poor pattern for imitation. If you were to come to regard him as . . . a sort of father, that would be – unhealthy. For both of you. It might be better to . . . be circumspect. That's all.'

I stared at her, at a loss as to how to respond.

She seemed to register my confusion, for she laughed a little, but her eyes stayed steady. 'I'm sure you think it's impertinent of me to say so when I've hardly known you ten minutes –'

In spite of myself, I said, 'Yes.'

'I know. It's perfectly insufferable, and none of my business, and naturally you'll ignore me,' she said.

'But I'm afraid I'm old-fashioned, and I can't help regarding it as my duty to . . .'

'To warn me off?'

She turned aside, as if my gaze was making her uncomfortable, and brushed her hair off her forehead. 'Yes. If you like. Yes.'

'Thank you,' I said. 'But I don't think I quite understand what you're getting at. You're his guest, too, aren't you?'

'Yes. I don't mean – it's simply that . . . Well, you're very young, and perhaps you might be out of your depth.'

'Because my father was a factory clerk?'

She shook her head with a quick, impatient movement. 'No, of course not. That's neither here nor there. Jack is . . . What can I say? He's used to getting his own way.'

I took a deep breath, feeling my shirt cling unpleasantly to my ribs. I wished, for a second time, that she hadn't come to meet me; the happiness I had felt at the station was tainted now. I said, 'I suppose you'd like me to turn round and go back to my mother.'

'Yes, perhaps.' She sighed, on the edge of a laugh. 'But I'm not such a fool as to suppose that you will.'

I waited; then, as she said nothing more, I started to walk again. A light wisp of cloud had drifted across the sun, and the brightness of the day had faded a little.

'Forgive me,' she said. 'I'm an interfering old besom.'

'Not at all. It's kind of you to . . .' I struggled for a courteous phrase, so transparently that she looked up and laughed; and her expression was simultaneously

227

so apologetic and so humorous that I couldn't help laughing too. 'I'm sorry,' I said. 'I'm sure you meant it kindly. But Jack is my friend.'

She blew a strand of hair away from her mouth. 'Let's not mention it again.'

'Never.'

We walked in silence for a few moments, until she pointed out the church tower, rising above the tree-tops, and slipped her arm casually through mine. I adjusted my step to hers, and answered politely enough to her chit-chat; but I felt a deep, childish resentment that she had spoiled my gladness, and it wasn't until we reached Tyme's End, and Jack came striding across the grass to meet me, that I could forget that unwelcome warning.

The house was dark inside, although every door and window seemed to be wedged open, and the air was fresh and sweet-smelling. I should have liked to explore it room by room, but Jack led me through without pausing, except to take my suitcase and drop it casually at the bottom of the stairs. Then we emerged from the back door on to a broad lawn, where croquet balls and mallets lay abandoned on the ground and a man was apparently asleep in the shade of a great bronze-leaved tree. I stood and took in the wide sweep of the lawn, the stone steps and sundial, filled with a strange ache that was half envy and half joy.

Jack walked over to the man lying on the grass, and said, 'Anthony,' and gave him a sharp kick in the ribs. 'Wake up. Let me introduce Oliver Gardner, one of Philip's protégés at Cambridge.' The man grunted and looked up, shading his eyes.

I held out my hand in his direction and said, 'How do you do?'

'How do you do?' he said, without moving.

'Gardner, this is Anthony Morton-Smith,' Jack said. 'He's exceptionally talented and exceptionally bad-mannered. I put up with the one for the enjoyment afforded me by the other.'

At that Morton-Smith grinned and sat up, affecting not to see my outstretched hand. 'So . . .' He tilted his head so that his hair fell across his forehead. He was swarthy and hadn't shaved; I could see a greasy gleam of sweat where his shirt collar was unbuttoned. 'Why are you here?'

'Because I was invited, I suppose,' I said, smiling.

'Of course,' he said, without returning my smile. He turned, pointedly, to Jack. 'I should have asked why you invited him.'

Jack glanced at me and said nothing but, 'Will you have a drink, Gardner?'

'Thank you,' I said, and stood awkwardly looking down at Morton-Smith while Jack strode back towards the house, whistling.

There was silence. Morton-Smith got slowly to his feet, bracing himself against the trunk of the tree and groaning a little. He looked me up and down, letting his eyes linger, finally, on my face. I tried to hold his stare, but I felt my face flush and glanced away in spite of myself.

He said, 'You're at Cambridge?'

'Yes.'

'Reading?'

'History.'

'Where were you at school?'

'I don't think you'd have heard of it,' I said.

He smiled, and his teeth glinted wetly. 'Try me.'

'Peltenshall Grammar School. It's quite small – I don't think it's –'

'Ah.' The smile broadened. 'A *grammar* school. That would explain the accent.'

'I –' I swallowed. 'I didn't know I had an accent.'

'Very well,' he said, 'the *lack* of accent, then. Don't worry about it. After all, why bother with an expensive education when one can produce nearly the same effect with elocution lessons? What does your father do?'

'He was a clerk.'

'Was he in the War?'

'Yes. He was killed.'

'What rank?'

'Private.'

He had rattled off the questions at me like a barrister interrogating a witness; but at that he paused and scratched his chin thoughtfully. 'I see,' he said.

'Do you?' I said. 'What?'

There was another beat of silence. Then he laughed. 'That Jack hasn't invited you for your social connections.'

'Is that why he invited *you*?'

'Or your charm.' He brushed a blade of grass idly off his shirtsleeve, then returned his gaze to mine. 'That leaves your intellect or your looks. Which is it, do you suppose?'

I turned aside and breathed in the scent of summer, letting my eyes rest on the bronze beech leaves against the high blue of the sky. I felt as if years had passed since I got off the train at Falconhurst station.

Morton-Smith seemed to take my silence as an attack. 'I'm intrigued, that's all. Please don't be offended. I'm as fond of the WCs as the next man.'

'The –?'

'Working classes, dear boy. Privates and all.'

'I don't think –' I stopped; then, against my better judgement, started to speak again. 'Look, I don't see what my father has to do with you, or – or anything. He's been dead for nearly twenty years – I never even knew him myself. And I'm not *your* guest. You needn't cross-examine me as if I've come here to touch you for a fiver.'

He raised his eyebrows, smiling gently, and opened his mouth as if to answer; but suddenly he seemed to think better of it.

Jack's voice came from behind me. 'Gardner. Your drink. Anthony, go and do something useful, there's a good chap.'

It surprised me that Morton-Smith should smile and obey him without a word, but he did. Jack watched him leave then turned to me, holding out a glass of whisky and soda. I took it and drank thirstily without thanking him, and he started to laugh. 'I believe you're already regretting having come.'

I looked at him and laughed too. 'I was. But I'm feeling better now.'

'He has that effect on most people. He talks an awful lot of rot.'

'He didn't understand why you'd invited me.'

'He doesn't need to.' A thought seemed to strike him, and he raised one eyebrow. 'Do *you* understand why I invited you?'

'I –' I took another mouthful of the whisky and soda; I was drinking it too quickly, but I couldn't help it. 'I hoped it was because you liked my company.'

He held my gaze. His mouth was in a half-smile, and his eyes were steady and amused. For a moment I remembered with unexpected vividness the first time I had met him, when I'd caught his eye at someone's idiotic comment and we'd swapped a look of shared humour; I remembered the hours that had passed like minutes as we talked, and the way that I had finally stumbled drunkenly back to my rooms, dizzy with euphoria and pride. I had forgotten how good-looking he was, and his air of holding the world in the palm of his hand.

He said, 'You're an idiot, Gardner.'

'Thank you,' I said, and drank again, until there was nothing left in the glass but ice. My lips made a slurping sound against the rim. When I looked up he was grinning, and even in the merciless summer light he looked hardly older than I was. I held out the tumbler, and added, 'If I can have another drink I won't regret having come at all.'

He took hold of my elbow. 'Come and get it yourself. Edie's inside – she burns horribly, it's the red hair – and she'll be a model of courtesy, I promise.'

I opened my mouth, wondering whether I should mention what she had said to me on the way from the station; but it was difficult, now, to remember exactly what she *had* said. In any case, there seemed to be no way of relaying it without giving it more importance than it deserved, and Jack was already propelling me gently but firmly towards the house. I leant into the pressure from his hand, feeling the same swell of delight and contentment that I'd felt on the station platform; and, as if he'd sensed it, he grinned at me.

'Happy?' he said. 'It's good whisky.'

'Yes,' I said. 'Yes. It is. I am.'

That night I woke sweating and struggling, hearing the silence ringing in my ears as if some loud noise had woken me. For a moment I was watching lines of grey men advance towards me over a moonscape of mud; and then I was staring into the dark, fighting to keep the nightmare at arm's length. I was tangled in the sheet, and it took me what seemed like an age of frantic effort to sit up and free my arms. I was wet all over with sweat and my pyjamas were clinging to my back and legs; but for all that I was cold, and I drew my knees up to my chest, shivering. I took deep breaths and concentrated on the moonlit room in front of me, making an inventory of its contents. I was at Tyme's End. I was safe. The terrible blank-faced figures surfaced again, and I pushed them away determinedly. In my dream there had been a smell like swimming baths and rotten meat, but now I could only smell the green, sweet smell of the garden outside. I dragged my fingers through my hair and wiped my hands on the pillowcase, steeling myself to lie down again and close my eyes.

There was a knock on the door. I said hoarsely, 'Come in.'

It was Jack. In the half-darkness I could just make out that he was still dressed. A golden edge of electric light was spilling through the doorway. He said, 'I thought I heard you call out.'

'No. I mean – yes, I probably did. Sorry.'

'Don't be absurd. What's up?'

'Nothing. A nightmare.' I laced my fingers together and stared down at them. There was a silence, and I heard Jack dig in his pocket and light a cigarette. The faint smell of tobacco mixed with the scent blowing in through the open window.

'You're too young to have nightmares,' he said.

'It's my father's,' I said, without thinking, and then realised how peculiar it sounded. 'I mean – it's about my father.' I glanced up, afraid that he wasn't listening, but he was watching me, his face intent. 'I dream I'm in the trenches, about to go over the top. And then I see the enemy walking towards me. They're . . . grey. The whole world is grey. I have a revolver, and I fire at them, but it doesn't stop them. All at once I realise they're already dead, but they carry on walking towards me.'

'And then?'

'Then I wake up.' I laughed, but he hitched up one shoulder and only smiled faintly.

'Do you want a cigarette?'

'No. Thanks.' I leant back against the head of the bed, and felt myself relax slowly. It was comforting to sit and watch him smoke in half-silhouette. 'It's queer. As if I've inherited my father's memories. I never knew him. He was killed before I was born, but I still dream about him. About the War. I know it's idiotic. I don't have any right to.'

'I don't think anyone's possessive about their nightmares.'

'At any rate, I dare say it was indigestion tonight,' I said, trying to laugh. 'The food in college is so rotten it must have come as a bit of a shock to my system, getting something edible. And the drink too, I suppose.'

'No doubt.' But there was a non-committal note in his voice. He'd finished his cigarette; he looked around for an ashtray, then came into the room, stubbed the end on the sole of his shoe and flicked the butt out of the window. He stood for a few moments looking out into the moonlight, so close I could have reached out and touched him. 'I'm sorry about Anthony,' he said abruptly. 'I don't blame you for thinking he's insufferable. And Edie and Philip can be tiresome. But they won't be here for long – only a couple of days, at the most – and then we can have a decent time.'

I said, 'I thought –' He looked round at me, and I saw the pallor of his teeth as he smiled. I said again, awkwardly, 'I thought . . . How long am I staying?'

'As long as you want,' he said.

'Oh. But the others –'

'Damn the others.' He leant out of the window so that his voice was low, meditative, and half lost in the silvery darkness. 'Compared to you, they're . . .' He said something indistinguishable.

I bent my head so that he wouldn't see me grin. I said, 'It's very kind of you to say so –'

'Nonsense. I'm glad to have you here. You were the only person worth listening to at dinner.'

I couldn't help laughing. 'Are you including yourself?'

'Certainly.' He brought his head back into the room and stood looking down at me, his face outlined by the moonlight. I couldn't see his eyes, and it gave me a strange, uncomfortable feeling not to know where he was looking. 'Do you want anything? Water? A bromide? Whisky?'

'No, thanks. I feel much better now.'

'Good show. Sleep well.'

I lay down, putting my hands behind my head. His face was a study in white and dark, inscrutable, like a mask. There was a moment when neither of us moved; then he reached down and tucked me in. He did it silently, with a brisk, businesslike efficiency. I lay frozen with surprise. Then, without a word, he left the room and shut the door.

I stayed still, watching the dim shadows of the ivy on the wall, feeling a sudden, childish desire to cry; but when I thought about it, I knew I wasn't unhappy but full of a raw relief, like an exile finally allowed to come home.

II

When I woke up the next morning it was still early, so early that the light coming through my curtains was greyish and chilly. I leant out of the window and saw that the sun was just beginning to filter through the trees. The sky was a hazy silver-pink that would be blue later. The birds were making a joyous, raucous racket that made me wonder how anyone ever managed to sleep on past the sunrise.

I felt surprisingly fresh and alert, and before I had time to think I had dressed and left my room, creeping down the stairs into the hall. I opened the front door and took a deep breath. In spite of the birdsong the world was very still, and every leaf and blade of grass seemed distinct, like a cardboard cut-out; the whole scene gave the impression of a stage-set, a silent entr'acte, while the lead actor waited in the wings. As the air filled my lungs I had a strange, expectant feeling, as though in a moment I should understand something I'd been struggling with. But it faded as suddenly as it had come, and I was jerked rudely out of my dream by the insistent note of a motorbike. It grew louder until I saw the bike itself come down the drive and brake a few feet away, and its rider dismounted, laughing. It was Jack, of course: hatless, taking his goggles off, his hair over his face. He gave me a mock salute, already digging in his pocket for his cigarette case.

'Good morning,' he said. 'Sleep well?'

'Yes, thanks,' I said, and looked away. I was obscurely ashamed of my nightmare, and I hoped that he wouldn't mention it; but somehow I was disappointed when he didn't.

'Splendid.' He lit his cigarette. 'Had brekker yet?'

'No. I've only just got up. And I wasn't sure –'

'Oh, it's Liberty Hall here – you must do as you please.' He put a casual hand on my shoulder. 'Completely, absolutely as you please. Fancy a spin on the bike?'

'No, thanks. I rather fancy going home in one piece.'

'Oh, well. If you change your mind . . .' I felt the warmth of his fingers through my shirt. He dropped his hand. 'I often go out on it early in the morning – you can get up to a respectable speed along the road to Tunbridge Wells. I recommend it.'

'My mother would never forgive me if I got killed.' I meant it in jest, but something about the solemn, early-morning calm, and the way he was looking at me, gave it a weight I hadn't intended. 'I mean –'

'My dear chap, neither would I.' He smiled. 'You're quite right. Don't play dice with death while you still have something to lose.'

There was a long silence. The sun had climbed, and now it was slanting through the trees into my eyes.

The sky had gone from ashes-of-roses to a pale, delicate blue.

'About last night –' I said, and stopped. Part of me wanted to pretend he hadn't seen me like that, sweating and unmanned by a bad dream, but the other part of me wanted to watch him remember, to know that he *had* been there and I hadn't imagined it.

'Yes?'

'Thank you. That is – thank you.'

He nodded, unsmiling, dropped his cigarette end on the gravel and stamped on it. 'Do you remember what you said to Anthony, yesterday? I overheard you. You said that your father didn't matter any more.'

'I don't think I said that ex—'

'Perhaps not exactly. But you were right. Why should you have his nightmares?' He turned on his heel as if to go into the house, and the gravel crunched under his feet. 'I've seen so many men ruined by their ancestors, in one way or another. You must leave all that behind. Leave *him* behind.'

'I know he wasn't rich –'

'That isn't what I mean. Oh, that's what Anthony would mean, or Edie. But no. I don't mean your father the factory clerk, although God knows he won't do you any favours – I mean your father the man. We're all the children of the dead, Gardner. Leave them where they are. We don't owe them anything.'

'But –' I hated saying *but* to him.

'What?' He laughed. '"If ye break faith with us who die/We shall not sleep"?'

Though poppies grow in Flanders fields . . . My

mind completed the lines, unbidden. 'I can't help dreaming about him.'

'No,' he said, and his voice softened. 'No, Gardner, you can't. But you can start to understand that all he did for you was conceive you.'

'All he did?'

'Gardner, you will be a great man. A scholar, a soldier, a poet, perhaps. But you don't owe anything to the past. You owe everything to the future. And that, at least, is a debt you can pay.'

I stared at him, torn between pleasure that he thought so well of me and a kind of unidentifiable discomfort. And as if he sensed both impulses, he grinned and jerked his head towards Tyme's End. 'Come on,' he said. 'Enough of this. Let's have breakfast.' He put his arm round my shoulders. I could feel the warmth of his body, and I was glad of it.

I nodded, and let him lead me back inside the house.

By eleven o'clock it was already hot. I had chosen a book at random from the shelves in Jack's study, but I found myself too sleepy and languid to read it, even in the relative cool of the drawing room. Edie had wandered in without a word and draped herself sideways over the armchair near the window; she was wearing pyjamas, and her hair was in a tousled mess that made her look more boyish than ever. She yawned, and when I yawned too she caught my eye and smiled. There was an easy, undemanding quality to her silence, and for the first time I could understand why Jack had invited her.

The door opened. Jack's voice said, 'What are you doing frowsting in here, Gardner? Do you fancy a bathe? There's a marvellous place on the riverbank, behind the house.'

Edie looked up, watched him for a moment, then turned her head away again.

I sat up. 'Yes, thanks. Let me get my togs.'

'No need. Edie won't be coming, will you, Edie?'

She met his eyes, and shrugged. 'No, I don't think I shall.'

'Good.' He looked back at me. 'I thought we might take a luncheon basket down with us.'

'That sounds delightful,' I said, glancing at Edie. Her face had a neutral, closed look, and she didn't return my gaze.

'Buck up then, or I shall be nothing but a smear of grease, like a melted pat of butter. I don't know how you can stand it in here.' He turned on his heel and I heard him whistling as he crossed the hall.

I said, 'Edie, if you wanted to join us, I'm sure you'd be most welcome –'

'Are you? How amusing.'

'I mean – that is –'

'Oh, Oliver, for God's sake,' she said, swinging her feet on to the floor and walking to the window. 'Jack is appallingly rude to me because he knows he'll get away with it, and it gives him pleasure. But it isn't your business.'

'Why do you let him?'

She reached out and pulled sharply at a tendril of ivy, peeling it away from the windowsill. 'I suppose you think you wouldn't?' There was a silence. 'Why don't you go and have your little picnic? I'm sure it'll be heavenly beside the river. I simply adored it the first time Jack took me there.'

'Edie –'

'I'll have Anthony to keep me company. Or even Philip, if he's finished his letters. Have a lovely time.'

I watched her for a few moments, then took my leave silently. I remembered what Jack had said: *They won't be here for long* . . . I couldn't help wondering why he surrounded himself with people like Edie and Anthony; it was as if an athlete should surround himself with cripples. But I pushed the thought away guiltily, because it was unfair to think badly of Edie and traitorous to think badly of Jack.

'Ah, Gardner. Give me a hand with this, won't you?' Jack was in the doorway with the luncheon hamper. He tilted his head over his shoulder at the bottles on the table behind him. 'Champagne, lemonade, ginger beer. Bring them all if you can't decide.'

'All right,' I said, laughing, loaded my arms with bottles, and went out after him into the sun.

We made our way to the far end of the lawn and through the trees, grinning and swearing as we caught our feet in the bracken and reeled under the weight of our burdens. After five minutes or so we came to the river and Jack led me downstream, to a place where the water rattled over stones and then widened and deepened. The banks sloped down to a wide, calm pool. The surface reflected the sun and the trees, so that the world was green and gold, muttering and chuckling to itself, smelling of moisture. I drew my breath in.

'Like it?'

I looked at him, and he grinned.

'Not too bad, is it? Put those bottles down – we can chill them in the water, over there, where it's shallow.'

242

He set the hamper down on the grass. 'Here's our lunch. Better bathe first, though.'

'This is – it's –' I shook my head. Edie had been right: it *was* heavenly. I could feel the sun on the back of my neck and sweat prickling in my armpits and groin, but the fierce heat was almost pleasant, like pain when relief is imminent. I sat down and started to pick at my shoelaces with damp fingers.

Jack was already in the river by the time I had undressed, and I felt myself honour bound, under his amused eye, to plunge into the river without hesitation. The first iciness of the water took my breath away, and I heard myself give a husky shout of protest, but after a few frantic strokes I found the coolness on my skin delicious, and I rolled over on to my back, gazing up at the treetops. Jack murmured something, but the water was rustling in my ears and I couldn't hear the words. I held my breath and sank, watching the sunlight fall into wrinkles as it struck the surface above my eyes; then I floated again, twisting and diving just to feel the water moving over my body. When I put one foot down the mud oozed between my toes. Jack drove a fan of dazzling drops into my face, and I splashed him back. For a little while we played like schoolboys, laughing and yelling, until I begged for pax so that I could catch my breath. Finally I collapsed, exhausted, on the grass, letting the sunshine dry my skin, and watched Jack wade over to the bottles and wrestle good-naturedly with the champagne cork. His hands were wet, and it took a good deal of time before he could get a purchase on the bottle.

I opened my mouth, but there was nothing I could

have said. I would have liked to tell him that I was perfectly, absolutely happy; I would have liked him to know that I had never expected to feel like a child again, irresponsible and safe, as I did now. But there was no question of putting it into words, even to myself. Instead I lay down, my chin on my hands, feeling the sun on my back, and inwardly thanked the world for existing.

We stayed on the riverbank for hours, slipping in and out of the water according to whim, eating a little here and there, as if the picnic were not lunch but rather an eternal elevenses, although we gave the champagne the attention it deserved. The morning turned into afternoon, and the sun swung slowly round, and we swam and read and dozed, hardly talking. I thought occasionally of the others, but it was only to be glad I was here, with Jack, without them. Sometimes, when I moved, I'd catch his eye and he'd smile at me. The champagne had gone to my head, and the ground beneath my hands tilted sleepily, first one way, then the other.

It was late afternoon. I drowsed, watching the blades of grass in front of my nose, feeling the new heat on my back as the shade retreated. Jack had been swimming, but after a few minutes I heard him get out of the water, and little flecks of cold landed on my shoulder blades. His shadow paused, and I started to turn my head to look up at him.

He said, 'Don't move.'

I paused, waiting. Then I felt something brush my ribs, just to the left of my spine – a little impact, like the tap of a finger – and then trace a light, ticklish line down my side. The grass in front of my eyes blurred,

244

filling my head with a green glow.

'Stay still,' Jack said. There was the crunch of dry grass under his feet and the sense of something warm close to me. Then he put his hand on my back, paused for a second, and rocked back on his heels. 'All right, you can move now.'

When I propped myself up on my elbows he was cupping his hands together. He opened them, tilting them carefully towards me, and I saw a beetle in his palm. It was a metallic green-gold, its carapace edged with a delicate fuzz. It waved its antennae with a dignified air, seeming to wonder what it was doing in Jack's hands. I leant over him to get a better look, and he looked at me and grinned. I said, 'Gosh.'

'It's like jewellery, isn't it?'

'What is it?'

'A rose chafer, I think. It must be rather confused, to end up here. They like flowers.'

I held my finger out to it, and let it examine my nail. It shone magnificently in the sun, like a squat, ponderous king wearing green and cloth-of-gold.

'We should probably go back to Tyme's End,' Jack said, his eyes still on the beetle. 'It must be nearly time for tea. Edie will think we've drowned.'

I got to my feet, taking in the debris that was scattered around us. 'Shall I pack the luncheon basket?'

'Yes. And perhaps you'd better get dressed too.' He glanced up at me, a glint in his eyes, and I felt myself blushing.

I pulled on my trousers and shirt, without bothering with my tie, and started to clear up the mess we'd made. Our glorious afternoon was over; there was nothing but the greaseproof paper wrappings and empty bottles to testify that it had happened at all. I passed Jack his clothes, but he continued to sit, intent on the beetle in his hand, without seeming to notice them.

I closed the hamper and strapped it shut, feeling my shirt graze the new sunburn on my shoulders. I had a sudden impulse to ask Jack why he had been so rude to Edie earlier; when I next saw her I wanted to know that he had explained to me, that I understood. I cleared my throat, but Jack didn't look up. He was frowning a little, concentrating, and his hand was still curled around the beetle. I started to smile at the childish, attentive look on his face; then I saw that he was pulling its legs off, one by one, with precise, deliberate fingers. As I watched, he flicked the last little strand of black away, leaving the beetle as nothing but a gold-green carapace, like the boss of a shield or a brooch. There was a pause while he tilted his head, like an artist considering the final details of a painting. Then he pinched the antennae delicately off the beetle's head.

I stayed where I was, silent.

I thought he would crush it to death then, but he only put it gently on the ground, smoothing a place for it between two tufts of grass. He looked up, saw me watching him, and smiled.

'Ready to go?' he said. 'You needn't wait for me.'

'I don't mind,' I said. I stood there, quiet, while he got dressed and gathered up an empty bottle that I had missed; and I let him put his arm over my shoulder as we walked back to the house together.

The rest of that afternoon passed in a hot, uncomfortable dream. My head was aching and my back and legs were burnt and raw. Jack had tea with the others, outside under the copper beech, but I had had enough of the sun and shut myself in my room. I tried again to read, but my sense of unreality was too strong, as though I had a fever. Once I smelt cigarette smoke drifting up from the drawing-room window below and heard snatches of laughter and male voices, but I was almost certain it was only Anthony and Langdon-Down. The sunlight played on the ceiling, reflecting off the ivy, honey-green.

It wasn't until after dinner, when the sun had gone down, that the clarity seemed to come back into the world. The heat had faded and Jack decided that we should take our brandy outside, in the cool blue evening. The swifts were looping and twisting between the trees and I stood watching them, half hypnotised by their grace and silence. Langdon-Down was delivering a donnish, soporific monologue on the Cathars – the conversation at dinner had touched on ideas of evil, and now he was examining, pedantically, the concept of the devil in European history – but the quiet monotony of his voice was easy to disregard. Anthony said something mocking, and Edie laughed, but I paid no attention.

Slowly I became aware of Jack at my elbow. When I looked round, he said, 'Something wrong?'

'No,' I said. 'Only sunburn.'

He laughed quietly. 'Idiot.'

'I know.' I hadn't realised that I was miserable until I felt the knot inside me loosening. He had spoken to me during dinner, of course, but that had been in front of the others; that was different. 'But you could have warned me.'

'That you're an idiot? Surely you knew that already.'

I punched him gently. 'That I'd get burnt.'

'As the moth said to the flame,' he murmured, and grinned. 'Is it my fault if you have no sense at all? Get Edie to give you some cold cream. No doubt she'll apply it for you as well, if you ask nicely.' He lit a cigarette, went to put the case back in his pocket and paused, holding it open. 'Have one.'

'No, thanks.'

'Go on. Have a cigarette.' There was a note in his voice that I hadn't heard before; or not when he was speaking to me, anyway. 'Have a bloody cigarette, Gardner.'

I held his look for as long as I could, and then took one. He leant forward to light it for me, his eyes intent. Then he squeezed my shoulder. It hurt, but I didn't say anything. 'Good man. But you're being unsociable. Come and sit down.'

I nodded, but I stayed where I was for a little while, unwilling to turn my eyes away from the swifts' mesmeric dance. The cigarette he had given me tasted bitter, like ash, but I smoked it obediently, without asking myself whether I was enjoying it.

When I did turn back towards the others it was because I had heard my name. Anthony smiled when he saw me move and raised his voice. 'I was saying to Jack that we shall have to find a way to amuse you tomorrow. He has grown-up business to attend to.'

Langdon-Down added, 'Gardner is a very resourceful and scholarly young man. As I was saying, in the twelfth century, the Bogomils . . .' but no one was listening to him.

'Yes, do be quiet, Tony. You're only jealous that you're not nineteen yourself,' Edie said. 'If anyone needs to be kept out of mischief it's you, not Oliver.'

'What business?' I said.

'I have a visitor,' Jack said.

'How long is he staying for?'

Anthony muttered something to Edie. She turned her head and hissed at him, and he laughed.

'He's not staying at all,' Jack said. 'He's a – well, not quite a friend.' There was a mocking note in his voice, but his face was thoughtful.

'Won't you introduce us to him, Jack?'

'I doubt you'd want to know him particularly, Edie. He's a bit of a poor specimen. He was at Cambridge with me, but I don't speak to him much.'

'Oh, Lord,' Anthony said. 'Not the chap who turned up just before Christmas?'

'That's the one. James Fraser. He's a queer fish,' Jack added, smiling at me. 'Rather pathetic, really. I shouldn't wonder if he meets a sticky end one of these days.'

'It beats me why you put up with him,' Anthony said.

'Oh, auld lang syne . . . He was at Emmanuel. I told you, didn't I? We had some larks together, but he got sent down. Then he was shell-shocked in the War. He's a sort of limpet, these days. Won't go away, and I don't have the heart to labour the point.'

'That's not like you,' Edie said. It was too dark now to read her expression.

'He was an entertaining chap when I knew him. We were good friends for a while. He was gratifyingly obedient.'

I sat down on the steps a few feet away. 'What was he sent down for?'

Anthony laughed, and Jack shot him a humorous glance, sharing the joke. Edie turned away, hunching her shoulders. I had the impression that this was a story they had heard before. Anthony said, 'Tell him. It's a scream.'

'We had a Viking funeral for the college tortoise,' Jack said. 'We poured kerosene over a punt and sent Plautus – that was the tortoise – down the Cam in it, blazing away. It was glorious.'

I laughed, and Edie turned sharply to look at me. She said, 'They should have sent you both down. Not just James.'

'They wouldn't have sent James down if he hadn't been such a damn' fool. In any case, it was trivial. We were simply high-spirited. And undergraduate-ish, I admit.' He glanced at me, a smile at the corners of his mouth. 'But then, so many undergraduates are.'

'They should have sent you both down,' Edie repeated, putting her glass down on the steps with a heavy clink. 'Poor Plautus.'

'Not many tortoises get such a spectacular valediction,' I said.

'Not many tortoises get burnt alive.' She stood up a little unsteadily, and made her way to the table to pour herself another drink. 'It was still alive, you see, Oliver. Viking funeral indeed! I think it's simply sick-making. The poor creature must have been in agony.'

There was a pause. Anthony said, 'Women are so sentimental.'

Jack was watching me. I didn't know how I knew, in the dark, but I could feel his eyes on my face. He reached out and tousled my hair and I bent my head, letting his fingers trace the vertebrae at the back of my neck. I closed my eyes and thought of the swifts, weaving eternally back and forth on the sky. I heard Edie drink her whisky in two or three gulps, stand up and walk away.

Anthony chuckled softly, without warmth. 'Isn't that just like a lesbian?' he said, twisting to stare after her. 'Call her a woman and she gets the black-and-blue, cameelious hump.'

'You don't know what you're talking about,' Jack said, his fingers tightening on the top of my spine.

'Oh, come on, Jack, she's positively –'

'Go to bed, Gardner,' he said, as if we had been sitting in silence. 'And put cold cream on your shoulders, or you won't be able to move tomorrow.' I looked up at him and he leant back in his chair, taking his hand away. 'Go on.'

'I'm not sleepy.'

'Oliver. Go to bed.' He held my gaze, without smiling, and his look was so level and intimate that it was as if there was no one else in the world.

I stood up, nodded goodnight to Anthony and Langdon-Down, and went into the house and upstairs. I stood at the window in my bedroom, breathing in the cool night air, and put my hand to my face. I could smell cigarette smoke on my skin.

It was the first time he'd called me Oliver.

I stayed where I was for a long time, whispering my name to myself over and over, trying to imitate exactly how he'd said it. It seemed absurd to me that it was only now, after nineteen years, that I truly believed that it was *my* name.

III

James Fraser arrived the next morning, after breakfast. Edie and I were playing chess on the front lawn and saw him come down the drive: an emaciated, shabby-genteel figure with thinning, colourless hair and a general air of being held together by his clothes. He glanced at us as he passed, and I had the fancy that his eyes lingered on me, but his manner was so furtive and ill at ease that it seemed bad form to look back at him. I turned my gaze deliberately back to the chessboard, and only heard the clang of the doorbell and the creak as the door opened.

Jack said, 'Fraser,' without any particular inflection.

'Martin.' His voice was thin and reedy, with a well-to-do accent that contrasted oddly with the wheedling tone. 'Answering the door yourself. Still can't get the staff, I suppose?' He gave an unpleasant, cut-off giggle.

'You'd better come in.'

The door shut. I moved a chess-piece at random, and when I looked up Edie was watching me, half smiling. 'Don't worry,' she said. 'It'll be over by luncheon, and then you'll have him back.' She took up her pawn, swapped it for my bishop, and dropped the larger piece into the grass.

'I don't know what you mean.'

'Check, by the way.' I looked down again, surprised, and she laughed. 'Excuse me. I should have said checkmate.'

'You're quite right,' I said, after a moment. 'Blast.'

She surveyed the board for a few moments, smiling, and then swept her hand across the configuration of pieces, knocking them into the grass with the others. 'You're a simply terrible chess-player.'

'No, I'm not,' I said absently, turning to look over my shoulder. 'I'm chivalrous, that's all.'

She snorted, and followed my gaze to the drawing-room window. She said, with uncanny perspicuity, 'There's no point staring. They'll be in Jack's study.'

'I wasn't.' I caught her eye, and gave up the pretence. I drew my knees up and laced my fingers between them, unable to account for my unease. 'I don't understand what business he could possibly have with Jack.'

'Why should you? You've only known Jack for a few months; it's not as if you're privy to every detail of his life.' She spoke sharply, but she didn't meet my eyes.

I said, stung, 'I only meant – he didn't *look* –'

'You don't own him, you know. Jack is perfectly capable of looking after himself. *Too* capable. And – honestly, for heaven's sake, as if *you* –' She stopped, as if she had caught herself just in time.

I said, 'As if I what?'

There was a silence. She picked up the chessmen and started to set them up. The two armies faced each other in perfect, hostile symmetry.

I waited, but after a while I knew she wasn't going to answer. I had brought my diary outside with me, and I reached for my fountain pen and forced myself to write a few lines, but it was no good. I couldn't concentrate. I found myself staring at a pale expanse of paper, my mind wandering. I couldn't explain what had put the wind up me, but it *was* up and blowing like a cold draught on the back of my neck, even in the heavy summer heat. If Fraser had only been different; if I could have seen at a glance why Jack chose to invite him to Tyme's End . . .

The white page of my diary glared at me in the sun, and a headache began to knock gently at my temples. Abruptly, I stood up. 'I'm just going inside, to –'

Edie leapt to her feet and took hold of my arm. 'Don't,' she said.

'Don't what?'

'Eavesdrop. Don't.'

I shook her off, rather more roughly than I meant to. 'I shouldn't dream of it. I'd like a drink, that's all.'

A second passed. She said, 'I'm sorry, that was a beastly thing to say,' but there was something in her expression that told me she hadn't been persuaded.

It was on the tip of my tongue to retort with a stronger term than *beastly*, but I swallowed the impulse and turned away without a word. I went through the side door into the scullery and poured myself a glass of water; I didn't let the water run, and it was warm and cloudy and tasted stale. Someone – probably Anthony – had taken the gramophone out of doors, and a catchy, irritating little melody was drifting in from the rose-garden. Rather than go back outside, I went through into the hall, shutting the door behind me; the music faded, and instead I could hear the quiet sounds of the house settling in the heat, and a murmur of voices from Jack's study. I stood irresolute, torn between wanting to step closer to the study door, and my pride. Whatever Edie said, I wasn't caddish enough to listen at keyholes, not even if I had a nagging sense that something was wrong. And if Jack caught me at it, I should never forgive myself.

Fraser raised his voice. The words were unclear, but the tone was unmistakably peevish, a thin, reedy petulance that set my teeth on edge. I was sure it was not one I would have employed with an old friend, whatever the circumstances.

But Jack laughed. It brought me back to myself: there couldn't possibly be anything wrong if he could laugh like that. I crossed the hall, treading heavily, and opened the front door. At the same time I heard the study door open behind me, and Fraser's voice muttering a few words that I didn't catch.

Jack said, 'Ah, Gardner. James, you haven't met Oliver Gardner, have you? A great friend of mine.' When I turned he was smiling at me, but there was a crease between his eyebrows.

Fraser shot me a glance that seemed at once troubled and wary. Now that I was closer to him, I could see that he had once been very good-looking. It made me uncomfortable; somehow, I thought, it would have been better if he had always been so unprepossessing. I didn't want to see, in this sneaking, threadbare man, the ruins of something else.

He said, 'Oliver Gardner,' repeating Jack's intonation exactly.

'How do you do?' I held out my hand, but he didn't take it. Instead he glanced at Jack, and although his face was hostile the look that passed between them contained a kind of understanding.

'I'll come back in a few days,' he said, 'when you've had time to think.'

'No doubt,' Jack said, with a half-smile.

'If you need to speak to me –'

'I shan't.'

He shrugged, but there was nothing easy or assured in the gesture. 'If you do, I'm staying at the Cloven Hoof, in Falconhurst. The public house, in the High Street.'

'Yes, I know it well. A pity you can't stay here, but I'm afraid –'

'I wouldn't stay here if you paid me.'

'Oh dear,' Jack said, 'not even then? That *is* damning.' He caught my eye, and his eyelid flickered in the merest suggestion of a wink. 'Well, I suppose we shall have to soldier on without you. And now, if you don't mind . . .' He gestured towards the open door, and Fraser shambled past me and out on to the doorstep. I smelt decay, and a whiff of spirits, and drew back; Fraser seemed to notice the movement and halted, looking at me. His eyes stayed on my face for longer than was comfortable.

Jack said, 'Come on, Gardner, old chap. Let's have a drink.'

I turned away. But I could not shake off the sensation that Fraser was still watching me; and even after he must have been long gone, I felt that look, and saw those eyes, filled with an unexpected, unwelcome fellow feeling.

I might have been imagining it, but after that encounter with Fraser it seemed to me that Jack's manner towards me changed. It was nothing that I could identify clearly: perhaps a softening in his face when he looked at me, or an affectionate, more possessive note in his voice when he spoke. When before he might have laughed as Anthony insulted me, he would quash him mildly; when he would have chaffed me himself, he only smiled. I was used to friendly mockery – after all, that was what, at school and even in my college, had formed the basis of most friendships – and I found this new consideration disconcerting; but nonetheless I couldn't help drinking it in, savouring it, like wine. That afternoon, after Fraser had left, when I lay dreaming under the copper beech, my hands behind my head, and Jack declaimed snippets of the Seneca translation he was working on, essaying the sound of the words – and later, that evening at dinner, when he quelled Anthony mid-mockery – I thought I perceived that new warmth, and it reassured me. The unease that lingered after Fraser's departure faded, and in my relief I shone in conversation and managed to say several things that made Jack laugh incontinently. I went to bed light-hearted, the morning's events quite forgotten.

And, as if to confirm my sense of a danger somehow turned aside, the next day and the next passed without incident, perfectly. I'd never been so happy as I was then: perhaps I'd never known it was possible. The weather was better than ever, and I seemed to move through a rich, indolent atmosphere, like honey. We read, bathed, smoked, played croquet and a kind of spurious cricket, talked, ate, drank – and every pursuit was the best, the only possible one. Edie and Anthony lost their sharp edges, softening in the sun; Anthony took photographs of us all, concentrating so hard he forgot to insult anyone, and for the first time I understood why Jack was fond of him. Even Langdon-Down, as he pottered about trying to reassemble his papers for his departure, managed to achieve a sort of uncharacteristic levity. It was as if the world had, for a few days, conspired to achieve perfection. And at the centre of it – at the centre of Tyme's End – was Jack, smiling at my enjoyment.

It was at breakfast, the day after that, that the first cloud covered the sun. After four or five cloudless days, even the faintest hint of grey felt oppressive, and that morning was almost completely overcast, the sun only just perceptible through a heavy haze. I had slept longer than I was accustomed to, and my eyes were sticky and swollen. I had dreamt again of my father; that is, I had had the same nightmare, only this time I had had the unpleasant sense, as I watched the men in grey advance, that I myself was culpable, that with a few words I could have averted the tragedy. I had woken suddenly, my mouth so dry it took an effort to open it, and, although I was glad not to have cried out, the nightmare clung to me, like a cobweb. It made me temperish and out-of-spirits. That morning, for the first time, I wished that Tyme's End had a proper complement of domestic staff; it irked me to have to assemble my own breakfast, and to sit surrounded by the debris left by the others. I found a letter from my mother waiting for me on the table, and I read it irritably, resenting her for her barely-concealed wish that I would come home, and her inconsequential news. I put it aside without finishing it, making a guilty mental vow to answer it that day, whatever other temptations came my way. As I slid it back into the envelope I saw another letter, addressed in a hand I didn't recognise, that had been concealed underneath.

Oliver Gardner, Esq., Tyme's End, Falconhurst.

I took it up, examining it with a mild curiosity. I had mentioned to several of my friends at Sidney Sussex that I would be spending part of the vac at Tyme's End, but I knew their handwriting, and the postmark was local and the envelope cheap and light-weight. I opened it.

I am aware that I am taking a colossal liberty in writing to you like this, but I ask for your forbearance quite sincerely. I know you will think this very bad form. I would have done so, once. But I ask you – no, I beg you, it will not surprise you if I do not stand on my dignity – to read this without throwing it into the fire. Read it. Throw it away if you must, but read it, first.

I sat very still, and it was some time before I could bring myself to read the rest. The writing was thin and pernickety, and I had never seen it before; but I knew, after those few lines, whose it was.

God knows what you thought of me, when we met a few days ago. I dread to think. At your age I would have felt nothing but contempt – or, rather, dismissed myself as an irrelevant sort of fellow, the type that other chaps might end up like. But I come from a good family, and I was – as you know, of course – one of Martin's associates at Cambridge. I was also very handsome. I mention that in the hope that you will see some similarities between my case and yours.

My friendship with Martin was probably the most intense of my life. He inspired me to everything I achieved, good and bad. He had a great power of influence, something which I see has increased with his age, especially now that he has attained some small measure of celebrity. Perhaps – no, certainly – you will despise me if I warn you against that. I mean, against him. But it is through no malice, no jealousy, that I urge you not to pursue his acquaintance. It is simply that I think if I had not met him, I would have been a better and happier man. I know it. I am not referring simply to the incident which led to my being sent down – if I am bitter about that, it is because Jack did not get sent down, not because I did. I mean that his influence, absorbed over a long period of time, is noxious, like one of those poisons which can kill while hardly making their presence felt.

The conventional phrases are not quite applicable. I don't mean they are not true. I could write to you of questionable moral character, or hidden scandal. But that is not what I am trying to tell you. It is old-fashioned to talk of Evil, particularly in reference to any one human being. Most of us who were in the trenches can no longer conceive of Evil as anything but that huge, impersonal horror. It would seem bathetic, almost obscene, to call a man evil. There was no room for men to be evil in that war – stupid, callous, cruel, but not the other. But I am unusual among my comrades. Martin is evil. That is the best word, and the only one.

Of course, being the young, intelligent man that you undoubtedly are, you will demand some evidence of this assertion. I am unable to supply any. There is no evidence, except what I and Martin both know to be true. Perhaps, one day, the world will learn what he is. Until that day, if it comes, there is nothing, either in his manner, his professed views, or his verifiable deeds to support my contention. In short, there is no reason to believe me, especially as Martin will – if you tell him of this letter, a course I again beg you not to take – attribute my position to nothing more than jealousy. He will probably laugh.

However, I am writing this in the hope that you will not communicate my anxiety to him. Believe me, it takes no little measure of courage and conviction to write this, and excuse me that I cannot write more plainly. This is the first unselfish action I have taken for more than fifteen years. You must forgive me if I cannot do it without flinching, a little. But I cannot put into words what I fear for you, if Martin begins to exert an undue influence upon you. Perhaps nothing more than disillusionment, perhaps something worse. When I knew him well he was dangerous. The War, I think, has hardened him, confirmed him in that venomous tendency. He is a great and deadly man. Most people see only the greatness, and most people, not attracting his attention, run no risk. But you are different. As I was.

I charge you, on your honour as a scholar and a
gentleman, do not let him know of this letter. Burn it
if you must. But keep it hidden.
I remain, etc., Jas. Fraser, Esq.

I looked at the paper for a long time. I couldn't bring
myself to read it again so I stared at the blotchy,
spidery signature. It was like Fraser himself: it hinted
at the ruins of something better.

The edge of a shadow that fell across the table
darkened and sharpened, and when I looked up I saw
that the sun had burnt off the clouds. From outside
there was the clack of a croquet mallet on a ball, and
Edie's voice raised in protest, strident, but seeming to
come from a long way away.

It was malicious, that was all: a childish, contemptible attempt to get at Jack through me. The
sheer melodrama of the language told me as much.
Dangerous? Venomous? It was so ridiculous I
propped my chin in my hands and laughed. A subtler,
more intelligent man might have done a better job. It
was unpleasant, of course – childish and manipulative
– and upsetting, my laughter notwithstanding. But I
had seen Fraser with my own eyes, and knew him to
be untrustworthy; and it would have been naive, I
thought, to be surprised that Jack had enemies. All
great men did.

Most people see only the greatness . . .

How could Fraser think that I would take his letter
seriously? What kind of man did he think I was –
what kind of man was *he*? I could only suppose that
he was desperate, throwing aside all concerns of
decency and self-respect. I looked again at the messy,

rather pathetic signature, and wanted to pity him. It was terrible, that a man could end up like that.

But I couldn't pity him. I remembered the way he'd met my eyes: as if he pitied *me*.

And for a moment my certainty was shaken. It was as if the room around me – the table, the chair I was sitting on, even the garden outside – trembled. Suppose the world I thought was solid was – not. Just suppose . . .

I folded the letter into two, and then into four, and shoved it deep into my pocket. I should tell Jack as soon as I saw him. Fraser was right: he *would* laugh. And that would make everything all right.

I had been halfway through a slice of bread and marmalade, but when I caught sight of it on the table it looked odd and alien, emphatically not the kind of thing I wanted to put in my mouth. I stood up, pushing my chair back, and went to find Jack.

But when I went outside Edie and Anthony were quarrelling, and Jack was nowhere to be seen. I hovered, impatient, while Anthony swung his croquet mallet carelessly, practising shots, and Edie stood with her hands on her hips, glaring. She was in the middle of a tirade – a long, fluent dissection of Anthony's manners, politics, appearance and parentage – that would have been amusing under different circumstances. Anthony glanced up and gave me a complicit smile that must have been calculated to infuriate her. He said, 'Edie, darling, is it my fault if you want to be something completely different from what *le bon Dieu* had in mind for you?'

'Oh, you smug little – jumped-up little – you're

simply insufferable. I suppose it's positively unthinkable that there's anything wrong with *you*. Well, let me tell you –'

'*Let* you? If only,' Anthony murmured, flicking me another look.

I said, 'Have you seen Jack?'

Edie said, 'You're a fool and a blackguard and a snob.' She turned to me. 'Yes – well, that is, no, he went into Falconhurst with Philip, to see him on to the train. He'll be back presently.'

'Oh.' I could feel the letter in my pocket, digging stiff edges of paper into me.

Edie watched me, brushing the tangle of reddish hair away from her face. 'I say, is everything quite all right?'

'Oh, yes, thank you.'

'Jolly good.' She turned back to Anthony, but the pause seemed to have taken the wind out of her sails. She opened her mouth, waited for a few seconds, as if for inspiration, and then closed it again.

Anthony said, 'Run away, Gardner. Edie and I are having a heart-to-heart.'

'So I heard.' I kicked a loose piece of stone that was on the terrace and it skittered and rebounded off the wall of the house. If Jack wasn't here, there was no use hanging around; I might as well find a book to read, or go for a bathe by myself, or . . . But I couldn't think of anything I wanted to do.

Edie's gaze had followed the stone as it ricocheted off the wall, and now she caught my eye. 'Ignore him, Oliver. Let's get a drink.' She walked past me, grasping my upper arm. I felt the dampness of her hand through the fabric of my shirt. 'Stir your stumps. It's terribly rude to keep a lady waiting.'

Anthony said, 'For God's sake, woman, it's hardly ten o'clock.' But by the time he'd finished his sentence we were inside, and Edie was making her way towards the decanter and soda siphon that were kept on a tray in the little sitting room. She poured two drinks, one much heavier on the soda than the other, and passed me the stronger one. I took it gratefully, and drank half of it in a gulp.

She sipped her own drink, watching me with her eyes narrowed. She said, 'All right, then, Oliver, what's up?'

'Nothing. Why should there be?'

She tilted her head towards my half-emptied glass with silent eloquence.

I felt my cheeks prickle as I flushed. I said, 'Very well, then. It's nothing, really, but I –' I stopped.

Edie held my look, her face unchanging.

'Edie, when you – the day I arrived, you met me at the station, and you warned me. About Jack. You said I should go home.'

'Oh.' She put her drink on the sideboard and strode back to the door, standing looking over the lawn with her hands in her pockets. Her hair was tousled and had lost its wave; from behind she looked like a boy.

'What did you mean?'

'What I said,' she said shortly. 'Look at Anthony playing croquet by himself. He's so desperate to *win*.'

'All right, but why?'

'No reason.'

'Edie, please.'

She glanced over her shoulder and paused, heaving a deep breath. 'I thought – I thought you'd be unhappy here. With Anthony making remarks about your – your father's profession, and –'

'It was Jack you were warning me about.'

'Nonsense. You can't be remembering it properly. You told me your father was a clerk in a factory, and I looked at you and thought you hadn't a chance, Anthony would tear you to pieces, like one of Actaeon's hounds. Was it Actaeon? Do you know? Never mind, I'll ask Jack, when he gets back. He loves being asked questions when he knows the answers, he might have been the Delphic oracle in a previous incarnation. It's funny, Anthony isn't a bit like that, he only likes questions to which he *doesn't* know the –'

'You told me Jack would be a very bad replacement for my father.'

'Did I? How terribly tactless.'

I pressed my hand against my pocket until the letter dug its little claws into me. 'Edie. Please tell me. What did you mean?'

'I –' She took another deep breath and sat down, reaching for her drink. It glowed amber in the sunlight from the window, and she stared into it as if it held a secret. She said, very slowly, 'If you don't know by now, then I was wrong.'

'I want you to tell me.'

Her eyes slid to my face and away again. She opened her mouth, and I noticed how neat her teeth were, how white and straight, like an animal's.

I heard a noise from the doorway behind me. Jack's voice said, 'Good Lord, is it time for whisky already? Just as well Philip's gone or he'd be horribly shocked.'

Edie stood up smoothly. 'Anthony and I had a bust-up, and Oliver has been too, too sweet. He's even drinking just to keep me company – imagine. You do have an eye for charming young men, don't you?'

Jack shot a glance at me, his mouth curved at one corner. 'I dare say,' he said. 'Gardner, will you come outside for a moment? I want to tell you something.'

I glanced at Edie. Her face was closed, her brows drawn together. I felt a rush of disappointment – or was it relief? – that Jack had interrupted her just as she was about to tell me . . . but it wasn't serious. I would have to ask her again; sooner or later she'd tell me whatever she had been about to say.

I drank the rest of my whisky and soda and followed Jack out on to the terrace.

IV

We walked across the grass, past Anthony's solitary game of croquet, towards the little copse of trees on the far side of the lawn. I glanced at Jack, but he was looking at the ground, his mouth in a half-smile. He had a pensive, absorbed air, as if he were alone.

After a while he seemed to remember that I was there. He looked at me and his half-smile turned into a grin. 'Forgive me,' he said. 'I'm in a brown study. Did you sleep well?'

It seemed so long since I had got up that it took me a moment to understand what he meant. Then, looking at his face, I was sure that he knew I'd had a nightmare. I'd been relieved that I hadn't shouted out when I awoke: but perhaps I had, without hearing my own voice. From the glint in his eyes, it appeared that I had. I said, 'Yes, thank you. Very well indeed.'

'I'm glad.' He knew I was lying, but there was nothing in his voice but amusement.

We carried on walking. I could feel the sweat starting out on my skin as the sunshine slid over me. I wondered if it would soak through my clothes, and cupped my hand over my pocket protectively. I was going to burn Fraser's letter, but in the meantime, I wanted to keep it intact, legible. I already had parts of it by heart.

Martin is evil. That is the best word, and the only one.

I said, 'Jack –'

He tilted his head back into the sunlight, closing his eyes. He said, 'Do you think this is beautiful? Do you think Tyme's End is beautiful?'

'Yes, of course.'

'You've been happy here?'

'Yes. You know I have. Jack –'

'Good. One day it'll be yours. I went to my solicitor this morning to change my will.'

I shook my head, laughing, momentarily distracted from what I had wanted to say. 'Well,' I said, 'in that case I shall have to start considering what bits of furniture I shall want to keep when I move in.'

'It may not be for years. And only if you outlive me, of course. But I have a feeling about you. I rather think you will.'

'I should hope so. You've got twenty years' head start. You could be my father. It's only fair that you should cop it before I do.'

'You ungrateful cub,' he said, punching me lightly. 'Aren't you even going to thank me?'

'For what?'

'For leaving you Tyme's End. And my not inconsiderable fortune, naturally. Although,' he added, 'by then I suppose it might be more inconsiderable.'

'All right. Thanks. Jack, this morning I –'

He started to laugh, turning on his heel to face me,

as if he wanted to see me properly. 'My God, Gardner, you're a cool customer, aren't you?'

'What?' I stood still and shoved my hands into my pockets, wishing he'd stop laughing and listen to me. 'Jack, I –'

'I had no idea you were such a serene young devil. Happens to you every day, does it, someone offering you riches beyond the dreams of avarice?'

'No, of course not, I simply –' I stopped, staring at him. 'You're not – Jack, you're not serious?'

'Certainly I'm serious.'

'You're going to leave Tyme's End to *me*?'

'Didn't I just say so?'

'But – you mean it?'

'I mean it.' He smiled into my eyes. 'I think you'll be happy here.'

'I can't. I can't let you. What about – you must have family, or –'

'No. My brother was shot as a deserter.'

I swallowed. 'I didn't know.'

He shrugged. 'Of course not. Why should you? Oh, don't worry about that, for heaven's sake. It was a long time ago. What I mean is, you're the right man for Tyme's End. There's no one else. I want you to have it.'

'I –' I turned and looked back at the house. The ivy riffled and shimmered in the breeze, and the light glinted on the windowpanes. I thought that I couldn't imagine being the master of Tyme's End, but the thrill of possession rose in my insides, like the fizz of champagne. *Mine* . . . I cleared my throat. 'But you hardly know me. What about your other friends?'

'I don't think any of them are as . . . suitable.'

'I can't accept it. I won't.'

Jack gave me a long look, then turned aside, smiling. 'When I'm dead you can refuse it, if you want.'

'It's not – please understand, I simply can't –'

'Then don't.' He was still smiling, as if he knew something I didn't. 'It's all right, Gardner. No one can make you take it.'

I struggled for words, torn between desire and duty and a kind of slippery unease that I couldn't quite put a name to.

I said, in a rush, 'You're not my father, Jack.'

For a few seconds I thought he hadn't heard. His gaze came back to my face and searched my eyes like a scholar looking up an entry in an index. Then he said, quietly, 'No, Gardner, I'm not. Your father was a clerk in a factory. Your father was an unremarkable, anonymous soldier who left you nothing but your good looks and a sense of inferiority. More to the point, your father is dead.'

I felt the air in my lungs thicken, as if it were suddenly liquid and not gas.

'What I am offering you is far beyond what your father could have offered you. I will be much, *much* more important to you than your father was.' He leant towards me, putting one hand on the side of my neck. 'Don't compare me to him again.'

I tried to hold his stare, but I couldn't. I glanced down at the grass, glowing green at my feet, and remembered the beetle he had torn apart. It should have made me want to pull away from him, but it didn't. I said, 'All right.'

'Good boy.'

He squeezed my neck and dropped his hand. Then we started to walk again. I could hear the rattling of river-water running over stones; it seemed implausibly loud, like a theatrical effect. The sunlight shone through the trees, emerald and gold.

I turned away and started to go back towards the house. Jack said, 'Oliver?' but I didn't reply. Although he started to say something else, I didn't look back, and he didn't follow me as I walked away.

I cannot put into words what I fear for you, if Martin begins to exert an undue influence upon you. Perhaps nothing more than disillusionment, perhaps something worse. When I knew him well he was dangerous . . .

I despised myself for reading the letter again, but it was irresistible, like picking at a scab. I couldn't leave it alone. I sat on my bed and spread the pages out on the nightstand, staring at the words as though I could make them unravel.

After a while I got my diary out, and sat with my fountain pen in my hand, trying to think of something to write. But nothing came. I shut my eyes and scrawled on the paper – meaningless shapes at first, and then, as words formed in my head, I found my hand starting to move in unconscious obedience. When I opened my eyes the page was covered with loops and waves, like a child's idea of the sea. A few words were just legible, although perhaps only because I already knew what they said. *Jack, Tyme's End. So happy here. Not my father.* And then, suddenly clearer, as if something had been guiding my hand, *dangerous*.

272

I read the word over and over until my heart seemed to beat in time to the syllables. I turned the pages back so that I wouldn't have to see it, and found myself looking at the entry I had written yesterday. It spoke to me in a dreamy, breathless voice: of a lazy day in the sun, bathing and three-man cricket, and the blue evening sky as I sat by the window in the drawing room to write. It made me feel weary and old.

There was a knock on my door. I ran my hand across my eyes, took a deep breath, and said, 'Come in.'

It was Edie. I'd looked for her earlier, after I'd left Jack on the lawn, but she'd been nowhere to be found. She had an odd, strained look on her face, and her eyes and nose were pink, as if she were hay-feverish. She said, 'I'm not intruding, am I?'

'No.'

'Jolly good.' She came in and closed the door behind her, leaning back against it as though someone might try to break it down at any moment. She held out her hand and I saw an envelope in it. 'You left this downstairs. Anthony started to read it aloud before I realised what it was. He's such a cad – I'm furious with him.'

My mother's letter. I took it, imagining snippets of it in Anthony's drawling public-school accent – or, worse, his imitation of mine. *Dearest Oliver . . . I must say I find the new vicar the tiniest bit unsavoury . . . I miss you, my darling, and it does seem rather hard that I might not see you before you go up again to Cambridge . . .* And would Jack have laughed when he heard it? I wasn't sure. I said, 'Thank you.'

'It simply isn't done,' Edie said. 'I don't know anyone else who would do a thing like that. I should have stopped him as soon as he picked it up, but I had no idea he would –'

'It's all right, Edie. I shouldn't have left it lying around. I know what Anthony's like by now.'

She gave me a brief smile, and came away from the door to perch on the back of the chair. My tie was dangling over it, but she didn't seem to notice. She said, 'Your mother sounds perfectly sweet.'

'She is,' I said, ashamed at how little conviction I could bring into my voice. Two weeks ago I would have said the same thing, and meant it. 'We're . . . very fond of each other.'

'It must have been hard for her.' Edie slid her fingertip over the edge of my dressing table, her eyes on the photo I'd leant against the mirror. 'Is that your father?'

I picked it up instinctively, and clutched it to my chest. 'Yes.' I felt foolish, so I laid it flat on the nightstand with my mother's letter on top. The return address caught my eye: *Mrs. V. S. Gardner, The Old Vicarage, Peltenshall*. The Old Vicarage was a grey, crumbling cottage, full of leaks and flaking plaster, so small it was astonishing how much money my mother had to spend to keep it standing. Compared to Tyme's End, it wasn't fit for human habitation.

Edie followed my eyes, and then looked away. She said, 'Well, I came to say toodle-oo.'

'Where are you going?'

'I'm off. Leaving,' she added. 'I've got thoroughly browned off. Oh, it's not your fault, or Jack's, or even Tony's. I've had enough, that's all. I shall be glad to get back to town.'

'For good, you mean?'

'I don't *live* here, Oliver.'

'Does Jack know?'

'Of course.' She snorted. 'He didn't object, naturally. Anthony's going later today, after they've finished taking photographs – *more* photographs, it's too tiresome – so you'll be alone here. With Jack, I mean. But you won't mind, will you?'

I opened my mouth and then turned to the window, letting my eyes rest on the treetops beyond the curve of the drive. Outside I could hear voices – Anthony and Jack, laughing. I spun back suddenly to look at Edie, and in the second before she had time to compose her expression I saw a hint of unease, even – I thought – of guilt.

She said, in a rush, 'Oliver, when you asked me earlier about Jack, it was only – that I thought you were so young, and we drink and smoke an awful lot, and Anthony sometimes takes snow . . . I'm sorry. It was jolly thoughtless of me. Your imagination must have positively run riot.'

'Langdon-Down isn't exactly dissolute,' I said.

She laughed unmusically. 'No. It was silly of me. What harm could you come to with your tutor here and Jack in charge?'

Her voice didn't ring quite true, but I didn't know what to say. I glanced involuntarily at Fraser's letter, where I'd left it on the nightstand, and felt a strange sense of humiliation. I moved over to it and slipped it into my pocket.

'Well. So long, old thing,' Edie said. 'I suppose I'd better be off, if I'm to catch my train. Pip pip.'

I nodded. My mother's address caught my eye

again, but this time, instead of seeing the Old Vicarage in my mind's eye, I saw her face: tired, a little gaunt, but smiling, as it almost always was. I pushed the letter aside and my father stared up at me from the photograph underneath, in black-and-white, eyes wide, looking more like me than I cared to admit.

I said, 'I think I shall come with you. If that's all right, I mean.'

'Of course,' she said, 'that would be delightful.'

'Would you give me a few minutes to pack?'

'To –?' Her expression changed.

'I'll be quick,' I said. 'I don't have much.'

'I thought you meant to see me off. Not to –'

I started to collect my belongings, dragged my shabby little suitcase out from under the bed and piled things into it higgledy-piggledy. Edie watched me, her mouth slightly open. My hands were shaking, but I kept moving. I was behaving abominably; no matter how much my mother missed me, she wouldn't want me to forget my manners or offend Jack.

Edie said, 'I'll wait for you downstairs.' She left the room, and I dragged open drawers, scooped my belongings into my arms, flung them into the suitcase. I knew that if I gave myself time to think I should change my mind. For the first time I was glad that I'd brought so little with me. In a few moments I had closed the case and was making my way down the stairs and outside. The sunlight hit me like a wall.

Edie was standing with Anthony and Jack, her weekend case in her hand, halfway through a sentence. She said, 'I shan't need them urgently, so have them sent whenever is convenient.' Then she glanced round.

Jack raised one eyebrow. 'Are you going somewhere, Gardner?'

'I – Jack, I'm so sorry, I have to go home. My mother –'

'Does she miss you too much, ducky?' Anthony said.

'She's had an accident. It's not serious, but she's hurt her ankle and can't walk. I'd rather not go, but there you are.'

Jack was giving me a steady look, but all he said was, 'Well, under the circumstances, of course you must go. Will you make your connection to Peltenshall?'

'I should do, thanks.' I couldn't meet his eyes; I wanted to drop my suitcase on the grass and blurt out that I was lying and in any case I'd changed my mind. 'You've been most hospitable. Thank you.'

Anthony said, 'I'll get the motor car out when I leave later. Perhaps you'd like to stay until then?'

'No, thank you. I don't have much luggage. Edie and I will walk to the station together.'

'Very well,' Jack said. 'I'm sorry you have to go, of course, but it can't be helped. I shan't forgive you if you forget to write to me, though.'

I cleared my throat, and then had to clear it again. 'I won't.'

'Good man. Well . . .' He glanced at Anthony and a look passed between them, too quick to read. Then his eyes dropped to Anthony's camera, and he said smoothly, 'I'll send on a copy of the photographs if you want. You were in a couple, weren't you, the other day?'

'I'd like that. Thanks.'

We stood awkwardly, looking at each other, until Edie said, 'Well, buck up or you'll miss your connection.' She kissed Jack's cheek, nodded at Anthony, and stood waiting for me a few feet away.

I shook hands with them both. Jack's handshake was cool and brief, but he said, 'I meant what I said, by the way,' before he turned back to Anthony, already grinning at something Anthony had murmured to him.

I said, 'Goodbye, Jack,' and followed Edie up the drive and out of the gates, leaving Tyme's End behind me.

We walked in silence. We were almost at the station by the time Edie said, 'What did he mean?'

'What?'

'Jack,' she said, looking up dreamily at the sky, as though she would hardly notice if I answered. 'What did he tell you?'

'Oh.' I shifted my suitcase into the other hand. The handle was sticky with sweat. I glanced at Edie, wondering if I was at liberty to tell her. Surely Jack would have told me to keep it under my hat if he hadn't wanted . . . ? But I said, 'Nothing, really.'

There was a silence. We turned the corner, made our way through the ticket office, bought our tickets and went through on to the sunlit platform; but when I caught Edie's eye she was frowning, as if she was still waiting for an answer to her question.

We sat down on the bench and I lit cigarettes for us both. I felt odd inside, as though I had swallowed a mouthful of ice. I said, 'I hope you don't mind if I catch a later train, so that I don't have to change at Tunbridge Wells West.'

'Of course not,' she said, taking the cigarette without looking at me. Then she seemed to register what I'd done and looked at me with a half-smile. 'What happened to the boy who didn't smoke?'

'Gone for ever.'

'Jack's doing,' she said.

There was a pause. There were only a few minutes left before her train. The air was full of birdsong, as it had been the day I arrived.

'He said he was going to leave Tyme's End to me,' I said, suddenly wanting to laugh. 'He said he'd been to his lawyer this morning to change his will.'

Edie turned to look at me sharply, but she knew immediately what I was talking about. 'He said *what*?'

'It's extraordinary, isn't it?' I said. 'I can hardly believe it myself.'

'Hardly? You mean you *do* believe it?'

'I don't think he was joking,' I said. 'I know what he's like when he's making fun. He was . . . different. Serious.'

'He can't possibly have been. *Tyme's End?* For God's sake, he's hardly known you three months.'

I said, stung, 'That's what I said.'

She gave a mirthless little giggle. 'Did he say he was in love with you?'

'No, of course he –'

But she ignored me. 'It's a rather cruel joke, that's all. How perfectly beastly of him. He must have thought that you'd get thoroughly overexcited.'

I closed my eyes. I said, slowly, 'I really, truly don't think he *was* joking.'

She twisted round to look at me. Then she leapt to

279

her feet, dragging her hair away from her face with one hand. She stared at me for a long time. 'My God,' she said, at last. 'You scheming little fiend.'

'I beg your pardon?'

'You vile, manipulative worm. My God, to think that all this time I thought *you* needed protection from *him*.'

'I didn't – Edie, I had no idea he was even considering it – and I told him I couldn't accept it –'

'Of course,' she said, spinning on her heel to glare at the opposite platform. 'Oh, of *course*. You won't accept it. Not even when you've had to work so hard for it – making him think you adored him, stringing us all along, playing the innocent to perfection. Honestly, I despise you. I suppose you think you have a right to it?'

'Edie, I don't understand – I swear I didn't –'

'You must have thought me a perfect idiot to try and warn you off when you knew precisely what you were doing.'

I swallowed. There was an edge to her anger that I didn't understand. I said, 'Edie . . . he hasn't disinherited you, in my favour, has he?'

She swung round, raising her hand, so that for a moment I thought she was going to slap me across the face. I flinched and she stepped backwards, but the fury was still in her voice when she said, 'How dare you, you gold-digging little sodomite? I am a decent, principled human being. I wouldn't stoop to –'

There was silence. She pressed her lips together, as if she didn't trust herself to finish the sentence.

I said, '*What* did you call me?'

She shook her head. Then she picked up her case,

strode to the other end of the platform and stood with her back to me, her hair blowing in the breeze, staring towards the curve in the railway line where the train would come into sight.

I thought, although I couldn't be certain, that she started to cry. I watched her shoulders shake. Then, as if in sympathy, I bent my head and covered my face with my hands; but it wasn't tears that welled up, but relieved, childish, irresistible laughter.

The train came. I watched Edie get on; she raised her hand in a gesture that might have been a wave, but she didn't look back.

I sat still. My train came and went.

After a while I pulled Fraser's letter out of my pocket and spread it on the bench, stroking the creases out with the flat of my hand. *Martin is evil* . . . The words seemed only pitiable now. I couldn't understand how I had been so stupid, so blind; but it was a relief. So Jack was one of those, and that was all. I had imagined something mysterious, unspeakable, infinitely worse.

The *fou rire* that had attacked me spilled over again. I felt tears running down my face, and little flecks of water landed on Fraser's writing, blurring the letters. I didn't dare to look round; no doubt I was attracting some attention, and no one could be blamed for thinking I was drunk. I bit my lip and tried to pull myself together.

Perhaps, one day, the world will learn what he is . . .
Fraser was blackmailing him.

The thought quelled my laughter instantly. What a fool I'd been, not to guess – but it explained so much.

I had been right to distrust him when I first met him. No doubt that was why his letter had been so circumlocutory: he was anxious not to jeopardise his negotiations with Jack. Good God, how low, how damnable.

But I couldn't quite take it seriously; the relief was still too strong. The whole affair was distasteful, of course, and dangerous for Jack; but I felt as if I had struggled out of a nightmare into broad daylight. I leant back on the bench with my hands behind my head, stretching. A woman on the opposite platform caught my eye and I winked at her; it was bad form, but I didn't care.

I lit a cigarette, went to put the lighter back in my pocket and paused, turning it over and over in my hand. It was Jack's; he must have forgotten to ask for it back and I'd appropriated it absent-mindedly. It was silver, and my fingers left smears on it.

I picked up Fraser's letter and read it one more time. It seemed as familiar as something I'd studied at school, but the words had lost their sting. I knew now that they couldn't touch me. *Evil* my foot.

I held the page by one corner and set fire to the bottom edge. The woman on the other platform glanced at me again, and I smiled at her. The flames rippled up the paper, consuming it, until I had to drop the last few inches on the platform. I waited until they'd blackened and curled up, and the fire died. Then I ground the ashes into a black smear with my heel, and made my way back through the ticket office, while another train came and went behind me.

V

I walked back along the High Street, my heart as light as my suitcase. I saw Anthony drive past in his motor car, looking like Mr Toad in his goggles and cap, but I drew back into the shade and he went past without catching sight of me. Now that Anthony had left, Jack would be alone at Tyme's End; but I dawdled, strolling along at my leisure, because there was no urgency. I wasn't sure how I was going to explain my lie earlier: I thought Jack would understand, but my stomach shrank a little when I racked my brain for what, precisely, I might say.

In any case, I was enjoying the walk. I felt a school-boyish pleasure in being alone and, as it were, out of bounds; paradoxically, because I knew I was going back to Tyme's End, I could revel in these last minutes of freedom. I started to whistle, but I was smiling too broadly to keep in tune.

I passed the public house; the sign swung above my head, creaking, and I glanced up at it as I went past. The Cloven Hoof. I was tempted to go in for a drink, but the name reminded me of something. I paused, staring at the sign, trying to remember. It was familiar, and not simply because I had walked past it.

I heard the door of the public house open, and caught a whiff of cigarette smoke, stale beer and stagnant warmth – the usual human fug – and a thin man hurried out, keeping his gaze on the ground. It was Fraser. I took an instinctive step back, ducking my head. I remembered, abruptly, that he had taken a room here: that was why I had remembered the name of the inn. When he had gone by, I raised my head again and watched him. He was wearing a coat despite the heat, and the seams glinted palely in the sun. His thin, colourless hair was plastered to his scalp with hair cream or sweat. He was hurrying, his shoulders hunched, like a man bent on an unpleasant errand. I despised him.

And he was going towards Tyme's End.

I waited until I was sure I could keep my temper. Then I set off after him. He walked like an old man, stiffly and slowly, so it was an effort not to gain ground, but I gritted my teeth and kept in time with his steps.

The walk seemed to take an eternity, but finally we went through the gates of Tyme's End. He went down the drive but I stood still, concealed by the trees, until I guessed that he'd had time to knock and be admitted. Then, gingerly, I emerged from my hiding place and made my way towards the house, keeping out of sight. I wasn't sure why I was taking such elaborate precautions, but somehow it seemed important that neither Fraser nor Jack should know I was there. I watched the drawing-room windows, making sure that the room was empty, and then abandoned caution and crossed the grass to the front door. Sometimes Jack left it open, in the heat, but it was shut. I guessed that they would be in the study, so I made my way round the other side of the house, to the back lawn. The croquet balls were clustered around the central peg; it looked as though Anthony had won against himself, after all. I eased the back door open and stood in the sitting room, listening.

I could hear voices, although they were a few rooms away and the words were indistinct. I walked softly through the dining room and stood in the hall, at the bottom of the stairs. They were in the study, and the door was ajar; now I could hear them perfectly. There was a sliver of daylight spilling into the hall, so that I could even see their shadows when they moved.

Jack said, 'Now, let's get down to business, shall we? Remind me of the figure you had in mind.'

'Ten thousand,' Fraser said, his voice tentative, as though it were a question.

'Ten thousand. That's rather a lot of money, James.'

'But you have it.'

'Certainly I have it. Whether I shall choose to give it to you is another matter.'

'You don't have a choice.'

'Oh, on the contrary. It's purely a question of generosity. Are you, I ask myself, a deserving case? Or will you blue it all on drink?'

'Stop it!' Fraser's voice rose and cracked. 'Stop laughing at me!'

'Oh, Lord . . .' I heard footsteps, and a shadow crossed the band of sunlight. Jack said, with a strange kind of tenderness, 'What else am I to do with you, Jimmy? You're a poor fish. You're of no great concern to anyone. Even your vices are mean and petty-minded. You might have money one day, if I give it to you, but you'll never amount to anything.'

'If it hadn't been for you I would have been –'

'What? Mediocre? Perhaps. Never anything more.'

There was a noise as if Fraser had stumbled away. 'This is all very well,' he said, a little breathless, 'but you're in my power. Don't forget that.'

'Oh,' Jack said. 'Yes, you're right. So, ten thousand . . .'

'Ten thousand five hundred,' Fraser said, his voice hitting a high note. 'I don't like being insulted.'

'I apologise,' Jack murmured. 'You must appreciate that my position is not without its . . . frustrations.'

There was a silence. The shadows crossed and re-crossed the light, and there was a scraping noise as the chair was drawn out from the desk, then the scratch of a nib on paper. Jack said quietly, 'And once you have this, you'll leave me alone and keep your mouth shut?' His voice shook a little and I clenched my fists.

'Probably.'

'Suppose I gave you another thousand? Would you give me your word of honour then?'

Fraser gave a gulp of laughter. 'My word of honour?'

'Yes, I suppose it wouldn't mean very much. Well, I suppose there's nothing I can do about that. Except – beg.' He paused. 'Would you like me to beg, Jimmy?'

'You can if you want.'

The chair creaked as Jack got up, and I heard him cross the room to where I imagined Fraser was standing. There was a crackle, so soft I could hardly hear it, like paper passing from hand to hand. The silence went on and on; I strained my ears, but there was no movement, not even a floorboard creaking.

At last Fraser said, 'What's this?'

'Your cheque,' Jack said. There was a note in his voice that I couldn't identify. 'Your ten thousand, five hundred pounds. What's the matter? Did I misspell your name?'

'But –' Fraser seemed to choke on his own breath. 'What's this?'

'Oh, I say, I am sorry,' Jack said. 'Come to think of it, I might inadvertently have misspelled my own name. Did I?'

Silence. I leant forward and closed my eyes, as if that would help me hear.

'It happens to me more and more as I get older,' Jack went on. 'I'll mean to write "H. J. Martin" and suddenly find myself writing "go to hell".' He added thoughtfully, 'I wonder what a priest would make of that.'

There was another pause. Then Fraser said, in a brittle, painful voice, 'Are you sure about this?'

'Quite sure.'

'I shall go to the police, you know. I wasn't bluffing. All this – you'll lose everything. I shall ruin you.'

'You think so, do you?' He laughed: a soft, pleased laugh, as though he had made a good croquet shot. 'You don't have a leg to stand on. Your word against mine, James. Imagine – who would be believed? Me, or you? Need I spell it out? *I* will ruin *you*, Fraser. Don't push me to do it. You know what I'm capable of.'

'I'd be telling them the truth.'

'That's entirely irrelevant. Now, I think we've

discussed this for long enough, don't you?'

'But why did you –' Fraser was almost crying out. I wanted to enjoy his misery but it was pitiful, not amusing. 'Why did you agree, and tell me to come back, and – you could have told me before. You knew I was right – you knew I *could* tell the police, that they'd believe me –'

'No.'

'Then – I don't believe you – *why* –?'

'I wanted you to hope. I find that hope is the most painful emotion that man is capable of. I wanted you to suffer. And you have, haven't you?'

'You –' His voice faltered; it sounded as though he had put his hands over his face. 'You are – evil. *Evil*.'

'Oh, but you knew that already, James.' A pause. 'And you're not exactly a paragon of virtue, are you? Blackmail is a very ugly word.'

'All this time you were –'

'Playing. Yes. I enjoy watching people like you squirm; I think you'll agree you had it coming. Now, really –'

There was a noise like someone stepping in a cowpat, and then a kind of choking; with a pang of disgust, I realised that Fraser was weeping. It went on for so long I wondered how Jack could bear it. Finally Fraser said, hoarsely, 'I'm sorry, I'm sorry –'

'Get out.'

'Yes, I'm sorry, Jack, I'm sorry, I'll go, forgive me . . .' The door jerked open and I just had time to draw back out of sight. Fraser was like a marionette whose strings had been cut; he had one hand over his face as he stumbled towards the door. Jack watched him from the doorway of the study, a quiet, satisfied look on his face. He waited until Fraser had scrabbled the door open and fallen through it, staggering and then running away like a child after a beating. Then he turned his head slowly to look at me. I met his stare, frozen, the blood mounting in my cheeks, but he only smiled. It seemed to last for ever. Then he moved to the front door, shut it, and walked into the drawing room. A few seconds later I heard the scrape of a match as he lit a cigarette.

I wanted to run away. There had been something in his gaze that had unnerved me, and not simply the fact that he hadn't been surprised to see me there. I was trembling. The sight of Fraser stumbling away like a broken man had shaken me.

The house creaked in the heat. It felt unfamiliar; it wasn't the place I had been so happy in.

Hesitantly, still carrying my suitcase, I went through the doorway into the drawing room. Jack was at the window, smoking. I sat down on the sofa and watched him. He was in shirtsleeves, and I could see his shoulder blades move as he exhaled.

He said, 'Oliver.' He didn't look round.

I opened my mouth to speak, but I didn't know what to say.

'Oliver. I knew you'd come back.'

'I'm sorry,' I said. 'I – I shouldn't have left so suddenly. My mother –'

He laughed. There was an edge of malice in it, as if he enjoyed my discomfort, but I clenched my hands together and told myself I was imagining it. He said, 'Gardner, honestly, you don't think I believed that nonsense about your mother? Anthony read us your letter, for God's sake. You couldn't have come up with a worse lie if you'd tried.'

'Then –' I wished he'd turn and look at me, but he was still watching the ivy on the windowsill flutter in the breeze. 'Then – thank you. For pretending you did. For making it easy for me.'

He shrugged. 'I knew you'd come back. That's all.'

'Don't you want to know why I left?'

He turned round. There was a strange expression on his face, as though his eyes were lit from inside his skull. He picked the packet of cigarettes up from the windowsill and threw it towards me. It landed on the sofa and I took one out and lit it, grateful for the diversion. When I put his lighter back in my pocket he noticed, and his mouth twitched.

He said, 'You can tell me if you want.'

I inhaled a lungful of smoke, blew it out through my nose, and tried to remember what I had decided to say. 'I – it's so childish, Jack, I'm sorry. It *was* my mother, partly; she's missing me terribly, and it's not as if she has anyone else –'

He shrugged my words away with one shoulder. 'And the rest? You said *partly*.'

'The rest was – Fraser sent me a letter. A vile, poisonous letter.'

'Ah.'

'I got cold feet. I should have known better. But it was –'

'May I see it?'

'I burnt it.'

He raised his eyebrows, tapping the ash from his cigarette into the ivy behind him, but that odd, elated expression was still on his face. 'What did it say?'

290

'That you were – Jack, you don't think for a moment that I –'

'Tell me what it said.'

'Nothing specific. Vague accusations that you'd corrupted him, that you were dissipated, and loose-living, and –' I hesitated. 'Evil. That was the word he used.'

'One of his favourite epithets,' Jack said. 'You heard him a few moments ago.'

'Yes.' I smiled at him, and for a second we were old friends, sharing a joke. But I still didn't feel quite at my ease. I glanced down at my suitcase, wishing I hadn't been such a fool. I said, 'And I came back because –'

'Oh, I know why you came back.'

I glanced up at him, taken aback. 'Do you?'

'Of course. It's perfectly obvious.' He ground the stub of his cigarette into the ashtray, rubbing the back of his neck with the other hand.

'Oh, God, no.' I checked an impulse to stand up, like an anxious child. 'It wasn't anything to do with Tyme's End – that is, you think I was frightened you'd change your mind, that I came back for that – truly, Jack, it wasn't –'

'That wasn't what I meant.'

'Then –'

He looked at me and smiled. 'Very well. Tell me. If you were so . . . afraid, why did you come back?'

'Because Edie told me – she didn't mean to, but she did – she told me that . . . She told me why Fraser was blackmailing you.'

He blinked. He didn't move, but his muscles seemed to tense. He stared at me until I felt my cheeks colour and had to look away; then he walked towards me, plucked the cigarette packet out of my lap and strode back to the window. He said, 'Edie has no idea why Fraser was blackmailing me.'

'Well –' I watched him light another cigarette, and felt glad that he had his back to me. 'She didn't say that exactly, only she told me about you, and then I realised –'

'She told you –?'

'That –' I had finished my own cigarette, and I wished he hadn't taken the packet back; I desperately wanted something to do with my hands. 'That you're – homosexual.' I wasn't sure I'd ever said the word before.

He laughed.

Of all the possible reactions, it was the one I hadn't anticipated. He threw back his head and laughed until the room rang with the sound.

I felt the blush on my face spread downwards, past my collar, across my whole body. I imagined a quick, clean death, and thought how grateful I would be for one.

'Homosexual,' he said, at last, correcting my pronunciation. 'With a short "o". It comes from Greek, Gardner, not Latin.'

'I didn't know,' I said.

'Why should you?' he said. 'I'm sorry for laughing, but you're absolutely priceless. Edie, too. As Anthony would say, you can trust a lesbian to bark up the wrong tree.'

'Then – you're not?'

He held my look for just long enough for me to realise what an impertinent question it was. Then he said, 'As it happens – no. At least . . . no. To tell you the truth, I'm not terribly interested in that sort of thing.'

I hadn't known it was possible to flush more deeply than I already had, but I did. For a few seconds I felt nothing but embarrassment, like a lobster in a vat of boiling water. I cleared my throat. 'Oh,' I said. 'Jolly good.'

He watched me, a smile tugging at the corner of his mouth. It would have been more humane of him to avert his eyes, but I supposed I had deserved it.

At long last he said, 'But you came back.'

I clenched my teeth together, caught his eye and looked away quickly.

'How loyal. Like a dog.'

'I'd imagined something so much worse,' I said, stumbling over the words.

His smile broadened, and he threw the cigarette packet back to me. I tried to field it, but my fingers only caught the corner. I bent down and blundered about for it on the floor, glad of the excuse to hide my face.

He waited until I'd got a cigarette out – the first one bent and crumbled in my fingers and I had to take another – and managed to light it. I drew in the smoke, glad of the bitterness, and felt my cheeks return slowly to their ordinary colour. Then he said, 'Would you like to know why Fraser was blackmailing me?'

I looked up, sharply. 'Only if you want to tell me.'

'Oh, I think I do.'

'Then – yes.' But I wasn't sure I was telling the truth. Of course it could be nothing serious – that Jack had disposed of Fraser so quickly reassured me of that – but all the same . . . I said, suddenly, 'No. No, Jack, it's none of my business. I don't want to know.'

It was as if he hadn't heard. He walked over to the gramophone and wound it thoughtfully, using one foot to leaf through a pile of records that someone had left on the floor. He said, 'Get a drink.'

'I'm sorry?'

'Get a drink. Get one for me too.' He glanced round, then crouched to pick up one of the records, turning it over to see the sleeve. 'Whisky and soda for me. You'd better make yours neat whisky.'

I stood waiting, although I wasn't sure what for, but Jack didn't say anything else. I crossed the hall, went into the kitchen and poured drinks for us both. I did it slowly, wondering at my own obedience. I had left my suitcase beside the sofa in the drawing room, but the warm air blew in through the window, tempting me. I still had the train ticket to Peltenshall in my pocket. I could desert without Jack even noticing, as long as I didn't mind leaving my things behind me.

But Jack had been so kind to me; it would be the basest ingratitude, and cowardly to boot.

I took a deep breath, drinking in the fragrance of the garden, and heard, as if from a long way away, the gentle creaking of the house as it settled in the heat. Yes, it would be cowardly to leave. And if I did, Jack might – *would*, almost certainly – disinherit me. That seemed, suddenly, to matter.

I poured more whisky into my glass, until there was a scant quarter-inch of space between the liquid and the rim. Then I took a deep breath, picked up both glasses and went back into the drawing room.

Jack said, 'Sit down.'

I sat down. I put my tumbler on the little table at my left hand. I said, 'Honestly, Jack, there's no need – whatever Fraser accused you of, I know you can't have done anything base or vicious.'

'Do you? How do you know that?'

I stared at him. 'Because I know you.'

He said, without ill will, 'Shut up, Gardner. I'm sure that's very touching, but you really know hardly anything about me.'

I picked up my drink – carefully, so that the liquid trembled below the rim, but didn't spill – and moistened my lips with it. I put the glass down again and sat with my hands folded. There was a breath of warm, sweet air from the window, the smell of summer.

'Now,' Jack said, and leant against the windowsill, watching me, as if it were I, not he, who had something difficult to say. Then, in a dreamy, pleasant tone, like someone at a cocktail party, he began to speak.

'I suppose you know a little of my war service in Arabia; of course you do – you read *The Owl of the Desert*, didn't you? That isn't absolutely . . . exact, but the details hardly matter; it's close enough to the truth to give you a decent idea of what I did. My life had a certain – glamour – that the trenches lacked. To the English, mud is regrettable, but sand has an inherent romance.' He smiled. 'Be that as it may . . . I worked for a little while in Egypt, and then I was appointed liaison officer between the Arabs and the British. That gave me some considerable freedom and I conducted my own operations, blowing things up, leading ambushes, organising assassinations of civilians.' I gave a start, and he laughed. 'Only a few, Gardner, and they were *very* efficiently carried out.'

I said, 'Is that what Fraser –?'

'No. There were . . . other things.' There was a silence. 'When one has absolute freedom . . . It's an extraordinary feeling. I could have done anything I wanted. At first there were no other British soldiers with me. And, in any case, I was producing very satisfactory results; it would have been foolish of my superiors to worry much about a few indiscretions here and there.'

I picked up my glass; when I raised it to my mouth the whisky slopped over the rim and ran down my chin. I swallowed and wiped my face with the back of my hand.

'But after a while,' Jack went on, watching me, 'I was sent another British officer, to tag round with us. It was a terrible bore. He was a little self-righteous Welshman – there was some story that his brother had been shot by our men at Gallipoli when they heard him speaking Welsh and thought he was a Turk – with a voice like a foghorn. To start with, I thought he might rub along with us quite amiably, but he turned out to be rather too naive for our purposes.'

'You mean –'

'I mean he had little conception of the necessities of modern warfare.' Jack shrugged. 'And unfortunately he wanted to impose his views on me, and my men. He was determined that we should play at war like gentlemen, as though it were cricket – only without enjoying it, naturally.' He lit a cigarette, shook the matchbox thoughtfully and smiled. 'You can keep that lighter of mine, by the way, Gardner. Where was I?'

'Disregarding the Geneva Convention, I think.'

He shot me a glance, but I avoided his eyes. I took another gulp of whisky, feeling it burn as it went down. He said, 'Yes, in effect. We had . . . procedures, with which Jones took issue. He made himself unpleasant.'

There was silence. I said, 'So, what did you do?'

'Nothing, at first.'

I looked at him, in spite of myself. 'Nothing?'

'We ignored him. We were perfectly civil and polite, and we acted as though he weren't there. We carried out our operations with the same enthusiasm as before. I ensured that he knew precisely what was happening. I listened to his outpourings of indignation with great courtesy and told him he was at liberty to report me. He threatened me with court martial. I was extremely patient with him. Then, a few weeks before he was due to return to Cairo, we came to a village – a sad, dirty little place – and my men found a group of women and children, hiding. I had one of the women brought before him, and gave him the choice between his life and hers. He chose his own. I went through all of them, one by one. At the end he was weeping like a baby, but he still chose himself over them.'

There was a silence.

I heard my voice say, 'You – went through –?'

'I shot them,' he said. He exhaled a long plume of smoke, and it hung in the air, grey-blue, until the

297

breeze blew it into nothingness. 'He watched them die in front of him. The first time I wondered if he might sacrifice himself; by the second I knew he'd plead, and blubber, and crawl, and choose his life over theirs, every time. He left that village knowing what sort of man he was. I had no trouble with him after that.' There was a pause. 'By the way, Oliver, do you know you're pouring whisky over your trousers?'

I set my glass down convulsively on the table, cracking the base. I looked at the damp patch on my knee. I heard a kind of sob, and thought I was laughing.

'He should never have survived; for a while I thought he might kill himself, but of course he didn't have the courage. He saw worse things than that later, and joined in; he had nothing to lose, you see. Perhaps he even enjoyed himself eventually. He couldn't report me – couldn't do anything in the end, he was a wreck – and so I didn't worry. And then he went back to Cairo. After the war he fell apart. He was a dipsomaniac – dropped dead a few years ago. But a few weeks before he died, he ran across Fraser in some sordid dive and told him the whole story – and Fraser knew me from Cambridge, and knew he was telling the truth . . . It was the damnedest luck.'

'Yes,' I said, in a low voice, 'the damnedest.'

Jack looked at me, his eyes narrowed. He said, 'Are you all right?'

I said, 'Tell me some of the other things you did.'

VI

It was one of the strangest things I had ever experienced, that Jack should talk and talk and I should listen without quite hearing what he said. A quiet, distant part of myself noted the phenomenon, while I sat blind and frozen, following the words with my mind and thankful that most of them meant nothing. The world intruded on my senses with an uncanny – almost absurd – clarity: the shiny leather of the sofa, the amber dregs of whisky catching the electric light, the smell of alcohol and roses, every creak and murmur of the floorboards as Jack moved. I heard the sounds his mouth made – the damp clicks of his tongue against his teeth, the suck of spit as he opened and closed his mouth – and the rustle of his shirt. It was as if I could have mapped the whole world from where I sat, knowing the exact location and movement of each atom, like a god. All the time there were words washing at me and images rising in my head; but somehow I couldn't see how the two were linked, I couldn't understand the process. Jack was a murderer, a torturer. That much I had gathered in the first few seconds. But his voice went on and on, and seemed to fade away, while the sensation of the smooth curve of my glass against my hand seemed to grow until it took up all my consciousness.

It was my name that brought me back to myself: my name, in Jack's voice.

'Oliver. You look like you're going to be sick.'

I said, with an effort, 'I don't think so.'

'Have you had enough?' He said it very gently.

I wanted to stand up, but my legs were numb, as if someone had cut neatly through my spine. I said, 'Please –'

'Have a cigarette.' He got one out of the packet, and lit it before he passed it to me. I took it and put it in my mouth, even though it had been in his first. He said, 'You poor, silly twerp.'

I shut my eyes. I was afraid; if the pictures were still there . . . but the darkness was blank, merciful. All I could see was the beetle he had torn apart, like a little green-gold potentate: and that seemed such a small thing, a foolish thing.

There was silence; blessed, blessed silence. It was like the silence after a nightmare, when I'd wake to find the roar of the guns was only in my head, and a few deep breaths would chase the terror away.

'Do you want more whisky?'

I wanted to look at him and laugh, but I couldn't remember how to do it. I couldn't believe I ever had done it. I said, 'No,' and held on to the maimed beetle in my mind's eye, because a beetle was insignificant, bloodless, incapable of crying out.

I should have known, when I saw him do that. I *had* known; or part of me had. But I had come

300

back to Tyme's End in spite of it.

All of a sudden I was cold. I saw my hands start to shake. My body was trembling so hard that the legs of the sofa were vibrating softly on the floor. My skin was crawling. The air around me was still and chilly; for a moment it was as if Tyme's End had disappeared and I was outside, alone, freezing, surrounded by space. I thought that if I opened my eyes I would see nothing but emptiness, grey emptiness, like one of my nightmares; but it wasn't no-man's-land, it was just . . . nothing.

I opened my eyes. Jack was in front of me. I stared into his face.

He said, 'You look terrible. You'd better go to bed.'

'I can't.'

'It'll do you good.'

'No.' I wasn't disagreeing, exactly, only trying to understand the words.

'Come on, Oliver. It's been a bit bloody for you, I know. But it'll seem better by and by. You mustn't take it too hard.'

I stared at him. Yes, he was like a father, comforting me after I'd been bowled out for a duck. I would laugh when I could remember how to. Jack, my father.

He reached out and held my shoulders in a firm, warm grip. I turned my head and looked at his hand. It was a sinewy, brown, long-fingered hand: a good-looking hand, as far as it went. A charming, secretive hand. I could probably have recalled every occasion on which it had touched me; I had probably listed every one in my diary.

Everything blurred. I was on my feet, staggering out

of the room and across the hall, punching a door open with my fists, leaning into a washbasin, watching whisky and bile splatter over the enamel. I was making noises like an animal, like a man sinking in quicksand. I was sliding down the wall because my knees had given way, and I was still retching, and there was the smell of acid, the stale stench of my own stomach. There was vomit on my chin and my trousers. I leant forwards, helpless, and the spasms seemed to go on for ever.

When they stopped, I got painfully to my feet. I bathed my face and rinsed my mouth. I met my own gaze in the mirror, and held it for as long as I could. My eyes were intent and unblinking; I was glad that I could keep them steady.

I went back into the drawing room. Jack looked round at me, and his eyes flicked down to my trousers, taking in the new stains. He said, 'Did you make it to the lavatory in time?'

I found my voice, and it was cool, dispassionate, the kind of voice I could admire. I said, 'Why did you tell me?'

He blinked. He shifted his weight, leaning back against the windowsill, one hand ruffling the ivy leaves as though they could feel his touch. 'You asked me to, Gardner.'

'I asked you not to.'

'Why did you come back to Tyme's End?'

'Because I loved you,' I said. 'Because you'd been kind to me, and I'd been happy. It was very simple. Why did you tell me?'

'Because I wanted you to know.' He smiled a little, watching me, and plucked an ivy leaf, twirling it in his

302

fingers. 'I wanted you to know what kind of man I am.'

'You wanted to destroy me,' I said.

'No.'

'You knew I'd grown to love you. I worshipped you. I wished you were my father. You waited until you were sure, and then you told me.'

'No,' he said again. 'Destroy you? No. I found you, Gardner. I chose you. When Philip introduced you, I *recognised* you. It was as though I already knew you. Why would I want to destroy you? You're my heir.'

I laughed involuntarily, and thought I might vomit again. 'Your *heir*? You don't think – oh, God. You think I'll take your money, you think I'll take Tyme's End, now that I know *this*?'

'Yes,' he said. The ivy leaf spun as he rolled the stem between his fingers. 'You're right, Gardner. I did wait until I was sure. I *know* you'll take my money, and Tyme's End. I know you'll stay here tonight, instead of running to the village inn, and when you wake up tomorrow nothing will seem quite as bad, and the day after that you'll start to remember how you felt about me, before you knew, and by the end of the week you'll be telling yourself that the things I've done aren't so bad, really.'

'No.'

He held my look, and then shrugged, with a curious, self-mocking quirk of the head. 'Won't you ask me why I did them?'

'Very well: why did you do them?'

'I wanted to see what would happen.' I heard myself make a harsh, disgusted noise, like a gasp, and he took a step towards me. 'I did them to see if I *could* do them. I wanted to know if I'd get away with it. I did them for the same reason that I cheat at croquet: because it's a game, and only a fool plays by the rules.'

'I didn't know you cheated at croquet,' I said.

He laughed, examining the stalk of the ivy he'd picked.

'Why,' I said, and my voice faltered for the first time. 'Why do you want me to inherit Tyme's End?'

The leaf fluttered in his hand like a scrap of dark green damask. 'Ambition,' he said, slowly. 'When I said I'd chosen you . . . I want to know that you'll be mine, even then.'

'I'm not yours now.'

He looked up, and smiled. 'Gardner, if you believe that, you're a greater fool than I thought. Why are you still here?'

'Did you –' I stared at the window. It was dark; I hadn't noticed the time passing. 'Did – you – ever –'

'Not really; I don't go in for loving people much.' A fractional pause. 'That was what you were going to ask, I take it?'

I sat down on the sofa and bowed my head. My father's suitcase looked even shabbier than usual in the electric light. My eyes blurred with fatigue. I said, 'Yes, that was what I was going to ask.'

There seemed nothing more to be said. I could feel Jack's eyes on me, but I didn't look up, and after a while he walked over to the gramophone. I heard a record sliding out of its sleeve, and then the clunk and crackle as he set the turntable going. It was the *Danse Macabre*. The twelve notes struck quietly, and then Death's solo violin came in, inviting the corpses to dance, the melody as catchy as a music-hall song. Jack whistled softly, sketching the tune. I would have hated him if I hadn't felt so exhausted.

The record finished. He wound the gramophone and put it on again. I thought I would never get it out of my head: the spooky, jaunty rise and fall of the strings, the triumph of Death. I had liked it once.

Jack said, 'Honestly, Oliver, you look done in. Go to bed.'

I shook my head.

'Stop being such a b. f. and *go to bed*.'

I raised my eyes to his, wondering if I should feel anything, but I didn't. He was right; I should go to bed. There was nothing else to be done.

'Is that it, then?' I asked. 'No more to be said. What will we do tomorrow? Bathe and play croquet and read in the sun?'

He held my look. He said, 'There's nothing to be afraid of.'

'I'm not afraid.' It was true. I was tired; only tired.

Jack glanced at the gramophone and started to whistle again. Then he seemed to remember what I'd said, a few moments ago. 'Yes,' he said softly. 'Since you ask. That's it. Over.' He took the needle away from the record, and the sudden silence seemed to illustrate his point. 'Or as over as anything ever is. I'm afraid no one escapes the past, Gardner; it's simply a question of how long the leash is.'

'It isn't my past, it's yours. It has nothing to do with me,' I said, trying to fan the spark of anger into a flame. 'You're not my father. This isn't my house.'

'Then why don't you leave?'

'I will, as soon as –'

'If you were going to leave you would have left

already,' he said, almost gently. 'You stayed to ask questions. You won't leave now. The desire to understand comes from the desire to forgive. This *is* your house, or it will be; and I might as well be your father.'

I thought I could still hear the melody of the *Danse Macabre*, very faintly, as if it had set up an echo in my brain. I said, 'You can go to bed, if you want.'

He hesitated, and shrugged. 'All right,' he said. 'I'll see you tomorrow.'

'Yes,' I said. 'Goodnight.'

I sat still, while he walked past me. I heard his footsteps going up the stairs, and the solid sound of his bedroom door closing. The noise was familiar. I had got into the habit of sitting on Jack's bed while he changed in the dressing room next door, leaving the communicating door open so that he could call through to me. I remembered being there a few evenings ago. We'd been laughing at something, although now I couldn't remember what it was.

I looked at my watch. It was very late, so late it was early. Jack must have talked for hours. Soon it would be getting light.

I bent to pick up my father's suitcase from the floor, laid it on the sofa beside me and opened it. My clothes were wound into a knot, and my father's picture was creased across the corner. I picked it up and turned it over. There had been a pencil wedged against the photograph, and it had left a dark scrawl across my father's chest. He looked at me, earnest and very young. I wondered whether I would have been different if he had lived; whether I would have been here.

Mixed in with a mess of shirt collars I found my diary. I looked at it, trying not to let myself remember, then gave up the struggle and flipped it open, wrestling with a dull ache under my heart.

Played cricket most of the afternoon – with much hilarity – and then adjourned to the terrace to try to establish the rules, once and for all. (To no avail.) Champagne, again. I changed for dinner and then talked to Jack while he dressed. There was a cartoon he'd found in Punch that looked like Anthony, and we were late coming down because we couldn't stop laughing . . .

Oh, God.

I turned the pages back. Here and there words caught my eye, but I couldn't bear to read any more; I knew what they said.

I looked at the window, seeing my reflection cut into pieces by the lead between the panes of glass. I heard Jack's voice again. *I shot them.* I sat as still as I had sat then, feeling the tears come into my eyes. Finally, when I blinked, they overflowed and slid down my face.

I closed the book and pressed it between my palms. I wanted to write the truth. I wanted everything he had told me to be there, in black and white. Lest I forget.

But it was impossible, and I knew it. Even if I could have found the words.

I opened the exercise book again, searching through the pages for the first time I'd said I was happy here, for the first time I had used the word *love*.

It came on the 17th of June. I ripped the page out, and the next, on and on until I came to yesterday's scrawl. I ripped that out too, so that there was nothing, after the 16th of June, but a fan of torn margins and a blank page.

I crumpled up the loose pages and put them in the ashtray. Then I set fire to them with Jack's silver lighter. They burned with a brighter, thicker flame than Fraser's letter had – although that had been in sunlight, a long time ago. He had been right, after all; I'd thought his turn of phrase exaggerated, even sensational, but he had simply been telling me the truth. I wished I could be grateful for that.

I watched the pages burn. They filled the room with whitish, acrid smoke that billowed in the breeze from the window and overwhelmed the scent of roses. When there was nothing left but ash, I took up the exercise book again, and the pencil. In a shaky, childish hand, I wrote:

21st June, 1936. Tyme's End.
REMEMBER.
I put my face into my hands, and wept.

The hours passed. When I raised my head, finally, the first thing I saw was my father's photograph. It gave me a kind of strength; for the first time in my life, I was glad that he had been ordinary, that he had died along with so many other men. I had never thought that it would be reassuring to imagine him shot down in Flanders mud, but now, somehow, it was.

I took the photograph in my hand, tried to smooth out the crease across the corner, and put it into my pocket. I closed my suitcase and ran my fingers over my father's faded initials. Outside, the sky was getting light behind the trees and the breeze coming through the window was cold and fresh, blowing away the smoke and the sweetness of the night air. I stood up and turned off the electric light. The room was dim, full of steady shadows. The world beyond the window was silent and touched with a silvery violet colour, like a painting.

I looked round, taking in every detail: the gramophone, the overflowing ashtray, the discarded newspaper on the sofa. I thought that perhaps I'd never be so happy, or so unhappy, as I'd been here. I wondered if I should ever see Tyme's End again and even now the thought made me sorry.

I picked up the suitcase and walked out into the hall. I felt light-headed and hazy, as if the world were not quite substantial. I fumbled at the front door, trying to open it quietly; my hands were cold and stiff, and I struggled to make them obey me. I wouldn't have been surprised to see my fingers pass through the latch, like a ghost's. When finally I managed to open the door I knew that despite my efforts I had made a lot of noise. I stood listening, but there was silence. I took a deep breath. The air smelt damp, like grass stains.

I had set my suitcase down, and now I took it up again. In this subtle daylight I could hardly see my father's initials, but I knew they were there. The case was light, but no lighter than it had been when I arrived: wretchedly poor and shabby, but no poorer or shabbier than it had been. It hadn't changed; and neither had I, or not much.

I shut the door behind me and set off down the

drive, walking on the verge so that my footsteps didn't crunch on the gravel. I didn't turn and look back, because I didn't trust myself.

I walked through the long grass, feeling the dew soak into my trousers. The birds were starting to sing. I had probably missed the milk train, and it would be hours until the next service; but I could walk to the next station or further – all the way to Tunbridge Wells West if I had to. I was in no hurry: all that mattered was that I was on my way home. I felt as if I could walk for ever.

There was a movement in front of me – a dark patch among the trees – that I took for a raven at first, but then I stopped where I was, staring through the undergrowth. It was larger than I'd thought: the size of a man. I stepped warily sideways, until I could see more clearly. It *was* a man, hurrying through the trees, ducking low branches, with one hand raised to protect his face. I thought I knew from the graceless-ness of his movements who it was, and then he lowered his hand to pluck a bramble off his sleeve and I was sure. It was Fraser. I could hear his breathing from here, a harsh sob in his voice as though he had been running for hours. I drew back behind the trunk of a tree and watched him as he scurried past, only a few feet away. When he reached the edge of the grass he reeled and almost fell over, like a sailor reaching dry land for the first time in a year. He looked over his shoulder, and then in the direction of Tyme's End, and I pressed myself against the bark of the tree, praying that he wouldn't notice me. The moment seemed to last for an hour. Finally he turned away and set off towards the gates. As he moved I caught sight of his face. He was weeping, his mouth open.

I relaxed, staring at his back. I could have called out, but there was nothing I wanted to say to him. I owed him thanks, but I couldn't imagine saying so; in spite of myself, I still despised him.

But what had he been doing here? Perhaps he had come to see Jack; but if so, why had he been running through the trees, in the wrong direction? I looked along the path he had taken, noting the trail of crushed bracken and broken branches. There was nothing there; I had wandered through the under-growth myself a few days ago, and the way Fraser had gone would lead to nothing but a little grassy clearing and the shed where Jack kept his motorcycle.

I put my suitcase down in the grass and took a few steps along the track Fraser had left. The birds were making a jubilant noise; when I advanced deeper into the trees they carried on singing, thoroughly undaunted by my presence. I followed the trail of trodden greenery, my nose full of the peppery smell of it, like perspiration. I went carefully, making as little noise as I could. If Jack were there . . . But I was certain, or almost, that he wouldn't be. He had wanted to hurt Fraser, to make his humiliation as final and complete as possible; there would be no advan-tage to meeting him at dawn, away from the house, like a lover.

But Fraser had been here, and he had been weeping as he ran away.

I made my way through the last few yards of bracken and brambles, and stepped warily into the open. Jack kept the grass mown short, and in places it had been worn down almost to bare earth by the bike coming and going. There was a bald trail, almost a path, that led away from me, curving back towards the drive. The shed was a little ramshackle production that might have been designed as a faux hermitage in the days when such things were fashionable, but it was as shipshape as it could be, and the door and window frame had been freshly painted. Jack was careless with most of his possessions, but he treated his bike as if it were animate and needed the best conditions to thrive. I had seen him stable it lovingly, attending to its every need, although he mocked himself for taking such pains.

The shed door was a little way open, swinging almost imperceptibly in the breeze. Jack never left it like that, unless he was inside . . .

I ducked sideways instinctively, out of sight of the shed's little window. Slowly I straightened up again and squinted at the window pane, trying to see past the reflections of trees and sky. I cleared my throat and said, 'Hello? Is someone there?' My voice was flat and thin in the open air. No one answered. I was alone.

I approached the shed like a schoolboy playing at soldiers, my heart beating harder than it should have. Nothing moved, except me.

I stood outside the door, and pulled it gently, to widen the gap between door and door frame. Then I peered inside.

There was nothing there but Jack's bike, covered by a tarpaulin, and the tidy shelves of tools. I hardly knew one end of a bike from the other, so I wouldn't be able to tell if anything was missing, but everything looked perfectly neat, the way Jack would have left it. I could smell something mechanical, like oil. I stood there for a moment, feeling a strange bewilderment. Perhaps Fraser hadn't been here at all; perhaps he'd been running from somewhere else. But the trail of trampled grass and undergrowth had led me here, and someone had left the door open.

It might have been Jack being careless. No doubt yesterday he'd had a lot to think about. But I didn't believe it for a moment.

I went out again into the sunlight and leant against the door, wondering.

I stared into the middle distance for a long time, then I shook myself and turned away. But something caught my attention, and I turned back. There were marks on the white paint of the door: three or four black smears on the edge, as though someone had pushed it open with dirty fingers. I touched them gently, and the dark stuff came off on my fingertips; when I raised them to my nose I smelt something like axle-grease or petroleum.

I imagined Fraser pushing wildly at the door, stumbling out, and forgetting to close it behind him.

He'd had oil on his hands.

I closed my eyes. I could see the bike, covered in its tarpaulin, and the rows of tools. I didn't know anything about bikes; I didn't know how easy it would be to sabotage one, or how likely the rider would be to notice that something was wrong before it was too late. I didn't know what Fraser had been doing, or trying to do.

But I could imagine.

VII

I stood and looked at the dirty marks on the door for a long time. The sun reflected off the white paint, and I could already feel it beginning to dry the dampness around my ankles. It was going to be another glorious day.

Jack would notice the fingerprints, and the door left open. Even if no one warned him, he'd know. He was one of the most observant people I'd ever met, and clever enough to be careful.

It would make a kind of peace between us, I thought, if I went back to Tyme's End and told him what I'd seen. There was no need to be dramatic. *I came back to say goodbye, so we didn't part on bad terms. Oh, and by the way, someone might've been fiddling with your bike – the shed door was open.* That would do the trick.

I took a deep breath. I raised my hand to my face, rubbing my fingers together, smearing the black grease into the whorls on my fingertips.

Peace between us. A *quietus*, a paying of debts. I wanted that almost more than anything. Even now.

I looked at the marks for a long time.

Then I wiped the door with my shirt cuff, polishing the paint back to shining whiteness; no one could have known there'd been a mark there unless they were looking for it. I shut the door properly, the way Jack would have left it, so that he wouldn't know the difference.

I walked back through the trees to where I'd left my suitcase. I picked it up and walked down the drive at an easy, leisurely pace, until I was outside the gates and I'd left Tyme's End behind.

I made my way east, along the long, straight road that ran from Falconhurst to Tunbridge Wells. It was still very early, and I walked in the middle of the road, looking up at the treetops that almost met overhead, separated by a ragged strip of sky. The sunlight cast a delicate net of light and shade over the tarmac. I felt more alone than I had ever felt. It was heady and rather frightening. Perhaps it was because I hadn't slept or eaten, but I couldn't help believing that, now I'd felt it, the sensation would never quite go away.

There was a hum of something behind me. I thought it was an insect buzzing, at first; then, with a cold spasm in my guts, I realised it was a motorbike, a long way away. I walked to the edge of the road, and looked round.

The road was almost perfectly straight, and I guessed that I could see for nearly a quarter of a mile, the level surface stretching away under the trees and narrowing to a point in the distance. There was a little road that joined it from the right, as I looked; that was the road I had taken, the road that led back to

Tyme's End. The insect-drone got louder, until it was unmistakably the sound of a bike. Then I saw the bike itself, coming over the lip of the smaller lane to join the road. It was still very distant, but approaching fast, and the road was so straight and the rider so steady that it seemed not so much to get closer, but to grow larger. It was Jack; I couldn't see his face yet, but I knew.

I stood still and watched him come closer. I wondered what he wanted. Was he coming after me? Or perhaps I was nothing to him, now, and he had other projects in hand, other ideas. All I could do was wait, and see if he stopped when he saw me.

If he stopped . . .

In my mind's eye I saw the door of the shed again, and the oily fingerprints. When I looked down I could see the stain on my shirt cuff, and the black grease ingrained in my skin. What had Fraser done?

Jack was only a little way away now: it would only be a matter of seconds before he reached me. I stayed where I was, as tense and immobile as an animal that scents danger. I didn't know if he'd seen me; in any case, he hadn't braked.

Perhaps he couldn't brake.

I watch him draw ever closer. I could have counted down: ten, nine, eight . . . The world slowed down around me. I could see his face, set and concentrated under his goggles. It was the same expression he'd had when he was pulling the legs off the beetle, on that heavenly golden day beside the river. I hadn't stopped him; I hadn't even said anything. I'd watched him quietly, because I loved him, and, after all, it was only a beetle.

I looked up, taking in the shining green of the trees above me. The motorbike was roaring towards me; in a few seconds it would have gone past. There was no time left to think.

I stepped out into the road.

Jack saw me, and his mouth opened. I looked into his face, but the goggles reflected sunlight and leaves, like the bulging, opaque eyes of an insect. For a moment I was standing in front of his bike while it hurtled towards me; suddenly, horribly, I felt how fragile I was compared to the terrifying momentum of metal and bone. I would have moved then if I could, but my limbs had frozen, too late. I watched my own death fly towards me, and thought of my father.

Jack swore, tried to brake, and dragged the handlebars round.

The bike skidded and screeched, the back wheel lifting away from the earth as though even gravity had failed. It seemed to pause, poised at an impossible angle, although the noise kept on, battering at my eardrums. I thought I cried out; then I flung my arms up to shield my face and dropped to the ground. In the darkness behind my eyelids there was nothing but the sound of crashing machinery, the bite of metal into flesh. I didn't know if the scream I could hear was Jack's or my own. I smelt rust and faeces. I waited for the pain.

It didn't come.

The world went quiet. When I raised my head there was no birdsong, or rustling in the undergrowth: nothing but the tick of cooling metal. The bike had skidded past me. It was dented and smashed, lying in the bracken as though it had tried to struggle home on its own, hopelessly wounded. I kept my eyes on it. There were stains on the body of it, dark brown against the metal, and I knew they must be blood; but slowly, as I looked, I realised that none of it was mine. It was strangely humiliating.

Then I made myself turn my head.

He was dead; Jack was dead. It was easy to see that. He was nothing but a stuffed, inanimate figure, like a guy, with one hand flung out to the side and his wristwatch shattered. It was half past five; it would never be any later. His skull had been smashed in sideways, and his temple had an odd, concave depression that trickled with blood and something whitish, like sperm. It was distasteful: not the stuff of nightmares, simply an unenviable state of affairs. I felt a faint sense of pity, as though he had walked into a crowded room with egg yolk on his tie.

But he had swerved.

He'd swerved to avoid me.

I stood up, picked up my suitcase, and walked a few paces. I felt fine: in fact, I was rather proud of myself for my composure, as though I had given myself a nasty cut while I was shaving and managed not to curse out loud.

He'd swerved.

If he hadn't swerved I would be dead; and he might not be.

My knees gave way. I folded awkwardly to the ground, shaking. I heard the crash again, saw it again. I pressed one hand over my eyes. Oh, God. He'd swerved. I hadn't expected him to swerve. Why had he . . . ?

318

I prayed, then. I wasn't especially religious, but I prayed that it had been reflex, and not a conscious choice; that he hadn't known what he was doing. I prayed that, if he'd thought about it, he would have chosen his own life, not mine.

Of course he would. I was sure – almost sure – when I thought about it, and that comforted me a little. It made it seem more like an accident.

But he had swerved, whether he'd meant to or not. I'd stepped in front of him and he'd swerved . . . The words went round and round in my mind, obsessive and relentless. He'd swerved, and I was glad he had.

I was glad he was dead.

I laughed, then, as though Jack were there to appreciate the joke. I laughed, and felt the tears start in my eyes, because I was alive, and unscathed, and free. Whatever had happened, I was going back to my mother in Peltenshall, back to Cambridge in October, back to the life I'd had. I felt an absurd rush of relief and triumph, as though it had all been a game. I had beaten him. I, Oliver Gardner, had beaten H. J. Martin. For no obvious reason, I remembered something I'd seen at school, in the Old Boys' match: our cricket captain bowling out his own father first ball, and the look on his face of pure, undiluted delight.

Then, for the first time in my life, I cried for my father.

After a long time I stood up, wiping my face. I looked back the way I had come. The sun had risen until it was shining full in my face, but even if it hadn't been, I wouldn't have been able to see Tyme's End from here. I shut my eyes and thought about it. I loved it; I admitted that to myself, now that I knew it was mine, and that I'd never live there. Jack had done his best to make me fall in love with it, and he'd succeeded. I'd never be as happy anywhere else. Wherever I was, whatever I did – if I married, and had children – I would think of Tyme's End. I wouldn't forget.

I swallowed. I'd go back one day. I promised myself that. Even if it wasn't for years and years, even if I was an old man. One more time.

It made it easier to turn away. I set my back to the rising sun, picked up my suitcase and looked down the road, towards the railway station and home. The sunlight filtered through the leaves around me, and the birds had started to sing again. It was over.

I started to walk. I wasn't tired, and I had a long way to go.

B.R.COLLINS

© Catherine Shakespeare Lane

'Collins is one hell of a writer'
Mal Peet

B.R. (Bridget) Collins is a graduate of both university and drama school. Her debut novel, *The Traitor Game*, won the Branford Boase Award in 2009 and was longlisted for the 2009 Carnegie Medal. Bridget lives in Kent.

For more information about Bridget, visit her on
www.jugjugjug.blogspot.com

EXCLUSIVE SNEAK PEEK!

If you dare, you win. If you fail, you die.

The extraordinary new novel from B.R. Collins.

ENTER THE GAME TO BEGIN: JULY 2011.

Visit www.bloomsbury.com/brcollins
to find out more